The Dilemma of Abortion

The Dilemma of Abortion

Edwin Kenyon MA, MD, FRCP, FRCPsych

faber and faber
LONDON · BOSTON

13008.

First published in 1986
by Faber and Faber Limited
3 Queen Square London WC1N 3AU

Filmset by Wilmaset Birkenhead Wirral
Printed in Great Britain by
Redwood Burn Trowbridge Wiltshire

British Library Cataloguing in Publication Data

Kenyon, Edwin
The dilemma of abortion.
1. Abortion
I. Title
363.4'6 RG734

ISBN 0-571-13935-3

Library of Congress Cataloging-in-Publication Data

Kenyon, Edwin.
The dilemma of abortion.
Bibliography: p.
Includes index.
1. Abortion. 2. Abortion—Great Britain.
3. Abortion—Moral and ethical aspects. I. Title.
HQ767.K46 1986 363.4'6 86-2145

ISBN 0-571-13935-3 (pbk.)

To all women concerned

Epitaph on a Child Killed by Procured Abortion

O thou, whose eyes were closed in death's pale night,
Ere fate revealed thee to my aching sight;
Ambiguous something, by no standard fixed,
Frail span, of naught and of existence mixed;
Embryo, imperfect as my tort'ring thought,
Sad outcast of existence and of naught;
Thou, who to guilty love first ow'st thy frame,
Whom guilty honour kills to hide its shame;
Dire offspring! formed by love's too pleasing pow'r!
Honour's dire victim in luckless hour!
Soften the pangs that still revenge thy doom:
Nor, from the dark abyss of nature's womb,
Where back I cast thee, let revolving time
Call up past scenes to aggravate my crime.
  Two adverse tyrants ruled thy wayward fate,
Thyself a helpless victim to their hate;
Love, spite of honour's dictates, gave thee breath;
Honour, in spite of love, pronounced thy death.

Anonymous, 1740

Contents

Preface

This book has been written in non-technical language in order to clarify the most important abortion issues facing us today – moral, political, religious, legal, medical and psychological – by presenting a critical study of how the current British Abortion Act is working, how it evolved and how it matches up to similar laws in other countries. Abortion raises the most fundamental issue of all, the nature of life and death, but has become associated in recent years with other equally perplexing and alarming concepts. We now have experiments on human embryos, 'test-tube babies', womb-leasing, sperm banks and genetic engineering, to name but a few. There has been a call for a halt to such advances until some ethical guidelines can be agreed. I have taken account of these recent controversies, especially in relation to abortion issues.

This is not an academic treatise nor a review of the literature. Nor is the account entirely theoretical, as much practical information is included – for instance, just how abortions are carried out, with the possible complications and the latest methods of diagnosing fetal abnormalities before the baby is born.

Modern medical advances, as well as improved conditions

generally, have brought their own problems, like that of overpopulation. This tends to be overshadowed by the more dramatic and tragic devastation brought about by drought and starvation, but in the last 25 years or so there has been a worldwide resurgence of interest in contraception and abortion. The task of co-ordinating published research from all over the world has been assumed by the International Reference Center for Abortion Research at the International Family Research Institute in the USA and Geneva. As an illustration of the number of works published, their 'Guide to the Literature' for the years 1968–1972 lists and annotates no fewer than 1,788 publications. I am particularly indebted to Francome's book *Abortion Freedom*, published in 1984, for information on abortion legislation in other countries.

I have devoted a whole chapter to describing the present state of abortion practice in various countries, notably the USA and our European neighbours. It is also interesting to note how many foreign women come to Britain for an abortion and from which countries they originate. For example, over 20,000 Spanish women came here in one year. This raises another interesting issue, that is, the effect of religion on abortion practice and particularly the relationship between church and state. I have tried to show, among other things, just how the Roman Catholic doctrine towards abortion has arisen and how various countries have dealt with this. As we live in a mixed society, it is also helpful to have some idea about the attitude of other religions towards abortion. The 'rights' and 'wrongs' of abortion can also be looked at from the point of view of moral philosophy, and I have given some account of this too.

Our laws are, of course, the ways in which our traditions, values and beliefs are finally codified and, ultimately, affect all our lives. They are in the nature of a compromise, hammered out in Parliament by democratically elected representatives. The Abortion Act 1967 was the result in the case of abortion and now regulates all legal abortions in this country. How this law evolved is described, as well as some much older laws that are still, surprisingly, in force today.

The crucial issue in this book is: Does the Abortion Act need changing and, if so, in what ways? In order to give an informed opinion on this one needs to know the details of the Act, how it is working in practice and what other people think about it, especially the professionals who are directly involved; also whether it is fair and available to all who need it, and whether there are any marked differences between abortions done privately and under the National Health Service (NHS).

In the end abortion is a medical matter but one bound by the ethical and legal rules of the time. This sometimes leads to difficulties, especially when what appear at first sight to be technical arguments, either medical or legal, are really nothing of the sort. A barrister has put it this way:

> Law and medicine do not happily coexist. Indeed, law and any professional discipline make extremely ill-suited bedfellows. But some of the least pleasant litigation and threatened litigation of the past few years has arisen out of attempts to apply the law to clinical situations. Often this is because the motives of those behind the case are fashioned by moral, political or religious beliefs which they consider should be compulsory.[1]

Women themselves, without necessarily calling themselves feminists, have been influential in changing both public opinion and the law. This has been particularly so in countries with restrictive laws based on religious ideas that are often inimical to that freedom of choice that so many women want. But what to some are reforms are to others anathema, like the recent 'Gillick affair' concerning the prescription of contraceptives or advice about abortion to under-age girls without parental consent.

My own position in all this will, I think, become clear from reading the book. My experience is based on 20 years as a consultant psychiatrist within the NHS with a special interest in both abortion and the care of mothers who become mentally ill after childbirth, whom I treated as far as possible without separating them from their babies. During this time I also held a clinical lectureship, which enabled me not only to teach and learn from generations of undergraduates and postgraduates but also to share problems with those from disciplines outside medicine, such as moral philosophy. All patients whose case histories I give were seen by me under the NHS; small details have been altered to preserve confidentiality, and for reasons of space complicated histories have had to be stated as briefly as possible. Many patients have multiple problems, unlike so many cases you see quoted in the abstract to further some cause.

A very brief outline of the book follows. The first chapter is concerned with the early stages of embryonic development, which it has been deemed permissible to interrupt with the latest research findings and the implications of the Warnock Committee Report.[2] Postcoital contraception and menstrual regulation are two techniques which fall into the grey area between contraception and abortion.

The next chapter outlines the contribution of moral philosophy and the development of our Judaeo-Christian tradition. Religious doctrines on abortion and related matters are given for Roman Catholicism, the Protestant Churches, Judaism, Buddhism, Hinduism, the faith of the Sikhs and Islam, with a concluding section on secularization and the psychology of religious belief.

Chapter 3 is concerned mainly with the evolution of our laws regulating abortion, from Anglo-Saxon times to the present. Separate sections deal with Scottish law and the complicated situation in Northern Ireland and the Irish Republic.

Chapter 4 is devoted to a detailed guide to legal abortion today, with a more thorough description of the main provisions of the Abortion Act 1967 and the four conditions under which abortions can now be carried out. The 'social clause' is fully explained, as well as the rights of the husband and the legal rights of the fetus itself. Basic statistics are given to show the actual numbers of abortions carried out, both legal and illegal, as well as such characteristics as age and marital status. The concluding sections deal with the special problems of teenage pregnancies and abortions. Some of the events and situations which lead women to seek abortions are also described in the concluding section of chapter 4. Their difficulties and delays in obtaining abortions are discussed, as well as some differences between NHS and privately done abortions.

How abortions are actually carried out, with the latest figures on the physical and emotional complications, are fully set out in chapter 5. The related issues of sterilization (male and female) and infanticide are also discussed.

Chapter 6 takes a wider view, looking at the problems of population control worldwide, the number of foreign-born women coming here for abortions, and the abortion laws and practices in the British Commonwealth, the Indian subcontinent, the USA, Latin America, France, Italy, Spain, Scandinavia, the USSR, China and Japan.

The final chapter contains details of the latest attempts to alter the Abortion Act, the anti-abortion lobby and some of the political and legal issues involved. Prevention of abortion is also mentioned, along with my personal views about possible future legislation.

For those who wish to read further I have indicated throughout the book relevant references by means of a superior number. They are listed in full on pages 268–78. They can be ignored without in any way affecting the content of the book.

I acknowledge permission from the Oxford University Press and the Editor of the *New Oxford Book of Eighteenth Century Verse* (1985) to reprint the anonymous poem 'Epitaph on a Child Killed by Procured Abortion'. I would also like to thank Mrs H. Ball for typing the manuscript and for helpful suggestions in its presentation.

Oxford
May 1985

I

When is an Abortion not an Abortion?

To the average layman the word 'abortion' is only too readily associated with illegal operations carried out in sordid circumstances. While its use is still maintained in the medical profession, the rather more neutral and clinical description 'termination of pregnancy' or 'termination' is often preferred. When a stigma becomes attached to something one way of trying to overcome this is to change its name. A notable example is to be found in the history of the mentally deficient, who were originally called 'idiots', 'imbeciles' and 'morons', then 'mentally deficient', which was changed to 'subnormal' by the 1959 Mental Health Act. However, this soon became 'mentally handicapped' until our latest legislation – the 1983 Mental Health Act – changed it yet again to 'mental impairment', if such patients are compulsorily detained.

For abortion the most generally favoured euphemism has been 'miscarriage'. Its use as a synonym for abortion dates back to the seventeenth century. It has been more usually equated with premature labour or an abortion which happens spontaneously, but think too of its other more general meanings, like miscarriage of justice, failure, error, act of going astray, many of which so aptly describe some of the explanations put forward for 'getting into trouble' and becoming a candidate for an abortion. The most modern popular usage for abortion is 'mission aborted' when the launching of a space rocket has gone wrong, a situation rich in sexual symbolism!

But finding a name for something is not necessarily the same as offering an explanation for it. Arguments over the precise meanings of these terms and how some of them have become incorporated in our law will be discussed later. As a general rule, throughout this book the terms 'abortion' and 'termination of pregnancy' will be used interchangeably unless otherwise specified and will refer to a legally performed operation carried out before the fetus has attained viability, that is, before it is capable of independent life. A legal definition of abortion is 'the intentional destruction of the fetus in the womb, or any untimely delivery brought about with intent to cause the death of the fetus'.[1] Viability is usually defined in terms of duration of pregnancy but sometimes by weight and length of the fetus. One reason for the recent concern about abortion legislation has been this very question of viability because with continuing advances in technology younger and younger fetuses can be kept alive.

Both abortion and infanticide (killing a baby after it has been born) have been practised since time immemorial, but the attitudes towards these held by any given society do not seem to be associated with its technological status, as there are no clear-cut correlations between 'primitive' societies condoning abortion and 'civilized' or advanced ones condemning it.

Four main methods of inducing abortions have been used by more primitive societies, namely, external treatments such as violent exercise or pressure on the abdomen, insertion of objects into the vagina or uterus, taking various substances by mouth (abortifacients) and the use of magic.

The variation in attitudes towards abortion is shown by cross-cultural surveys carried out by social anthropologists and others.[2] The well-known work by Devereux, *A Study of Abortion in Primitive Societies* (reissued in a new edition in

1976)[3], demonstrated the amazing diversity of attitudes and practices concerning both abortion and infanticide in 400 pre-industrial societies. Penalties among disapproving societies ranged from a scolding to a death sentence.

The attitude towards abortion takes on a particular intensity when it becomes a matter of religious rather than secular concern. In our time much anxiety has also been expressed over possible physical consequences, especially when abortion has been either self-induced or performed by unqualified people. Although individual catastrophes and 'horror stories' have been well documented, such fears are probably much exaggerated. The very fact that a substantial number of societies have condoned and practised abortion suggests that overall results are not usually serious, especially as undesirable or tragic consequences are rarely mentioned.

In modern times, at least in Europe, four basic grounds have evolved for recommending an abortion. These are, first, medical, including psychiatric; secondly, eugenic (originally concerned with breeding a healthy stock); thirdly, humanitarian; and, fourthly, social. These, under various names and guises have been championed, reviled or disputed by various societies at different times.

Drawing the line

For some (the absolutists) there is no room for manoeuvre or argument – an inflexible doctrine is adopted which appears to them to be self-evident and 'natural', such as 'It is always wrong to take human life.' This type of approach can also lead to extensive semantic arguments and philosophical speculations, such as what is meant by 'life' and 'human'. These matters are taken up in more detail in chapter 2 of this book. When it is accepted that some intervention in human reproduction is indicated, the next question is: at what stage might this be done? And then what justifications are offered for intervening at this particular stage? In other words, at what particular developmental stage should a line be drawn beyond which a very much more serious view is taken of interfering with the pregnancy or beyond which it is absolutely or conditionally forbidden?

Looked at historically, some very surprising and diverse lines have been drawn, varying in time from before conception has even taken place to after birth. Methods both advocated and condemned have encompassed the four basic ways for regulating the number of children born, namely, contraception, sterilization, abortion and infanticide.

A brief outline summary is given below of the differing views as to when and how a pregnancy might be interrupted, to be followed in the rest of this chapter and the next by a more detailed discussion of the issues raised.

(1) Before the union of sperm and ovum. This may include artificial methods of contraception and sterilization.
(2) At conception (fertilization). This for some is when 'life' begins and should be neither artificially prevented nor interrupted at any stage of development.
(3) Through interception – prevention of implantation of a fertilized ovum (postcoital contraception).
(4) Through menstrual regulation – evacuation of the uterus within 14 days of a missed period, before pregnancy can be reliably diagnosed.
(5) On the implantation in the uterine wall of a fertilized ovum (nidation) (up to about one week after ovulation).
(6) On the acquisition of a soul.
(7) Up to 14 days' development – recommended by the Warnock Committee as the crucial time for implantation, twinning and appearance of the 'primitive streak'.
(8) At the change from embryo to fetus – after about the fourth month.

(9) On the acquisition of human form (which has been interpreted as at 120 days' gestation).

(10) When the fetal brain has developed to a certain functional level – a situation analogous to brain death (i.e. 'brain life' – at about 8 weeks' gestation).

(11) When the fetus is sentient, that is, capable of sense perception, especially pain. The timing of this is not precisely known, but if it depends on having a functioning nervous system, it would be somewhere around 14 to 18 weeks.

(12) At or after quickening. 'Quick' originally meant 'alive' but in this context refers to when fetal movements are first felt, usually between 16 and 20 weeks.

(13) On viability (the ability to survive outside the uterus), traditionally taken to be at 28 weeks or corresponding to a fetal weight of about 1 kilogram (kg) (2.2 lb). For comparison the ideal body-weight for a full-term newborn baby is 3.4 kg (7.5 lb).

(14) At birth or during delivery – the special legal category of 'child destruction'.

(15) Following birth (infanticide or murder).

The early stages

Before trying to tackle the much more complicated definitions of life and such matters as when a fetus becomes a person, the apparently more straightforward ones, such as what constitutes a pregnancy and a miscarriage, will be discussed. The revival of interest in these basic topics was started by the introduction of new methods of postcoital contraception, with concern being expressed over its legal status. The *Shorter Oxford English Dictionary* defines pregnancy as 'Condition of being pregnant or with child or young; gestation'. It is the 'with child' bit which causes the difficulty – when is a tiny conglomeration of cells, embryo or fetus a child? Doctors get round the semantic difficulty of the very early stages of pregnancy by talking about the 'products of conception'.

There are also difficulties over the term 'miscarriage'. Presumably, before you can miscarry you must 'carry', which implies that pregnancy does not 'really' begin until nidation – when the implanted fertilized ovum is carried in the uterine wall – so that only *after* this has happened can we speak of an abortion or miscarriage. Thus the contemporary consensus view that is now backed by legal authority would suggest that any interruption of development before the stage of implantation would be considered a form of contraception and not abortion and hence, by implication, not subject to the Abortion Act 1967.

These views have been, and still are, challenged from semantic, moral, religious, legal and commonsense points of view. There is obviously a continuum of life, but to call any interruption of this 'unnatural' or 'contrary to nature' is to ignore what often happens naturally.

Natural wastage

When considering intervention of any sort as being against nature and the natural order of things (sometimes expressed in theological terms as contrary to God's intentions or some similar phrase) it is as well to remind ourselves of what the 'natural' processes are. It is immediately obvious that nature herself often intervenes, and there is a great deal of what might be called natural wastage. Indeed, nature's prodigality is observed right from the start. For example, of the 500 million or so sperms that are deposited after each ejaculation, only a few hundred reach the Fallopian tube where fertilization occurs, and usually only one sperm finally unites with the ovum. Therefore, millions of live sperm (? human life) are continuously produced and, in the procreational sense of the word, 'wasted'. A woman's ovaries contain thousands of potential ova, which are already formed and present at birth, but only one is released each month (ovulation) throughout her reproductive life from puberty to the menopause.

Further it is often assumed that conception – essentially a *process* lasting about five days from fertilization to established implantation – always leads to pregnancy. This is not so. Even when this does happen, as many as half of these conceptuses are normally lost with the next period and a further 20 per cent or so in the early weeks of pregnancy. Failure of implantation is, therefore, a common process in nature and is probably one way in which abnormally developing (potential) fetuses are eliminated.

A lot more research is required to explain fully the early weeks of pregnancy. A study in the *Lancet* concluded that about 8 per cent of human pregnancies are lost at such an early stage of development that the women concerned are unaware that conception has occurred.[4] They do not seem to suffer any ill effects subsequently. Looked at in another way, the predicted future of an individual ovum has been summarized thus: '16 per cent of ova do not divide, 15 per cent are lost during various pre-implantation stages in the first postovulatory week, 27 per cent of ova abort during implantation in the second postovulatory week, and 10.5 per cent of ova surviving the first missed menstrual period subsequently abort spontaneously'.[5]

Also, in so-called ectopic pregnancies fertilized ova may implant in the wrong place. This is usually a Fallopian tube (oviduct) instead of the uterus, the place where fertilization generally takes place. These again are 'wasted' pregnancies, as normal development and delivery cannot take place.

There is, too, the matter of spontaneous abortions, which in many cases also serve to eliminate grossly abnormal fetuses. An estimated 5 per cent of all recognizable human conceptuses have a chromosome abnormality, but because of the selective deaths of embryos and fetuses with such abnormalities, the proportion of affected conceptuses drops to 4.2 per cent at eight weeks' pregnancy and eventually down to 0.6 per cent in live births.[6] Most spontaneous abortions come about before the end of the third month of pregnancy. Some unfortunate women have recurrent or habitual abortions. In one investigation of a number of such cases[7] the probable causes were found to be genetic abnormalities in 25 per cent, uterine abnormalities in 15 per cent, hormonal abnormalities in 23 per cent; the causes were unknown in 37 per cent.

The 'human life' which begins at fertilization may not be a single one, not only in the possible development of twins but also in other ways. For instance, when two separate ova are fertilized at the same time, one may absorb the other to produce a human chimera containing a double genetic component. Also an embryo may suffer resorption in the uterus and may either cease to exist or go on to form the placental tissue called a hydatidiform mole with no trace of an embryo. From all this it can be seen that the situation in nature is vastly more complicated than most people realize. It will also become obvious, in the next section, that planned embryonic loss is an important feature of 'test-tube' baby programmes, which in this respect may only be mimicking nature. Those who take an absolutist view of the 'sacredness' of human life from the beginning do not always know the biological facts such as spontaneous loss being a random but unavoidable feature of natural reproduction in human populations. Does this also justify research on human embryos?

Embryo research – for and against

The subject of embryo research has engendered such public controversy that before considering the arguments for and against it in more detail and proposals for regulating it, I would like first to summarize the fundamental issues involved. The main aims of embryo research are not to provide further grist for the mills of theologians, philosophers, lawyers and politicians, although all have important contributions to make, but to help infertile couples have children, to prevent the birth of mentally and physically handicapped children and to further understanding of our own early development. Medical experts themselves differ about the best ways of achieving these aims. To put all of this into perspective, I will first briefly mention the seven techniques which are (theoretically) available for helping infertile couples:[8]

(1) *In vitro* fertilization or IVF. *In vitro* is Latin for 'in a glass', and in this context it means that eggs are removed from the woman and then fertilized with sperm in a laboratory glass dish. Following this they are replaced as embryos in the mother's womb. Overall at present there is about a 15 per cent chance that one or more of such replaced embryos will eventually give rise to a live child. The first such 'test-tube' baby was born in 1978, and up to February 1983 more than 80 children had been born in Britain following IVF.

(2) Spare embryos. These are the embryos fertilized *in vitro* but not yet replaced in the womb.

(3) Embryo freezing. Embryos formed *in vitro* can then be stored pending further transfers. They are frozen and preserved in liquid nitrogen at temperatures of around 200° below zero Centigrade.

(4) Surrogate motherhood. A normal, healthy woman becomes pregnant by being artificially inseminated by the sperm of a man in an infertile partnership. The baby, when born, is handed over to the infertile couple. There are other possible variants, but this is what is usually meant by surrogacy.

(5) Womb leasing. Similar to surrogacy except that a healthy woman carries an embryo which has been fertilized *in vitro* from the egg of a woman whose womb could not sustain a full pregnancy and the sperm of her partner.

(6) Ectogenesis. An unlikely possibility of an *in vitro* fertilized embryo growing to full term in an artificial womb created in the laboratory.
(7) Embryo donation. An egg may be removed from a fertile woman, then fertilized *in vitro* with the sperm of a man whose infertile partner then has the embryo implanted in her womb.

One of the main arguments in favour of continuing research with human embryos is to improve on existing 'test-tube' techniques.[9] Estimates vary as to the success rate. In the early 1980s women undergoing treatment had only a 3 per cent chance of giving birth to a 'test-tube' baby; since then the success rate has multiplied nearly five times. In fact (paradoxically), further improvements in this area could eventually do away with the necessity for embryo experimentation. In the meantime it is worth recalling that there are about 900,000 people in Britain who are infertile and that at present less than one half will conceive.

Frozen embryos, thawed and replaced in the womb, have given rise to healthy babies. The first such embryo, in Australia, produced a healthy 6-pound baby girl. Britain's first frozen embryo baby was born in Manchester in early 1985; this time it was a boy, and he was able to leave hospital six days after delivery. The very latest discovery is a method of freezing eggs – up to now only sperm and embryos could be frozen successfully – which can later be thawed and fertilized. If this promising early work is allowed to continue and is successful, it could eventually remove the need to freeze embryos for 'test-tube' baby treatment.

Further controversy has surrounded the production and use of 'spare' embryos. There are two possible sources for these, one being the 'spares' produced by fertilizing a greater number of eggs than are necessary to ensure a pregnancy in an IVF programme to help an infertile couple. Such 'spares' may be frozen for subsequent implantation if the first attempt is unsuccessful. Should this not be necessary, society must face up to the possible fate of the embryos. (In one case both parents were killed in an air crash, thus posing the problem of who 'owned' their embryos.)

An alternative source of 'spare' embryos could be eggs taken from ovaries removed for medical reasons or even donated after death. Given the woman's permission, such eggs could be fertilized, or even stimulated to develop without fertilization, and used for research purposes. Their use would not have the same moral implications, since they would have no 'parents' and no potential for becoming human beings or even fetuses. Arguments have ranged from the viewpoint that only one egg should be taken, fertilized and implanted at a time, to medical views stipulating that the best results can be obtained by implanting two, three or more eggs.

Another cogent reason for encouraging embryo research is to help understand and prevent many of our inherited and congenital abnormalities. Chromosomal abnormalities are being better understood and charted, and are present in, and probably cause, a high proportion of early spontaneous abortions. It has been estimated that up to 60 per cent of affected early embryos are lost and another 15 per cent (100,000 pregnancies a year) end in early abortions. The best-known result of a chromosomal abnormality is Down's syndrome (previously known as mongolism).

Overall about 75,000 British women suffer a miscarriage annually, with all that means in terms of emotional, physical and economic cost. Even more tragic are those unfortunate women who have recurring miscarriages, some 15,000 annually. Recurrent miscarriage is defined as three or more consecutive spontaneous miscarriages. There is still a lot to be learned about the precise causes of these miscarriages.

There are now about 1,500 disorders known to arise in the genes, often accompanied by subtle biochemical disorders. These can account for something like 7,000 affected babies a year born in the United Kingdom. Indeed, if one takes the whole range of congenital (that is, 'born with') defects, then something of the order of 14,000 British babies are born annually with such defects, about one half of which may die soon after birth.

Another possible benefit of embryo research would be fewer induced abortions. Two examples spring to mind. First, instead of aborting a fetus that may develop into a handicapped child, the abnormality could be diagnosed better at an earlier stage of development and perhaps treated while the baby is still inside the womb. Secondly, sex-linked genetic disorders, such as haemophilia, might be prevented by pre-implantation gender identification (that is, after *in vitro* fertilization, embryos of the sex associated with the inherited disease would not be transferred into the womb).

Other medico-social advances which could come out of embryo research are improved methods of contraception – for instance, some sort of vaccine; help in understanding male infertility, which may be responsible for reproductive failures in anything up to 50 per cent of cases among the 250,000 or so infertile couples in Britain. Finally, there is the possibility of growing spare organs or particular body tissues which could later be implanted, rather than relying on donors. This perhaps lies in the area of fetal rather than embryo research.

Inextricably linked with these 'medical' arguments are a whole range of moral, ethical[10] and religious views, many of which are discussed in more detail in the next chapter. Here only a few points will be stressed. Not all medical scientists are in favour of embryo research, although it seems to me, with a few notable exceptions, that those who speak out against using human embryos do so not on strictly medical grounds but on moral or religious ones. A case in point is the group of Fellows of the Royal College of Obstetricians and Gynaecologists who wrote a letter to *The Times* in February 1985. They put forward strong views against embryo research on the grounds that it reduced the human embryo to the level of an experimental animal and contravened a code of medical ethics. It is not clear which 'code' is being invoked, but what is significant is that their address is given not as the College but as the 'Order of Christian Unity'.

One notable exception, opposing such research on purely technical grounds, is the distinguished French worker Professor J. Lejeune (*The Times*, 26 March 1985). He poses and answers (in the negative) two basic questions. First, is it demonstrable that no equivalent research could be performed on laboratory animals rather than on early human beings? He answers no to this because already very refined protocols have been used in mice experiments, leading to great achievements. Second, is this type of experiment on early embryos the most appropriate way to learn about the causes, the mechanisms and, possibly, the prevention and/or cure of genetic disabilities like haemophilia, muscular dystrophy and Down's syndrome? He again answers no because maturation of the blood, of the muscles or of the brain cannot be observed in human embryos less than 14 days old. Hence troubles afflicting these tissues must be studied in subjects that have already developed the relevant organs. I must point out, though, that Professor Lejeune is in a minority among experts in this field.

A reasoned reply by the President of the Royal Society (*The Times*, 6 April 1985) pointed out that although much can be learned from animal experiments, there are still essential steps to which tests on human material are indispensable. He gave as an example the original IVF experiments, in which it was necessary to check, before reimplantation, that there were no chromosomal abnormalities in human embryos. He also remarked that it was still important to continue experiments on human embryos less than 14 days old to elicit further information about genetically transmitted diseases. An example of this is recent work on nucleic acid, which may eventually be used to distinguish between early embryonic tissue which is normal and that which carries a genetic defect. When this has been achieved, it will be possible to fertilize an ovum outside the body and to reimplant it only if it has been shown to be free of a genetic defect known to be carried by either or both parents. This would be a tremendous advance on alternatives such as selective abortion.

Another, more obvious, argument against only using animals is that animals do not suffer from the same genetic and hereditary disorders as we do, so that to investigate uniquely human conditions requires human embryos.

It has been suggested, too, that research on the gametes (that is, the sperm and eggs) before fertilization, when many ethical problems would not arise, could eventually provide most of the answers being sought. From the opposite point of view it could be argued that it is unethical *not* to use 'spare' embryos generated in IVF work for research, treating them as effectively subject to the same wastage as we see in nature, and that if they were used, it would not be necessary to generate embryos specifically for research.

Most other arguments can be boiled down either to agreeing or not agreeing with the proposition that human life is unique or sacred from the moment of conception and on no account should be tampered with. Some people mistakenly believe that ethics is the same as right or wrong, that it is somehow mixed up with God and that all that is necessary is the belief that man is special. Here we get on to dangerous semantic ground – just what is meant by 'special', for instance? So much depends on which words and phrases are used in presenting an argument. Language can be used in such emotive ways.

Strangely, recent research has added a new twist to the age-old philosophical question: when does life begin? This was summarized by Clifford Longley (*The Times*, 30 July 1984), who pointed out that a new distinction along the developmental continuum had been made inadvertently by the technique of freezing embryos. As he put it:

> It is that early embryos are capable, like corpses, sperm and ova, but unlike developed fetuses, babies and adults, of deep freezing. A conceptus can be kept in suitable conditions at the right temperature for a very long time, probably many years. Freezing halts the cell multiplication process, which can be resumed long afterwards. Those who believe the conceptus is already human life, not to be discarded or altered destructively, have to justify themselves in the light of this revealing fact. What kind of life is it that can be thus arrested? Is it life

> at all? Is a totally passive and inert deep-frozen embryo actually alive? To argue that it is, is to extend the definition of 'life'; it cannot, on the other hand, be deemed 'dead' . . . A clearer definition of life is needed, making explicit what has hitherto been taken for granted, such as 'Life entails continuous organic processes which once halted, cannot be restarted' . . . an organism whose organic processes can be discontinued would not therefore possess 'life' . . . it does not have one of the essential properties of life, an imperative continuity of basic biological functions.

A good example of the emotive use of terminology is to refer to every embryo and fetus as an 'unborn child'. An embryo is a fertilized egg, not an unborn child. It has no organs, no sensations, and it is not capable of an independent existence. All right, it is 'alive', but so are sperms and ova. Again, to say that such an embryo is genetically unique is to beg the question; so is each sperm and egg. A human embryo is without consciousness, sentience, movement, articulation and final individuation. It may have a great potential but is singularly empty in actuality.

Nor does either nature or society, for that matter, have a high regard for human embryos. We have already seen how high is the natural wastage of 'unborn children'. Many thousands of women rely on methods of contraception which, partly or exclusively, act by preventing the implantation of embryos. (Further details on postcoital contraception are given later in this chapter.) Also, there are no church rites for an embryo's entrance and exit. There is no burial in sacred ground, nor is registration of a birth required until 28 weeks' gestation.

It could be argued that embryo research is dedicated to the creation, not the destruction, of human life and that more thought should be given to the quality rather than the quantity of such life. We should draw a distinction between human material and human nature; sensibility determines the respect we give to living things. To say, with Lord Denning, that the only logical point at which the law could start is the moment of fertilization is entirely legalistic – simply convenient but neither logical nor appropriate.

The Warnock Committee and proposed legislation

The Government had been under increasing pressure to allay public anxiety about the future of embryo research and other related matters. It seemed that research findings and their practical implementation were progressing too quickly and were outstripping their ethical and legal implications. It was therefore proposed to set up a Committee of Enquiry to make recommendations which could eventually be turned into legislation.

The Committee, chaired by Lady Warnock, was set up in July 1982 with the following terms of reference: 'To consider recent and potential developments in medicine and science related to human fertilization and embryology; to consider what policies and safeguards should be applied, including consideration of the social, ethical and legal implications of these developments; and to make recommendations.' The Report[11] was published in July 1984 and immediately stirred up many of the old controversies.

Apart from the Chairman, there were 15 other members (four of whom were women) representing various disciplines, such as psychiatry, social work, obstetrics, general practice, philosophy, theology and the law. The Committee made 63 recommendations. For present purposes, the ones most concerned with embryo research will be briefly summarized.

(1) A new statutory licensing body should be set up to regulate infertility services and research on human embryos produced *in vitro*.

(2) Artificial insemination by donor (AID) and IVF should be 'generally available', i.e. without restriction on whose sperm or eggs were used and regardless of whether recipients were married – subject to the control of the licensing body and to point 10 below.

(3) Egg donation, sperm freezing, multiple fertilization

of eggs resulting in 'spares' which were not transferred to the womb and the freezing of human embryos produced by IVF should be accepted as recognized techniques.

(4) The sale and purchase of eggs, sperm and human embryos should be permitted but controlled by the licensing authority.

(5) *In vitro* human embryos should not be kept alive for more than 14 days. Research on them might be conducted up to that time under licence and, where possible, with the consent of the couples who generated them. Human embryos might be produced specifically for research.

(6) It would be a criminal offence to keep a human embryo alive *in vitro* after 14 days.

(7) The human embryo should be given some protection in law.

(8) Embryos resulting from trans-species fertilization should not be allowed to live beyond the two-cell stage, and to transfer a human embryo to a non-human uterus should be a criminal offence.

(9) No embryo that had been the subject of research should be transferred to a woman.

(10) No male or female should provide sperm or eggs for more than 10 children, but otherwise there should be no restriction on the supply and use of donated eggs, semen and embryos.

(11) It should be an offence for any agency or professional third party to assist in providing for a surrogate pregnancy, but surrogate motherhood itself should not be an offence.

(12) Children produced by AID or egg donation should be legitimate in the eyes of the law but at 18 years old should have access to ethnic and generic information about the donors. The latter should have no rights or obligations in respect of the children concerned.

Not all the members of the Committee were agreed on every recommendation. Of the 16 members three signed a minority report recommending a ban on all experiments on human embryos, and another four signed a minority report recommending a ban on experiments on human embryos 'brought into existence specifically for research'.

While the Committee agreed that once fertilization had occurred, 'there is no particular point of the developmental process that is more important than another; all are part of a continuous process' and 'biologically there is no one single identifiable stage in the development of the embryo beyond which the *in vitro* embryo should not be kept alive,' they none the less took 14 days as the decisive period. This was chosen for three principal reasons.

First, at this stage there appears what is called the 'primitive streak'. This can be taken to be the forerunner of the central nervous system as well as 'the beginning of individual development of the embryo'. By this is meant that certain cells now develop special functions instead of being 'all-purpose', undifferentiated ones. This also implies that before anything resembling a nervous system and brain develops, the embryo is incapable of feeling pain. However, not all scientists equate an anatomical nervous system with the capacity to experience pain. For example, lower protozoa have some sort of sensory perception and will react to painful stimuli.

Secondly, this is the last moment when twinning can occur. Thirdly, implantation of the embryo in the womb ends at this point.

It is not surprising that the anti-abortion lobby has latched on to the uncertainties of the 14-day ruling. Its logical inconsistency is stressed: if it is not permissible to experiment on or 'kill' an embryo after 14 days, why is it legally permissible to 'kill' a much older fetus by aborting it under the 1967 Abortion Act? They further argue that many aborted fetuses have well developed nervous systems and question whether there is any fundamental difference between *in vitro* 'pain' and *in utero* 'pain'.

This argument was not considered by the Warnock Committee, as abortion and contraception were not in its terms of reference, but on page 64 of the Report there is an interesting footnote on possible implications for research on aborted fetuses:

> The focus of this [Report] is on the very early human embryo. Almost all of these embryos will result from *in vitro* fertilization, although some may be obtained from uterine lavage. We are conscious, however, that there are other whole live embryos and fetuses of greater gestational age, which may become available for research following termination of pregnancy. We recognize that both abortion and the Code of Practice contained in the Report on 'The Uses of Fetuses and Fetal Material for Research' (the Peel Report)[12] are very much outside our terms of reference. Nevertheless it seems to us totally illogical to propose stringent legislative controls on the use of very early human embryos for research, while there is a less formal mechanism governing the research use of whole live embryos and fetuses of more advanced gestation. Although we understand these mechanisms have worked well, we consider there is a case for bringing any research that makes use of whole live aborted embryos or fetuses – whether obtained from *in vitro* fertilization, uterine lavage or termination of pregnancy – within the sort of legislative framework proposed in this report: we suggest that this be given urgent consideration.

The Committee recommended legislation to ensure there is no right of ownership to an embryo, but parents could give informed consent to use for research or disposal wherever possible. The freezing of sperm, eggs and embryos should be permitted, but the frozen deposits should be reviewed every five years and the parents or originators consulted about whether they wanted them kept, destroyed or donated. Frozen embryos should be stored for a maximum of 10 years.

The anti-abortion lobby, having been unsuccessful in getting the abortion laws modified or rescinded, is now vigorously mounting a fresh attack via embryo research. The type of criticism and argument put forward can perhaps best be exemplified by quoting objections raised to the Warnock Report in the pamphlet entitled 'Warnock Dissected'.[13] The final page is headed 'Summary of Life's Commentary on the Report' and gives an eight-point critique:

> 1. The Warnock proposals are a betrayal of human life in its earliest stages. However urgent the need to relieve human infertility, the principle that all human life should receive the full protection of the law must never be violated.
> 2. In particular, we oppose the technique of selecting the 'best' embryos for transfer to the womb, throwing away, freezing and experimentation on 'spares' and the use of *in vitro* embryos for supplying replacement organs for adults.
> 3. The Report is often evasive and muddled. Its fundamental weakness is its failure to give due weight to the significance of fertilization (p. 6).
> 4. The Report often caricatures or ignores the pro-life case (pp. 7 and 14).
> 5. On the crucial issue of the moral status of the human embryo the Report abandons 'moral reasoning' and resorts to mere assertion – and 'the more generally held opinion'. Apparently the embryo is a 'sort of' human being, to be accorded some protection in law, but the Report is very obscure at this point (p. 9).
> 6. The majority recommendation that human embryos should be kept alive up to 14 days seems to rest on the alleged fact that the 'primitive streak' [misunderstood here] occurs then, and that this is the latest stage at which twinning can occur (pp. 11–14). But the 'twinning' argument is false. Reference to the time of implantation in the womb confuses the issue further (p. 14).
> 7. In fact, the Report shows scant regard for the dignity and right to life of the human being in the embryonic stage. It would permit sale and purchase, freezing and experimentation on embryos (as well as sale and storage of gametes). It shows only passing concern for the children 'produced' by IVF (pp. 17–18).
> 8. Warnock was at most times guided by considerations of utility and cost-effectiveness rather than moral principle. Despite its rejection of the commercialization of surrogate motherhood and its proposal for a licensing authority to oversee IVF practices, it opens the door to wholesale manipulation of human life *in vitro* and further debasement of human sexuality (pp. 18–19).

Warnock has also been accused, among other things, of arriving at utilitarian judgements; but it is precisely this type of judgement that determines the great majority of our social laws. In this case the benefits of the treatment of infertility and the advancement of medical science more generally are regarded as outweighing any measurable harm implicit in the practice. This view can, of course, be countered by an intuitive morality that to treat human life – any human life – in that way is intrinsically wrong.

Another example of the Committee's allegedly muddled thinking on the moral issues is its use of the concept 'human' in trying to draw the line between very young beings who might in certain circumstances be killed or allowed to die and those who have a right to life, to whom this should not happen. Such distinctions, according to the Report, would require the fetus or embryo to be 'plainly human' (in this context meaning that it is able to experience pain and to perceive its environment) and a 'full human being' without further defining what is meant by this. Although it is declared that 'human' is a biological term, this cannot in itself, without some additional moral criterion, provide the basis for the 'supremely important' moral principle that was sought. If the principle is simply pro-human in a biological sense, this means all human beings are of equal moral importance, but Warnock rejects this. Nor, morally speaking, is there anything specifically human about feeling pain and perceiving the environment. If, however, the capacity for sentience and perception are to be used as the moral cut-off points in the development of the human embryo, this is no longer relying on specifically human attributes, as claimed, nor is any moral justification offered for rejecting the same moral cut-off points in relation to other animal species.

For all this, what seems to have captured the public imagination – perhaps fanned by a certain type of journalism – is the surrogacy question. One criticism of the Warnock Report approach to this is that the Committee is against selling one human being for the benefit of another (commercial surrogacy), yet the whole Report attempts to establish guidelines for using 'children' as treatment for other people's problems. Although infertility is a great sadness and burden, it could in one sense be said to be made worse by aborting those children who would otherwise have been available for adoption. Against this would be the chance of overcoming the infertility and having their own children.

The whole surrogacy issue was made more urgent in early 1985 by the 'Baby Cotton affair'. An American father provided sperm for the (paid) English surrogate mother. In the end the baby was made a ward of court, and care and control were granted to the natural father and his wife as long as they were able to take the baby back to America. However, this 'happy ending' required a complex series of moves involving the parents, the courts and the local authority. It began with Barnet social services department applying to a local magistrate for a 'place of safety' order, a move almost unanimously criticized in legal circles. Before the order could be reviewed by a juvenile court (the options were that the baby could become a ward of court or be taken into care), the natural father successfully applied for the baby to be made a ward of court. This took the matter out of the hands of the local magistrates, as it was then a matter for a High Court judge to deal with.

Mr Justice Latey decided that the key issue was the baby's interests and that these could best be served by handing her over to the commissioning parents, but this does not answer the general criticism of the law, as set out in the Children and Young Persons Act 1969, that place of safety orders were being abused. There is also the question of adoption. Section 50 of the Adoption Act 1953 makes it an offence to pay for an adopted child or for an adoption to be arranged. In this case the natural father paid about £13,000 in fees to the surrogacy agency. Were he to attempt to adopt the child, he would be liable to prosecution in the United Kingdom for this offence. This also places the baby in a legal limbo. Because the natural father and Mrs Kim Cotton, the surrogate mother, are not married, the child is illegitimate, and as the only way to legitimacy is through adoption, the problem becomes an insolubly circular one. The American-run surrogacy agency may also be in trouble, both because Mrs Cotton has apparently agreed to sell her story to the press for £20,000 and because it has paid her fee of £6,500, as criminal charges could be brought against her. There are the (legal) possibilities of avoiding both the Adoption Act and the common-law offence of 'baby-selling'. 'Rent-a-Womb' schemes will need to be made illegal, and, indeed, this is what Warnock has recommended.

The Government's answer to all this was a promise of comprehensive legislation based on the Warnock Committee's recommendations, but as this would need very careful drafting and further consultations, it would take about a year before it could be laid before Parliament. In the meantime three things have happened: the introduction of legislation to ban commercial surrogacy, the setting up of a voluntary body to advise on embryo research and an attempt to pre-empt further legislation by a Private Member's Bill.

On 16 July 1985, the Surrogacy Arrangements Act received the Royal Assent and came into force immediately, extending to the whole of the United Kingdom. The Act prohibits commercial surrogacy agencies from recruiting potential surrogate mothers, negotiating surrogacy agreements or advertising. The Act has four sections. Section 1 defines the terms employed in the Act and specifies the exact constituents of a surrogacy arrangement. Section 2 gives a list of commercial activities relating to surrogacy which are prohibited. Surrogate mothers and commissioning parents are exempt from prosecution. Section 3 makes it an offence to publish advertisements of or for surrogacy services. Section 4 outlines the penalties.

In order to allay fears about research on 'spare' embryos, the Royal College of Obstetricians and Gynaecologists, with the Medical Research Council, has organized a Voluntary Licensing Authority for doctors and scientists engaged in this work. It will be chaired by Dame Mary Donaldson, and its membership will comprise four nominees each from the Council and the College, along with four non-medical representatives.

The Private Member's Bill was introduced by Enoch Powell as the Unborn Child (Protection) Bill. The precepts underlying the Bill were that human beings were never to be treated by one another instrumentally; that life was to be respected and protected for its own sake; and that life began at conception, from which point it developed, in continuity, to maturity and beyond. From all this it followed that the manipulation of human embryos was licit only if directed to the continued life and true development of that embryo. The Bill 'prevents a human embryo being created, kept or used for any purpose other than enabling a child to be born by a particular woman. It would be an offence to fertilize a human embryo *in vitro* or possess one so fertilized without leave of the Secretary of State, who would give his permission only for this specific purpose.'

On 15 February 1985, on a free vote in the House of Commons, the Bill was passed by a majority of 172 in favour of a second reading. (The actual division was 238 to 66 in favour.) The free vote split not only the Cabinet but also party, Ministry and even family. However, the Bill was talked out at a later stage, and then it seemed unlikely it would ever again see the light of day. Much to everybody's surprise, a rarely used loophole was found in the procedures for introducing Private Member's Bills which would have enabled the Powell Bill to be resurrected. While this still remained a possibility, a further flood of rhetoric was released. In the end the parliamentary ploy failed, and on 7 June 1985, by means of further procedural manoeuvres, the Bill was finally lost.

There remain, however, certain grey areas which need further clarification, and I propose to devote the rest of the chapter to discussing two of them, namely, postcoital contraception and menstrual regulation.

Postcoital contraception

This method of contraception is sometimes referred to as 'the after-sex pill' or the 'morning-after pill', but effective postcoital techniques can also include the fitting of an intra-uterine contraceptive device (IUD). These techniques are now being made better known, and more readily available, as emergency methods after unprotected sexual intercourse.

A conference on the subject was held in London in 1982 and the proceedings subsequently published in 1983 by the Pregnancy Advisory Service.[14] It was this that sparked off another round of correspondence in *The Times*, raising again some of the fundamental issues already discussed.

The main questions posed were: How do these techniques work? When or how should they be offered? And are they legal (abortion or contraception?)? As a mark of their ambiguity they have sometimes been referred to as 'interception', as, strictly speaking, they are not forms of contraception – the prevention of fertilization – but stop the (possibly) already fertilized ovum from implanting in the uterine wall. It has been argued by some that the effective beginning of life is not fertilization at all but implantation, and that before that point there is no 'carriage' and therefore no miscarriage (abortion). Others argue for the uniqueness of the potential being which comes into existence at fertilization.

What is now known about the techniques of postcoital contraception, and what are the hazards involved? There are three main methods of postcoital contraception, two of which are currently in use and available only as emergency methods within strictly prescribed time limits and carried out under medical supervision. The one not at present available uses prostaglandins – naturally occurring chemical compounds – some of which can be synthesized, or substances very similar. They are partly responsible for initiating uterine contractions, and it is possible that at some future date a similar compound might be available either as a pill or as a vaginal pessary.

The method most favoured, using the postcoital pill (strictly, pill*s*), is the one originally introduced by the Canadian gynaecologist Yuzpe in 1977. The pills must be taken within 72 hours of intercourse: two tablets of Ovran,

Eugynon 50 or PC4 straightaway and two tablets 12 hours later. These are the trade names of combined oral contraceptive pills which contain the right proportions of the two hormone types oestrogen and progestogen. To minimize nausea and vomiting the pills are best taken after meals and without alcohol. This is not a 'do-it-yourself' technique, as even with low-dosage oestrogens there are possible risks and complications which only a doctor can advise about.

The possible side-effects and complications are nausea (60 per cent), vomiting (24 per cent), breast tenderness, headache, withdrawal bleeding and dizziness. There may be individual medical reasons why oestrogens should not be taken. The failure rate is about 1 per cent, and if a pregnancy does supervene, there is about a 10 per cent chance that it will be an ectopic one.

What about the possibility of fetal abnormality? A World Health Organization survey carried out in 1981 showed that ordinary doses of progestogens and oestrogens given in early pregnancy do not lead to malformed fetuses, but that this can happen if they are given in high, continuous dosage in the later stages of pregnancy. In any case it must be remembered that about 2 per cent of all pregnancies end in some abnormality in the baby.

The period is not 'brought on' by the treatment, but it may be earlier than usual, so that a further pregnancy is still possible. It is advisable then, if further acts of intercourse are to take place, to use other contraceptive measures until the onset of the next period. All those receiving postcoital pills should be seen again in three weeks for further counselling and a check-up.

How do the pills work? It is not known for sure, but probably in three different ways. First, they produce changes in the lining wall of the uterus, which is then made inhospitable for implantation. Secondly, they suppress the function of an important part of the ovary (corpus luteum). Thirdly, they interfere with ovulation, as sometimes the hormone peaks in the bloodstream at mid-cycle are abolished or delayed.

The second available method of postcoital contraception is by fitting an IUD within five days of sexual intercourse. This is the preferred method when the woman presents later than 72 hours after intercourse, when the pill is contra-indicated, following unprotected intercourse on more than one occasion during the cycle in question (multiple exposure), or when the IUD is the preferred method anyway for longer-term protection. The failure rate is very low – in one series no pregnancies in 700 insertions – although pregnancies have occurred with an IUD still *in situ* and have gone to term normally.

An IUD works by preventing implantation but can also be effective after implantation which would be equivalent to an early abortion. Side-effects and complications can involve difficulties over fitting the device; this is sometimes painful in a woman who has never borne any children. Occasionally a faint is induced on insertion and very rarely the heart may be affected (cardiac arrest). There is a risk of introducing infection or causing a flare-up or spread of infection acquired at the time of intercourse. Future fertility may be impaired, especially when inflammatory disease is present or, perhaps, an existing early pregnancy. It is best avoided in those who have never had a child.

The legal uncertainties over postcoital interception have now been clarified. In May 1983 (as reported in *The Times*) the Attorney-General, in a written parliamentary reply, ruled that using the 'morning-after' contraceptive pill was not a criminal offence and that no further action would be taken in the four cases referred to the Director of Public Prosecutions (DPP), two of them by the anti-abortion organization Life. The Department of Health and Social Security (DHSS) had already issued informal guidelines to all doctors on the subject, and it is understood that it is now updating and revising its 'Handbook of Contraceptive Practice' (1984) to take account of this new ruling.

From the legal point of view the sole issue was whether preventing implantation of the fertilized ovum constituted procuring a miscarriage within the meaning of the Offences Against the Person Act of 1861. (A more detailed account of the 1861 Act will be found in chapter 3.) Interpreting statutes required that the words used should be given the meaning they bore at the time the Acts were passed, and since the words were in a general statute, they were presumed to be used in their popular, ordinary or natural sense. The Attorney-General stated: 'It is clear that, used in its ordinary sense, the word "miscarriage" is not apt to describe a failure to implant, whether spontaneous or not. Likewise the phrase "procure a miscarriage" cannot be construed to include the prevention of implantation.' Whatever the state of medical knowledge in the nineteenth century, the ordinary use of the word 'miscarriage' referred to interference at a later stage of pre-natal development than implantation.

Even though the legal situation is now much clearer, there still remains a number of medical, legal and ethical problems concerning the use of postcoital contraception. The actual timing of implantation is variable, and there is no on-the-spot test that I know of that gives an objective and precise measure of this. Theoretically it could be as long as two weeks, but it is usually reckoned that if implantation is going to occur, it will take place between five and eight days after ovulation – an average three days for transport of the fertilized ovum down the Fallopian tube into the uterus and then two days in the uterus before final implantation in the uterine wall. Ovulation can be detected and various stages in the menstrual cycle can be identified both by hormonal changes and by changes in the composition and the appearance of the vaginal mucus, but a woman may refuse examination. Therefore much depends on her medical history, what she says about when she has had intercourse and how often and so on, this information, of course, being open to falsification.

There is the problem that a woman may be untruthful, may visit different centres on many occasions and may come to rely on instant postcoital contraception as a long-term and repeated back-up instead of using it as an occasional emergency procedure only. Little is known about the long-term effects of using the pill in this way. Strictly speaking, the use of high doses of contraceptive pills for this purpose is not specifically licensed under the Medicines Act, although the pills are licensed for general contraceptive purposes. (Following the favourable legal ruling, the matter was referred to the Committee on Safety of Medicines so that it could give an authoritative medical view on the risks and benefits involved.)

Another question is how often, or in what circumstances, these pills should be presented to a woman who wants them 'just in case' – for instance, on holiday, when she might be raped or assaulted or have a failure with her usual contraceptive method and not be able to get postcoital contraception in time. How far should it be regarded as a woman's right to be able to carry them around in her handbag to take when she sees fit? There are also the women who, for various reasons, do not have a regular sex life, so do not need constant contraceptive protection. There is, finally, the prospect of unscrupulous operators in the private sector who would, in fact, be producing early abortions but who might claim that they thought implantation had not yet occurred.

Two remaining legal points are discussed by Ian Kennedy in the PAS publication already mentioned.[15] Is there any question of legal liability on the part of the individual doctor or the agency if postcoital birth control is used but is not effective? And if it proves not to have worked, what risk is there of fetal damage? Would this impose any legal liability if it occurred? Kennedy stresses the need for informing the woman fully that no method is foolproof and that she needs to arrange a follow-up appointment for a check-up. If at that check-up she is found to be pregnant, he suggests that it would be both lawful (under the Abortion Act) and appropriate to offer an abortion. If she decides against this and wants to continue the pregnancy, then it would be the duty of the doctor and the agency to ensure that she receives all appropriate care during her pregnancy, including counselling and further advice about the possibility of fetal damage.

Menstrual therapies

This leads on to a consideration of another 'borderline' procedure, which does not seem to have been covered by the Attorney-General's ruling. The borderline or ambiguous status of this procedure is well exemplified by the number of different names it goes by. The *Lancet*[16] refers to 'menstrual therapies', but other names are 'menstrual regulation, induction, extraction or aspiration', 'mini-abortion' or 'mini-suction'. They all refer to the same thing, namely, evacuation of the uterine contents within 14 days of a missed period, before pregnancy can reliably be diagnosed. At the time this procedure was introduced there was no reliable pregnancy test before the twelfth day after a delayed period (the fortieth day of amenorrhoea). However, newer tests can now be used to diagnose pregnancy reliably as early as 10 to 14 days after conception, that is, before the first day of an expected period.

The procedure can look like an ordinary, minor operation, such as the routine dilatation and curettage (D and C) used to 'investigate' possible causes of a missed period (amenorrhoea) before it is certain whether or not a woman is pregnant. This gives two possible ways round the moral and legal prohibitions in countries with strict anti-abortion laws and no freely available contraceptive advice: first, by arguing that pregnancy really begins only after implantation and, secondly, by invoking the idea of 'intent' – can an abortion be performed on a non-pregnant woman or at least when it is impossible to prove pregnancy? If clear proof of pregnancy is needed first, then no offence is committed, this being the view adopted in some parts of Latin America. In northern Nigeria, Pakistan and India there are laws dating back to 1860 which state that a woman cannot be prosecuted for aborting herself unless pregnancy is proved, but in some legal systems if the intention is to procure an abortion (and that in itself is illegal), it does not matter whether the woman is pregnant or not.

The method usually used for menstrual regulation now is vacuum aspiration, which is safe and effective and does not usually require dilatation of the cervix or a general anaesthetic. Medical methods using prostaglandins or similar substances may eventually become the preferred method.

The legality of menstrual regulation has never been tested in the courts, but the Lane Committee[17] did recommend in 1974 that it should be incorporated into the 1967 Abortion Act; this was not implemented. In our legal system a defendant is presumed innocent unless the prosecution can prove all the elements of a crime, namely, the wrongful act (*actus reus*) and the wrongful intention (*mens rea*) beyond reasonable doubt. When menstrual regulation is undertaken before pregnancy can be proven to this degree of certainty, no prosecution can realistically be brought for unlawful abortion. It is very doubtful if a charge of attempted abortion would stick either.

However, some official legal guidance was given by the law officers of the Crown in March 1979. It was their opinion that menstrual regulation was legal when used within the terms of the 1967 Abortion Act and that 'termination of pregnancy', as used in the Act, means steps taken that are 'intended to terminate a pregnancy which two practitioners in good faith believe to exist'. This opinion was given in a letter from the then DPP, Sir Thomas Hetherington, to Mrs Renée Short, MP, on 13 March 1979.

Further research

One of the 'spin-offs' from human embryo research has been a greater understanding of the physiology of early pregnancy. This in turn has led to earlier and more reliable methods of diagnosing pregnancy; in more accurate timing of ovulation and implantation and finally in the development of new ways either to prevent conception or produce a very early abortion.

As soon as the fertilized embryo implants in the uterine wall the tissue immediately surrounding it (trophoblast) secretes a hormone called human chorionic gonadotropin (HCG). It also produces, in increasing quantities, another hormone, progesterone.

HCG is excreted in the urine and forms the basis for the early detection of pregnancy which has now been further improved by the use of monoclonal antibodies. These antibodies behave like chemical detectives in that they can recognize and bind to HCG. The technical details are very complicated but the whole thing can be put together in a home test kit for the rapid detection of early pregnancy. Using similar principles, tests are also becoming available which can give a woman 24 to 36 hours' warning of impending ovulation which can then be used as a more accurate aid in 'natural' birth control by identifying the 'safe period'.

However, the detection of HCG does not absolutely guarantee that a live pregnancy is forthcoming as certain tumours and moles can also produce it. The best known of these is a hydatidiform mole.

Another area of progress has been in developing agents which counteract the progesterone produced, this being an essential hormone for the development of the embryo. This, in turn, could eventually lead to a 'do it yourself' pill which would, in effect, produce an early abortion. One such anti-progesterone pill, code named RU 486, is already undergoing clinical trials in Scotland, America and elsewhere.[18] It might be used as a once a month contraceptive pill when a woman would not know whether or not she was pregnant. Clearly these new developments will raise fresh legal and moral dilemmas.

Because interrupting embryonic development at this stage is such a novel procedure, it has been suggested that a new name is required to describe it, namely 'contragestion'. In an effort to clarify terminology the following outline scheme has been suggested:[19]

Contraception – before the gametes fuse.
Postcoital procedures – between fertilization and implantation (6th – 13th day after fertilization).
Contragestional agents – from implantation to the time organs are formed (organogenesis or up to 6 weeks after fertilization).
Abortion – up to 12 weeks after fertilization.
Late abortion – after 12 weeks.

2

Values, Morals and Religion

Many of the arguments surrounding abortion are not about facts – often in short supply – but about values, opinions, attitudes and beliefs. However, such 'facts' as there are can be slanted, disputed or presented in an emotive way to promote a particular cause. Francome[1] outlines four main disputes about facts: (1) the effects of abortion on attitudes to life, (2) the effect of legislation on 'back-street' abortions, (3) the medical effects of abortion, (4) public opinion on abortion.

Even the doctor who may think he is making a detached clinical judgement about the 'facts' in his very decision-making becomes involved, either explicitly or implicitly, with value judgements. Trying to duck the issue by saying it is the patient's beliefs, attitudes and values which are of paramount importance does not entirely work either because the doctor can accept or give more weight to some and not to others. In clinical terms 'therapeutic indications' for termination imply a series of steps. There exist at least two possible actions, one of which is given preference in terms of motivation, which is explicitly stated and which is deemed to be valid and legitimate in terms of some value system whose order of priorities

is revealed by one's choice. ('Value' here means a hierarchy of choices.) Callahan[2] puts it this way:

> The problem is most fundamentally a moral problem; what one makes of questions and answers concerning abortion 'indications' will be a reflection of a moral stance, whether recognized or not. The laws that one thinks good or bad, wise or unwise, progressive or retrogressive, will be a function of what one thinks important or unimportant for society. In all its vagueness and the disagreements it engenders, the principle of the sanctity of life is still serviceable in trying to develop some moral concepts and attitudes about abortion . . . Abortion decisions need to be made in the light of moral policies and a 'moral policy' is best conceived of as the decision to move in one possible general direction rather than another . . . A policy points a way . . . but does not lay out a moral blueprint, with every eventuality determined in advance . . . Abortion does not seem the kind of moral issue which is just 'solved' once and for all; it can only be coped with . . .

Moral philosophy

The original function of philosophy was to clarify concepts and critically evaluate assumptions and arguments. Plato (in the *Republic*, 352D) described moral philosophy as enquiring 'how we ought to live', but we must question certain older views that there are basic moral principles that are absolute and objectively valid for all time and all peoples. For example, 'It is always wrong to take another's life.' This may well be modified in wartime (e.g. the 'Just War'), for capital punishment or in dealing with terrorists. Some tribes approve of killing old and weak members: the Spartans exposed sickly infants to death on the mountainside, and it has been alleged recently that in parts of modern China the killing of substantial numbers of female babies was allowed as part of a population policy.

Arguments continue to this day about the merits of one or other school of absolutism or relativism. The absolutist position is that certain laws governing the conduct of individuals or societies are permanent, objective, universal and divine; for all men, in all places at all times. And that certain acts are wrong regardless of any good that may come of them. On the other hand, relativists hold that all consequences of an act should be taken into account in assessing its rightness. Laws can be derived from other sources or can be rejected, with particular cases being decided on their particular merits.

The classic case, already mentioned and much to the fore in the abortion debate, is the absolutist doctrine that taking human life is always wrong. Yet even some 'absolutists' will still make exceptions, for example, to defend yourself or your country, capital punishment for murder and so on.

The dangers of absolutism are that it can breed fanaticism and bolster dictatorships, and is immediately divisive. How many murders have been committed in the name of 'faith' with the certainty that God is on your side? Absolutists know they are right and superior, and that their victims are wrong, inferior and alien. Even though morals and ideologies can get confused there can still be some terrible 'means' allowed to justify certain 'ends'. Belief in an order of values higher than the individual can sometimes lead to the view that tolerance, appreciation of circumstances, relativity and concern for others, is more important and more difficult to attain than the comforts of moral certainty.

On the other hand, purposeless relativism can also be dangerous and can lead to such things as the devaluation of life with further disastrous consequences. However, relativists do not necessarily deny any permanent moral principles or a natural law valid irrespective of human provisions. Nor is it incompatible with the view that each person has rights that are not to be over-ruled for the benefit of society as a whole. War could be justified by relativists if it prevented more evil than it caused; the war against Hitler would not be a 'just war' according to the absolutists as it was undertaken not merely to defend life itself.

Just as the law distinguishes between motive and intention, so do moral philosophers. There are three main branches of moral philosophy.[3] The first is concerned with logical issues, essentially problems posed by moral concepts and judgements, such as the terms 'objective' and 'absolute' or 'subjective' and 'relative'. The second is concerned with criteria, standards of moral judgements, such as what makes a good thing good. The third is concerned with the consistency of moral thinking with other bodies of thought, as, for instance, possible conflicts between natural science and theology.

The editor of the *Journal of Medical Ethics*, Raanan Gillon, wrote a series of useful summary articles for the *British Medical Journal* (May–June 1985) in which he mentioned four basic moral propositions which have been used to decide between the moral worth of different sorts of being, e.g. embryo, child, person.

(1) The Benthamite position, so called after Jeremy Bentham (1748–1832), the English writer on jurisprudence and utilitarian ethics. He argued that sentience – the ability to experience pain and pleasure – was the fundamental moral criterion and that all others were ultimately reducible to it, so that suffering rather than reasoning was the important distinction. If, then, all sentient beings are morally equivalent, whether or not to kill them depends entirely on calculations of the pleasure and pain of all those potentially affected.

(2) Arguments over 'speciesism' – for example, to help differentiate animals (one species) from humans (another species) because, after all, most animals can also be shown to be sentient. The question is: Does being a member of the species *Homo sapiens* confer a unique moral importance, so that all (living and innocent) human beings have the moral right not to be killed and not to be denied appropriate help when in life-threatening situations? One religious answer to this is to say that only humans possess a soul and that this in itself confers uniqueness. Others differentiate

humans by reason of their having various capacities such as self-awareness, language, complex forms of communication, to name just a few.

(3) The concept of 'viability' and the view that all viable innocent human beings have a right to life. There are many difficulties, both legal and medical, with the definition of viability, even though it is operationally defined and used in British abortion legislation. One weakness of the concept of viability is that it depends so much on technology, at least when used in the sense of a fetus being viable when it is capable of living an existence independent from that of its mother. In theory any human embryo, at any stage of development, is viable with appropriate technology.

(4) Granted that sentience is morally important, there may still be a special sub-class within the group of sentient beings which is morally more important than others in the sense of having priority where the right to life is concerned. One such sub-class, much discussed by philosophers, is 'personhood' or being a human person.

Immanuel Kant (1724–1804), the German philosopher of the 'idealist' school, maintained that it was rational, willing agents who provided the criteria for moral obligations. Such rational willing agents he called persons. On the other hand John Locke (1632–1704), the English physician-philosopher and the principal founder of philosophical liberalism and (with Bacon) English empiricism, had a different view. He considered the ability to think, combined with self-awareness over time, to be the essence of personhood, although it was Descartes who devised the famous aphorism 'Cogito, ergo sum' ('I think, therefore I am').

However, adopting any of these positions leads to difficulties because some human beings (e.g. very young infants, brain-damaged adults) would not qualify for inclusion, thus making personhood a discontinuous concept as well as playing havoc with the closely related idea of personal identity. Three broad approaches have been advocated to overcome these problems.

First, there is dualism, perpetuated in medicine by the use of the term 'psychosomatic'. It is postulated that both bodies (organic substances) and minds (spiritual or some non-material substances) coexist and are in some way interrelated. Dualism is often referred to as Cartesian, after René Descartes (1596–1650), the French philosopher and mathematician known as 'the father of modern philosophy'. The important point here is that mind and body are made of different substances that are ontologically (by the nature of their existence) distinct.

A second way of dealing with the dilemma is to use some variant of identity theory whereby persons are identified by either their bodies or some other part of them, usually their brains.

The third approach is to deny personhood as the intrinsic property of any human being and to see it instead as a social construct, that is, an attribute socially conferred on some, but not all, human beings by other human beings.

All these approaches have been applied to sexual problems in general[4] as well as to the abortion debate,[5] with the most favoured 'model' being some form of utilitarianism. Utilitarianism generally states that an act is good so far as it leads to the greatest good of the greatest number of people. It is sometimes divided into classical or hedonistic utilitarianism, the latter having pleasure (happiness) alone as the 'good' end or ideal, the former admitting, in addition to happiness, ends such as virtue, knowledge, love and beauty as 'good'. Both are utilitarian in the sense that both claim that an act is right only by virtue of its utility, its usefulness for producing results that are good in themselves.[6]

In essence, when considering the greatest good of the greatest number, in the abortion issue the rights of certain groups have to be considered – the mothers, the fetuses and the community. In order both to highlight and to be more specific about related problems, a brief summary of these is given below under five headings. Many of the issues mentioned will be discussed in more detail later.

(1) The mother and associated issues such as women's rights and autonomy, abortion on demand or only under special conditions (e.g. health, rape).
(2) The fetus and such issues as the sanctity of life, when life begins, what constitutes a human person, the right to be born wanted, loved and healthy, the quality of life and so on.
(3) The family and possible effects on, or the rights of, the putative father, husband, grandparents or in-laws and other children, and legal problems over property ownership and inheritance.
(4) Society, population policy, economic and social factors; possible 'brutalization' and abortion equated with murder, which could then lead to infanticide and euthanasia; political and legal aspects; the conscientious objection or religious views of minority groups.
(5) Doctors and nurses involved in abortion; the divisive issue of whether to opt out or not; effects on recruitment, staff morale and other patients; the burden on resources, especially the National Health Service.

One of the ways moral philosophers have helped to clarify decisions about abortion is by trying to abstract the central issues and to express them as questions that are answerable. (For instance, one popular question, 'When does human life begin?', does not make for a fruitful debate; neither do arguments over the definition of a person. If, as already noted, this implies a developed capacity for reasoning, willing, desiring and relating to others, it cannot apply to any stage of embryonic or fetal development.) The central issue, according to Sumner,[7] is not even whether fetuses are human but whether all human beings, including fetuses, have the same moral status. In other words, species membership or, indeed, belonging to a particular race or sex, is not a morally relevant characteristic. There must be some other morally relevant characteristic that makes it wrong to take human life.

Sumner adopts a modified utilitarian stance, somewhere between the extreme conservative and liberal views. Previously Tooley[8] had suggested that the key characteristic was self-consciousness, the ability to appreciate that one is a living being with a possible future. In his opinion, only a being with this ability has a serious right to life. However, this seems to me to be a very sophisticated ability, which may not develop until late childhood, so it immediately blurs the distinction between abortion and infanticide. Every liberal view must meet the conservative challenge to point to a morally significant difference between an eight-month-old fetus and a newborn baby. In a later book[9] Tooley gives an extensive and closely argued account of all the traditional moral arguments.

This work is extended by Sumner but without accepting infanticide. His criterion is sentience, or the capacity for feeling, so that, in his view, to count morally a being must at least be capable of experiencing pain or pleasure. Rather more speculatively, this also includes animals who possess a central nervous system akin to ours.

He agrees with the liberals that an early abortion, before the fetus becomes sentient (and, in his view, has moral standing), is permissible and is on a par with contraception. The fetus is presumed to become sentient some time in the second trimester of pregnancy, at around 14 weeks. Thus early abortion prevents the emergence of a new being with moral standing but does no wrong to any existing being with a right to life.

A late abortion must be judged differently. It does violate the rights of a being with moral standing, but this does not mean it is always wrong. The fact that the fetus is still totally dependent on its mother's body makes abortion easier to justify than infanticide, but it still needs a serious reason such as a threat to maternal health (mental or physical) to justify it. A case-by-case approach is recommended.

While this seems to me to be a sensible compromise, there are some criticisms which can be made, notably the problem of the precise determination and measurement of sentience and the question of whether sentience would be so important if abortion procedures could be shown to be painless. So are Sumner's arguments more concerned with *methods* of abortion? And if some method were devised which did not cause pain to the fetus, would his arguments still stand? (As, in fact, practically all abortion operations are carried out under a general anaesthetic, the fetus does not in any case feel any pain.) There is also the 'academic' problem of the equation of contraception with early abortion, as any utilitarian should advocate the production of as many beings as possible as long as they can be happy without detracting more from the happiness of others than the total sum of their own happiness.

There are a further two general points which might be made against a wholesale acceptance of a relativist utilitarian approach. First, preoccupation with the benefits to the majority might eclipse minority rights. Secondly, there is the 'slippery slope' situation – the fear that things could go too far (for example, agreeing on a 14-day limit for embryo research but later extending this further for other 'good reasons').

Organized religions

As our legal system is based on, and derived from, not only certain ethical principles, often of a social utilitarian kind, but also on the Judaeo-Christian tradition, some understanding of the latter is helpful. As we now live in a pluralistic society, some knowledge, too, of non-Christian religious attitudes is essential. This can also be very relevant in assessing both a woman's likely emotional reaction to abortion and the attitude of her family and immediate subculture.

The International Inventory of Information on Induced Abortion[10] summarized the position:

> While popular opinion suggests that there exists a clear-cut opposition to abortion on the part of some religious bodies and a categorical support by others, it appears, in fact, that representatives of a variety of positions can be found in each of the major religions and that the historical picture is also varied: that is, some religious bodies have changed . . . their position over the centuries or in recent years, rather than maintaining a single unbroken history of opposition or support. It is undoubtedly misleading to present 'positions' on abortion in isolation . . . that is, apart from related cultural values.

Many people make their moral judgements on religious grounds, but this deduction can be shown to be fallacious. The argument is not that they are mistaken in their religious beliefs but that no moral judgement can be founded on authority. Bertrand Russell put it succinctly when he wrote: 'Theologians have always taught that God's decrees are good and that this is not a mere tautology: it follows that goodness is logically independent of God's decrees.'

In a more detailed critique of theological arguments about abortion Sumner[11] shows the need to fulfil three main requirements: they must be grounded in orthodox canons of inductive and deductive logic; personal feelings or sentiments cannot themselves count as reasons in favour of a moral view of abortion; and any facts marshalled in favour of a particular view must be publicly accessible, so they must be subject to some form of empirical verification. He further argues that unless some form of natural theology is correct, religious beliefs cannot count as reasons in favour of a moral view of abortion, but if a natural theology *is* correct, then religion is part of science and its claims are empirically testable, otherwise its claims are supernatural, beyond confirmation or refutation. Such claims cannot be impersonal reasons, since it is not irrational or unreasonable to deny them. If reasons are to be impersonal, then what is a reason for the believer must also be a reason for the unbeliever. Religious commitments may serve as reasons for 'tastes' but not as reasons for moral values.

Early Christianity

In spite of this, Christian viewpoints (there is no single coherent Christian position but many differing sectarian ones) are still powerful influences.[12] In essence, the 'traditional' Christian stance against all forms of abortion seems to have been founded on a confusion over purification rites after childbirth (Leviticus), a mistranslation and misunderstanding of Exodus, which was then further modified by the Hellenistic schools of thought and other philosophical traditions.

The Book of Exodus, alone in the Bible, deals with abortion but then only in the context of compensation for injury to the mother: that is, punishing a man who injures a pregnant woman and not the fetus. Exodus 2: 22–4, in the New English Bible translation, reads: 'When, in the occurrence of a brawl, a man knocks against a pregnant woman so that she has a miscarriage but suffers no further hurt, then the offender must pay whatever the woman's husband demands after assessment. Whenever hurt is done, you shall give life for life, eye for eye . . .' The implication is that if no harm comes to the woman and if the *husband* is not aggrieved – no mention is made of the woman herself (she being his property?) – then no punishment is called for.

One important debating point among the early Church fathers was the question of when the fetus acquired a soul. There were three main traditions to define this stage. Traducianism promulgated the doctrine that the human soul was transmitted by the parents to the children. For some this was restricted to the physical act of generation; others refrained from being dogmatic on this point, and this version of traducianism was collectively styled 'generationism'. Traducianism was advocated by Tertullian (*c.* 160–*c.* 220) in order to explain original sin, and also by St Augustine (354–430), although he understood it as a spiritual generation. The third doctrine was creationism: this taught that God created *de nihilo* a fresh soul for each individual at his or her conception or birth. This was opposed to traducianism as well as to any doctrine of the soul's pre-existence. Creationism was upheld by St Jerome. (It is not clear how identical twins or quadruplets acquired their souls.)

It was at one time further disputed whether male and female fetuses received their souls at the same time. For over 600 years it was believed that males received theirs on the fortieth day after conception but females had to wait for 80 days! This maintained the already well established tradition of male domination and superiority, coupled with a general misogyny in early Christianity. Later (1869) 40 days was adopted for both sexes.

This curious anomaly seems to have been derived from Leviticus 12: 2, 4 and 5:

> When a woman conceives and bears a male child, she shall be unclean for seven days, as in the period of impurity through menstruation . . . The woman shall wait for thirty-three days because her blood requires purification: she shall touch nothing that is holy, and shall not enter the sanctuary till her days of purification are completed. If she bears a female child, she shall be unclean for fourteen days as for menstruation and shall wait for sixty-six days because her blood requires purification.

Tertullian, the African Church Father, made erroneous deductions because he knew no Hebrew and blindly followed an inaccurate translation of the Septuagint. He perpetuated the distinction between an 'animate' and an 'inanimate' fetus instead of, as in the Book of Exodus, between the injured and unharmed mother. He declared that the seed itself contained the future life. He also used much ingenuity in ascertaining when the fetus actually became 'animate' (i.e. literally 'alive' but, in this context, signifying the point at which it acquired a soul), finally promulgating 40 and 80 days respectively. His strong condemnation of abortion is contained in his *Apologeticus* (9), written some time in the third century: 'Prevention of birth is a precipitation of murder; nor does it matter whether one takes the life when formed or drives it away while forming. He also is a man who is about to be one.' He had an evangelical need to preserve the faith and encourage believers to multiply. His views eventually gave credence to the idea that the Bible held abortion to be a crime.

One modern commentator[13] makes the rather acerbic observation: 'Though the error has long since been exposed, the Church still maintains this position, and it has become incorporated in the law of the State, which beautifully demonstrates that moral laws are not really derived from biblical authority, but that biblical authority is sought to justify regulations which, because of unconscious prejudices, seem "natural" and "right".'

So the deduction must be that the early Christians accepted an interpretation of the old Mosaic law as forbidding abortion.

There seems to have been little discussion of this issue among succeeding generations, when the Christian doctrine was being spread throughout the Greco-Roman world. Even St Paul refrained from preaching on the subject. It was only much later, and in quite different circumstances, that St Augustine revived the Old Jewish ban on abortion and condemned all forms of contraception.

St Augustine, who had a pagan father and a Christian mother, built up the doctrines of Hell and original sin. The latter could be countered by baptism, with the implication that the souls of the unbaptized were lost. St Thomas of Aquinas (*c.* 1225–74), the Dominican philosopher and theologian, introduced the principle that life is related to movement and therefore life starts not at conception but at the moment of quickening. He also suggested the possibility of salvation for infants dying before birth.

It seems that over a long period of time two aspects of the issue had become confused, the moral-religious and the social-political, with contrary ideologies eventually causing dissension and division. For example, the Children of Israel had been commanded to multiply, and in Christ's day the strictly orthodox Jews had obeyed, even when an increasing population became a burden.

The Greeks also had limited territory and were afraid both of overpopulation and of being burdened with handicapped children. It was to Pythagoras (sixth century BC), the greek philosopher and mathematician, that the doctrine of the transmigration of souls was attributed. Plato (427–347 BC), in his *Republic* (V, 460), commended the killing of imperfect children and those born of depraved citizens, and he proposed that 'when both sexes had passed the age assigned for presenting children to the State, no child is to be brought to light'. He admitted the mother's right to decide on abortion but also said the question should be settled as early in pregnancy as possible.

Aristotle (384–322 BC), following Plato, was mindful of the practical issues and also wanted to keep the population at an optimal level in order to avoid poverty, sedition and other evils. He stated in his *Politica* (VII. 16, 1335) 'The number of children allowed to each marriage shall be regulated by the State, and . . . if any woman be pregnant after she has produced the prescribed number, an abortion shall be procured before the fetus has life.' Both Plato and Aristotle also held that a woman should abort her pregnancy if she conceived after her fortieth year.

Among the Romans abortion became very common, with Roman Law declaring that the fetus became a fully human being only at birth, but in accordance with their patriarchal tradition it was the father, not the mother, who had the right to make the decision. There are no traces of penalties for abortion until about AD 200; the first Roman jurist who denounced it seems to have been Ulpian. Previously Seneca (*c.* 4 BC–AD 65), the Roman moralist, had spoken about abortion being practised by fashionable women simply to preserve their beauty.

However, the views of Tertullian, St Augustine and others prevailed and were perpetuated in the Decretum of Gratian (1148), which in turn became the first section of the Corpus Juris Canonica.[14] Thus Canon Law became consistent with Roman Law, perpetuating the difference between *embryo formatus* (with a soul) and *informatus* (without a soul). The death of the *embryo formatus* entailed a life for a life, but in destroying the *embryo informatus* only a fine was imposed.

Roman Catholicism

The absolutist position of the Roman Catholic Church on abortion is well known, but it is perhaps not so well established or as consistent as many people think. The strict interpretation rests on the doctrine that the soul enters the embryo at the moment of conception, so that the gravity of an abortion is unchanged regardless of the timing of it. However, between 1211 and 1869 it was taught that the male fetus was 'animate' at 40 days and the female at 80. The date 1869 is a crucial one, as some allege that up to that date, when Pope Pius IX effected sharp changes in Church law, abortion up to quickening was allowed. He abolished the distinction between the 'formed' and 'unformed' fetus, and abortion was prohibited even to save the life of the mother.

In actual fact, the time of 'ensoulment' or 'hominization' has never been definitively fixed by the Catholic Church and is still argued about today. According to one authority, Father John Mahoney, the Second Vatican Council deliberately set aside the question of when the spiritual soul was infused. Also, the Roman Congregation for the Doctrine of Faith acknowledges disagreement about this point and does not adjudicate, yet Roman Catholics are required to behave as though ensoulment occurred at fertilization. Mahoney, himself a Jesuit philosopher and theologian, further argues in *Bio-ethics and Belief*[15] that ensoulment at fertilization is highly improbable anyway. It is better understood as a process that must occur at or after the time at which (a) the developing embryo is no longer able to divide into twins, (b) the coalescence of embryos is no longer possible and (c) cell differentiation, rather than mere cell division, has started.

Other Roman Catholic theorists, deploying classical arguments going back to St Thomas Aquinas, have stated that ensoulment cannot happen until even later, perhaps after the development of neural tissue, and if some such happening is accepted, it raises once again a version of mind–body dualism against which there are powerful philosophical arguments. Counter-claims have either denied the need for dualism or used it to suggest that the soul takes on a particular 'form' of human body. This latter view encompasses the Aristotelian theory of hylomorphism, according to which the actual specific reality of a physical thing is the *forma*, while the *materia* contributes to its being only potentiality and limitation.

In spite of all these doubts and difficulties, the papal encyclical 'Humanae Vitae' of 1968 states: 'The direct interruption of the generative process already begun, and, above all, directly willed and procured abortion, even if for therapeutic reasons, are to be absolutely excluded as licit means of regulating birth.' The encyclical also restated the traditional Catholic teaching on contraception – that the use of artificial birth control is a grave sin.

One distinguishing feature of the Roman Catholic religion as compared with Protestantism is the crucial place of sexuality in both theory and practice. It is noteworthy that its sexual doctrines – a high value on virginity and celibacy and the primary purpose of sexual intercourse being the procreation of children – are promulgated by those who have chosen an abnormal (in a statistical sense) lifestyle by foregoing marriage and intercourse. Artificial birth control is regarded as against the will of God; indeed, the present Pope in 1983 equated the use of contraception with 'the denial that God is God', while in the 1930s it was often looked on as murder. However, with changing attitudes and the acceptance of the 'safe period' the Church's concern with contraception has diminished.

Nevertheless, both abortion and contraception have been favourite themes of Pope John Paul II ever since his election in 1978, and his strong and reiterated condemnations have been seen by many to be out of keeping with modern Catholic thought and a grave embarrassment to the Catholic hierarchy. This has been met, at least in this country, by a conspiracy of silence until recently, when the Duke of Norfolk and the influential Catholic paper, the *Herald*, condemned this teaching. As one commentator expressed it, the real issue was not sexual morality at all but the continuing imbalance in the relationship between the papacy and the remainder of the Church, where one opinion (because it is the Pope's) prevails over all others in the formulation of public teaching.

The Pope's 1982 visit to Britain failed to galvanize the anti-abortion movement. Indeed, at that time a Gallup poll showed widespread support for abortion and indicated that Catholics here did not agree with official Church doctrine. Seven out of 10 Catholics supported the woman's right to choose (*Daily Mail*, 27 May 1982).

Just how well founded is the Catholic teaching on abortion, and is it regarded as infallible? As regards the latter, this is disputed. In fact, the doctrine of papal infallibility dates only from the nineteenth century. It was declared to be dogma in 1870 by the First Vatican Council, and it can act retrospectively. The Pope is deemed to be infallible when speaking *ex cathedra*, but it is not clear how often this has actually happened. Some maintain that Paul VI's encyclical 'Humanae Vitae' is an example of infallibility, although the majority of Catholic theologians will deny this. Two examples which are not disputed are the doctrines of the Immaculate Conception, promulgated by Pope Pius IX in 1854, and of the Assumption (the doctrine that the Virgin Mary ascended bodily into heaven), ratified by Pope Pius XII in 1950.

The doctrine that the human embryo has absolute protection 'from the beginning' has recently been shown by Dunstan,[16] a distinguished Christian (Anglican) theologian, to be a modern invention. He argued that the Christian tradition had, until the late nineteenth century, attempted to grade the protection given to the nascent human being according to the stages of its development. What he actually wrote was this:

> The aim of this paper has been, not to claim contemporary relevance for either an outmoded embryology or an outmoded philosophical speculation on the soul and the time of 'entering' (if it does) the body; nor yet to ventilate again the licity of abortion. It has been to recall a moral tradition expressed in terms of these three things, persisting to the end of the nineteenth century, and, for those cognizant of the arcane casuistry of medical practice, well beyond that date. The tradition attempted to grade the protection accorded the nascent human being according to the stages of its development. The tradition is challenged today by those who claim absolute protection 'from the moment of conception' and so would forbid forms of postcoital contraception (like hormonal compounds or intra-uterine devices which inhibit implantation), and any use of ova fertilized *in vitro* not directed towards their being implanted and brought to term in live birth.

Carried to its logical conclusion, not only would this prohibition put paid to much modern research and practice, but it could even lead to the idea that if an *in vitro* fertilized embryo were observed to be defective, it should still be implanted. However, this has been disputed, as has Professor Dunstan's interpretation, in that he provides no unequivocal authorization to destroy an embryo which is understood to be both live and human.

The official line was given, once again, in response to the Warnock Report on the future of embryo research. The Roman Catholic response, authorized by the Bishops' Conference, simply declared: 'The destruction of human embryos . . . is the killing of human life.' Even this absolute position at least allows the so-called 'simple case' – one ovum from a married woman, fertilized *in vitro* by the husband's sperm and returned to her womb. It would also seem to allow the attempted fertilization of two or more ova, if it is intended to return to the womb all that are successfully treated. But the moral judgement becomes more complicated when doctors start to make calculations based on the average rate of success. If they try to fertilize five ova, expecting to succeed with two (which they will implant) and in fact fertilize all five, it is not clear what they must do. To quote the religious affairs correspondent of *The Times* (19 November 1984):

> [The Doctor] is probably left trying to make a subtle distinction between killing and letting die, being under no obligation, from whatever moral position he argues, to take extraordinary means to keep an inevitably doomed embryo alive by all means for as long as possible, and the distinction, in such a case, between observation of the embryo and experimentation on it is also not so clear clinically as it is in moral theory . . . The Roman Catholic Church, outside the Establishment, seems to see itself as raising a flag in the name of the sanctity of life, insisting that detailed moral judgements are subordinate to the upholding of certain moral absolutes.

There is, however, another aspect of Catholic teaching which can be used to soften this uncompromising line, and that is the use of casuistry in what has been called the 'double effect'. This is well described by Sumner,[17] who calls this, and the argument from self-defence, 'tempting ways of moderating a harsh and inflexible morality': killing an innocent being is sometimes permissible as long as the killing is indirect. The origin of this is in Aquinas' justification of killing in self-defence. This has been refined by Catholic moralists into an elaborate system. When an act will produce two effects, one good and one evil, the act is permissible when all the following requirements are satisfied:

(1) The intrinsic quality of the act – the act itself, and independently of its effects, is not impermissible.
(2) Causality – the evil effect is not the means of producing the good effect.
(3) Intention – only the good effect is intended, the evil effect is merely tolerated.
(4) Proportionality – the good and evil effects are more or less equally balanced in importance.

When these conditions are satisfied, and when the evil effect is the death of a being with moral standing, it is a case of indirect killing. When one or more conditions are violated, it is direct killing.

Some hypothetical clinical examples will show certain practical applications of this. Direct abortions would be:

(a) if the mother is suffering from malignant hypertension (severe high blood pressure), which could lead to her death by the time the fetus was viable;
(b) if a hydrocephalic fetus (one with an abnormally large skull and 'water on the brain') is diagnosed in labour, when both fetus and mother would die by normal delivery and neither would survive a caesarean section. The only way to save the mother's life is to perform a craniotomy (to crush the skull), thus permitting vaginal delivery of a stillborn child.

Indirect abortions would be:

(a) if during early pregnancy the mother was found to have cancer of the cervix and would stand a good chance of surviving only if a hysterectomy were performed;
(b) if an early ectopic pregnancy (in the Fallopian tube instead of the uterus) is found and unless this is dealt with by abortion or salpingectomy (removing the tube), it will rupture and the mother will die from shock and peritonitis.

That the appeal to the 'double effect' would justify fewer abortions than even the strictest rendering of the right of self-defence is doubtful (in Sumner's view) if the principle enables one to draw a moral distinction between the cases. The medical procedure involved produces two effects – the death of the fetus and the preservation of the mother's life – it is disconnecting the fetus that is causally indispensable, not killing it. As the medical procedure is not impermissible in itself, it will both kill the fetus and save the mother's life, and the death of the fetus will not itself be a means of ensuring the mother's survival. The result is guaranteed by the fact that it is only the termination of pregnancy, and not the securing of the death of the fetus, that is essential to abortion.

There are two possible counter-arguments to this inflation of the class of indirect abortions. In the indirect case it is not the fetus that threatens the woman's life – for instance, the woman with cancer of the cervix would be in danger even if she were not pregnant – whereas in the direct cases it is the pregnancy itself which is the threat. However, the distinction between the cases cannot depend on whether the fetus threatens to be the cause of the woman's death. Further, the causal connection between the medical procedures in the direct cases and the death of the fetus is too intimate for them to count as indirect killings. It is not inherently impossible for the fetus to survive a hysterectomy (it could not survive the other destructive procedures), and if the technology for fetal transfer were available, such fetuses could be saved.

It is possible to extend the 'double effect' to other 'good' like the mother's health and not just her life, save for the proportionality condition. For example, if the fetus would survive if the abortion were not done, to contend that therefore the greater good (fetal life) is being sacrificed to the lesser (the woman's health) is not justified. So where does one strike the balance? A life for a life? Perhaps one could extend the principle to injuries to the woman such as permanent disablement or psychotic illness, so that in effect it would be possible to have a range of permissible abortions depending on how strictly or loosely the proportionality principle was interpreted.

On the self-defence argument the fetus is seen as the intruder and parasite, and in defending the woman against this 'threat' it could be said that both parties are innocent, so neither occupies a privileged position. The deciding factor, then, would be the balance of benefits and burdens for both parties.

Others have argued that abortion need not also be illegal – a sin is not necessarily a crime – and that restrictive abortion laws should be repealed, or that in cases of irreconcilable conflict, when the woman and fetus are in equal jeopardy, the decision should always be in favour of the mother, so that abortion should be permitted to save the mother's life. Still others have even made a plea to return to the old belief in delayed 'animation', which held that a rational human soul is not present until some weeks or months after conception, pointing out that the Catholic Church has never decided the matter definitively, as her canons on baptism and abortion are really procedural directives based on the pragmatic assumption that from the moment of conception the embryo is a living human person.

The many inconsistencies in the doctrine have often been noted – like the attitude towards 'natural' wastage, spontaneous miscarriages, ectopic pregnancies and early stillbirths. Greer,[18] in her trenchant style, puts it like this:

> thus the ethical problems posed by abortion go far beyond the relatively few cases of deliberate interruption of pregnancy, which are in themselves so variable and so subject to factors beyond the individual's control that each case must be taken on its merits, which cannot themselves be understood without an understanding of the whole spectrum of abortion. A genuine attempt to disentangle the complex ethical questions involved in pregnancy termination would benefit us all, for individual women are struggling, with very little help from their spiritual mentors, to confront a genuine problem. Catholic opponents of reproductive freedom for women remain fixated on the minority of cases of induced abortion, incurious about the vast majority of cases and unable or unwilling to understand the morality of actions taken because the individual came to the conclusion that she had no choice. Their interest is predominantly legalistic, for they concentrate on preventing the existence of adequate facilities for pregnancy termination, and not on the souls of those trying to live in the most responsible and conscientious way. The problem with the machinations of the Catholic lobby against abortion is not that they are bigoted or fanatical, but that they are frivolous.

Not that the Catholic Church is impervious to change, although it fights hard to stem this. While it has always favoured a close relationship between State and Church, this has often led not only to conflict but also to involvement in politics. Nineteenth-century liberal Catholicism and the more extreme Modernist Movement (condemned in 1907) attempted theological adjustment to modern science and history.

Since Vatican Council II (1962–5) there has been a ferment of change in most areas of Roman Catholic life, including worship, Church relations, social reform and the more active participation of laymen. More recently so-called liberation theology has come under fire. This movement grew up in the mid-1960s in an effort to understand the Christian Gospel in terms of current needs for establishing human freedom. Four areas of oppression were identified: economic exploitation in less developed countries, sexual prejudice against women, racial discrimination and political tyranny. In Latin America, where there is so much overcrowding, poverty and illegal abortions, some priests have taken a very radical stand, even to the point of being actively involved with revolutionary groups.

In more developed countries surveys and opinion polls have often shown a wide disparity between official Catholic doctrine and the beliefs and practices of the laity. There are now more open divisions, and in the USA there are actually two Catholic organizations which are pro-abortion:[19] Catholics for a Free Choice, a Washington-based group, which includes a former Jesuit priest among its members, and Catholic Alternatives, based in New York, which calls itself a lay organization that supports Catholics in their use and choice of birth-control methods and/or termination of pregnancy.

Protestantism

There are said to be about 343 million Protestants in the world today, compared with 806 million Roman Catholics. The Protestant Reformation was essentially a movement for theological and moral reform in the Western Christian Church during the sixteenth and seventeenth centuries. It was an attempt to recover what was considered to be the teaching of the Bible and early Christianity, as opposed to tradition and the papacy. Salvation was to be sought through faith rather than by works (solifidianism).[20] Martin Luther triggered the German Reformation in 1517, backed by German princes' 'protestations' against Roman Catholicism in 1529. Numerous subdivisions subsequently developed – Lutheranism, Calvinism and so on. In Britain the Reformation was rather slow to develop and less radical, but the religious changes were accompanied by social and political upheavals, leading to a permanent split in Western Christianity. Separate established Churches developed as the Church of England and the Church of Scotland (Presbyterianism). The Anglican Church was disestablished in predominantly Roman Catholic Ireland in 1869 and strongly Nonconformist Wales in 1920.

Modern Protestantism has been especially vulnerable to secular thought and has emphasized life within this world, but it embraces extremes of religious outlook from conservative fundamentalism to extreme liberalism in theology. Some try to make a distinction between private or personal moral views and approval or otherwise of certain legislation. Many statements by religious bodies have combined the two, supporting legislation that conforms with their moral position. Methodists in both Britain and the USA have supported liberal laws and opposed attempts at restriction.

The 1960s saw the beginning of the 'permissive society', with a marked decline in religious influence. For instance, by 1962 nearly one-third of all weddings were civil ceremonies, and Church of England attendance declined, while at the turn of the century nearly 70 per cent of couples had been married in an Anglican church. There was also a change within the Church itself, exemplified by the publication of Bishop John Robinson's influential book *Honest to God.*[21] This challenged many religious assumptions, including premarital sexual relations. About the same time was also published *Towards a Quaker View of Sex*,[22] which challenged the traditional approach of the organized Church to morality and urged more tolerance and understanding towards homosexuality and both premarital and extramarital sex.

The initial view of the British Council of Churches, in its Report of 1962, was to take implantation as the time when biological development had reached the stage at which it should be treated as human life. For the Church of England the Board of Social Responsibility issued a pamphlet, *Abortion and Ethical Discussion* (1965), which suggested that risk of deformity, rape or incest were not in themselves sufficient grounds for terminating a pregnancy. These views were re-examined by the Synod in 1975 in response to what was considered to be too permissive legislation. In 1980 the Board issued a statement which brought it nearer to the Roman Catholic position, stating: 'The right of the innocent to life admits surely of few exceptions indeed.' It added that it could not issue authoritative statements committing all members of the Church of England, noting that deep divisions of opinion concerning abortion existed in the Church.

The Church of England then (1984) published its response to the Warnock Report, as before prepared by the Board of Social Responsibility. It was close to the Warnock view that there was a real difference between an embryo at its earliest stage of existence and from about 14 days onwards. A minority were in favour of the Catholic position that human life started at conception. The Anglican majority, however, strongly denied this and stated: 'While a fertilized ovum should be treated with respect, its life is not so sacrosanct that it should be afforded the same status as we afford to human beings.' But they were against the creation of 'spare' embryos, although they could envisage spare embryos being created by other means (an unintended surplus) and felt that for up to 14 days it should be permissible, under strict control, for experiments to be performed on them. These embryos were, in effect, bound to die eventually, and the Board considered that they could be put to some use beneficial to humanity while they lived.

The Church of England felt it had a definite role to play in implementing some of the Warnock recommendations and tried to answer the questions raised point by point, thus demonstrating its role within the Establishment as inculcator of moral precepts (*The Times*, 19 November 1984).

One fundamental concept, rarely challenged or even thought about, is our Christian tradition of monogamy. The opening paragraph of an interesting article on the subject by Clifford Longley (*The Times*, 21 January 1985) reads:

> The one common thread running through a variety of contemporary issues, surrogate motherhood, the remarriage of divorcees in church, changes in sexual ethics, is whether monogamous marriage must be maintained as an absolute and inflexible model, or whether it can survive the making of exceptions. Arguments commonly supposed to be about morality are in fact about monogamy, whose origins in the Judaeo-Christian tradition are far from clear.

Judaism

Judaism is the oldest of the three Western religions – Christianity and Islam both sprang from it – and was founded some 4,000 years ago by the Hebrew chieftain Abraham. It is estimated that there are 14 million Jews in the world, 450,000 in Britain. The Jews were expelled from England in 1290 by Edward I and not allowed back until Oliver Cromwell lifted the ban in 1650. It is interesting to note in passing that Shakespeare (1564–1616) would have had no personal experience of Jews, so that Shylock was both derived from and continued to propagate the popular but prejudiced stereotype of the Jew.

Judaism is the form which the religion of the Jews took in the era after AD 70 and differed in its ritual from that of the Bible, the latter becoming the outlook of the Pharisees.[23] It was a shift from a temple cult to a religion of the home and synagogue. The role of the priest virtually disappeared, the Rabbi becoming a teacher and an authority on the sacred Scriptures. The Commandments were derived from the Pentateuch (the first five books of the Old Testament), which is their most important religious text. Devout Jews obey no fewer than 613 Commandments, including the 10 of the Christian faith.

The word *Torah* has different meanings; it is used in the narrow sense of the teaching of divine origin that is contained in the Pentateuch but also for an oral tradition as well as for some other books of the Hebrew Bible. Further, it is used in a broad sense to signify the whole of traditional Jewish law and teaching. The divine teaching is sacrosanct and cannot be changed, although it can be interpreted by competent authorities. The Talmud is the main text of rabbinical Judaism and is a wide-ranging commentary on the Mishnah. In general it can be divided into Halakhah, legal and ritual matters, and Aggadah, theological, ethical and folklorist matters. The former is binding on all traditional Jews; while the latter is not binding, it is essential to later Jewish theology.

The Commandments of God (Mitzvah) contained in the Torah determine Jewish mores and extend into every facet of the life of the individual and community. In the nineteenth century various reform movements sought to modify some of the beliefs and practices of traditional Judaism, which led to the setting up of Reform and Conservative Judaism as separate religious movements.

The Jewish Community, or Kehillah, usually centres on a synagogue, to which all committed Jews will belong. Although the family is the most important unit of Judaism, much of the religion is dependent on communal life. It is a positive duty for Jews to marry and have at least two children (one of each sex) in accordance with the commandment (in Genesis) to 'be fruitful and multiply'. For a marriage to be dissolved a religious divorce ceremony is used in which the husband presents a specially written bill of divorce to his wife. A woman's role is primarily that of wife and mother; she is not bound to keep all the Commandments as the male is. Reformed Judaism has given women a more public role.

The Talmud, historically following the Old Testament, mentions that the fetus can be sacrificed to save the life of the mother. Generally speaking, Orthodox Jews support a restrictive position on abortion, while Conservative and Reform Jews a more liberal one. There are gradations of opinion that range from the view that abortion is permissible 'only to save the mother's life' or 'for the sake of her mental and physical health', to a desire to reform all existing restrictive abortion laws, to the claim that any abortion may be performed for any reason prior to birth, as no 'person' is believed present until 30 days after birth.

However, recent controversy in England over abortion, embryo research, the Warnock Report and surrogacy have tended to widen the splits. Perhaps the first recorded example of surrogacy was the case of Abraham and Hagar. There are many myths and legends surrounding Abraham's life, but one detail which does seem to be well established is that his wife, at least initially, was unable to bear him a child. He then had one with Hagar, variously described as his wife's handmaiden, his bondswoman or an Egyptian concubine. One version is that his wife, called Sarai (Sarah), was also his half-sister. Famine in Canaan drove Abraham to Egypt, where for convenience he called Sarai his sister. His first son, Ishmael, was born of Hagar. In his hundredth year God changed his name from Abram to Abraham, and in her ninetieth year Sarai's name was changed to Sarah and she was promised a son. Abraham was incredulous and laughed, hence his son's name Isaac, from the Hebrew verb 'to laugh'. Hagar was driven into the wilderness by Sarah's harshness before her son was born, hence her son was called Ishmael, meaning 'outcast'. 'Hagarenes' was the old name for the Saracens, Arabs or Moors who were supposed to be descendants of Hagar.

The most recent rifts were brought to the public's attention by some remarks of the Chief Rabbi, Sir Immanuel Jakobovits, in his article in *The Times* (15 December 1984) and subsequent correspondence, summarized in another *Times* article (11 February 1985). The Chief Rabbi is the leader of Britain's Orthodox Jews, the United Synagogue, who make up about four-fifths of the Jewish population. The remainder belong to Liberal, Reform and Progressive synagogues, but by an understood arrangement Sir Immanuel speaks for all of them on national issues, and he is trusted to do so by the Board of Deputies of British Jews. On this occasion he had accused some non-Orthodox Jewish leaders in England of betraying Judaism.

Apart from general disagreements over policy and interpretation, there were specific points related to marriage and sexuality. In response to his statement welcoming the Court of Appeal verdict concerning contraceptives for under-age girls, Rabbi Julia Neuberger, a progressive, said in her letter to *The Times*: 'To describe, as Sir Immanuel does, the rise in the abortion rate and unwanted pregnancies (as rightly predicted by the British Medical Association) as "unfortunate" is callous in the extreme, and clearly against the strong life ethic in Judaism.' Following this Sir Immanuel replied in the *Jewish Chronicle* that Rabbi Neuberger's support for surrogate motherhood, her description of pregnancy as 'a loathsome burden' and her stating that she had been sterilized were an 'obscene perversion of Jewish values'. Her letter condoned promiscuity and invalidated the duty to honour parents 'in order to enable these children to promote immorality'. A leading article in the *Jewish Chronicle* described the controversy as a 'war of religion', with the prospect of two bitterly hostile camps and the opening of a communal divide. It contrasted what was happening in Anglo-Jewry with the opposite tendency in the Christian Churches, the Church Unity movement.

Given this diversity of opinion in Britain, it is perhaps not surprising to find a similar situation in Israel itself, yet the general tendency seems to have been for Jews to help in the liberalization of abortion laws in other parts of the world. In Israel, as long ago as 1952, the District Court of Haifa ruled that abortion openly performed on *bona fide* medical grounds was permissible, and from then on doctors were not prosecuted. Pressure came from feminists to change the law to the 'right to choose'. This was supported by the left but opposed by Orthodox religious groups, the right wing and the Israeli Society of Gynaecologists.[24]

The argument used was that of the 'suicide of the nation': there were too few Jews to fight for the cause and liberal abortion laws were compared with the decimation of the Jews by the Nazis. The weakness of this argument is that it is not absolute, as many young girls and women who have an abortion may very well have children at a later date.

A law was passed in 1977 which required the permission of three members of a panel consisting of two doctors and a social worker. The grounds for an abortion were that the mother was over 40, or under 18; incest or other illegal sexual acts; fetal abnormality; and danger to the life or health of the mother. There was also a 'social clause' for adverse family and social circumstances. Abortions were running at about 18,000 a year. In 1979 the 'social clause' was voted out, the actual vote being made a measure of confidence in the Government. In practice this does not seem to have made a great deal of difference to the number of abortions.

Buddhism

Buddhism was founded about 2,500 years ago by Prince Siddhartha Gautama (his clan name), who lived *c.* 563–483 BC in Northern India. He was known as 'Buddha', a Sanskrit title meaning the 'Awakened' or 'Enlightened' one.[25] Strictly this is not a proper name; it denotes rather a state of being. According to legend, he led a life of luxury as a young man, and after he had married and produced a son, he left his family and wandered off in search of enlightenment. About six years later he found it. There are said to be about 256 million Buddhists in the world today.

He taught four Noble Truths, the last of which was the

affirmation of a way of deliverance from the endless round of birth and death. The Buddhist way is threefold – morality, meditation and wisdom – but in fuller form is described as an eightfold path:

(1) right understanding, as taught by the Buddha;
(2) right purpose, necessary moral resolve;
(3) right speech, avoiding defamatory talk;
(4) right bodily action, avoiding excessive sensuality, dishonesty and actions injurious to others;
(5) right means of livelihood, a trade or occupation which does not entail violence or hurt to others;
(6) right endeavour or effort, avoiding morally unwholesome states of mind.
(7) right mindfulness, constant awareness of one's actions, intentions and feelings;
(8) right concentration, the practice of bringing consciousness to a single point in meditation.

In later centuries the teachings were elaborated into various sects and schools by philosopher-monks. For the lay follower, who does not become a homeless wanderer, the Buddhist life consists in taking the three refuges: the pursuit of morality, especially generosity; keeping special days and festivals and pilgrimages to sacred places; and social responsibilities. The latter are set out in the Sigalovada Sutta, which codifies the ethical and social duties in common human relationships such as parent–child and husband–wife.

In theory, contraception may prevent the beginning of the Buddhist lifecycle, which starts at conception. As Buddhism prohibits the taking of life and places emphasis on compassion, abortion is unacceptable.

Hinduism

Hinduism is the European name for the Sanatana Dharma, the 'Eternal Law'. The name is derived from the Sanskrit meaning 'river', the Hindus being the inhabitants of the 'land beyond the Indus River', so called by the invading Muslims who entered India in the eighth century.[26] There are about 500 million believers, and in the 1971 census in India Hindus constituted 83 per cent of the total population.

The earliest Hindu text, the Rig Veda, dates from before 1000 BC. Hinduism covers a wide range of cults, beliefs and practices. What is common to most schools is the belief in the 'release' from the repeated cycle of birth and death, but there are variations not only from one region of the country to another but also from village to village. Generally the belief is in the reincarnation of the self in successive bodies – whether for the better or the worse is held to depend on one's merit. There is the further complication of the division of the population into castes.

In the West the most misunderstood aspect of Hinduism is its treatment of sensuality and eroticism. The erotic temple sculptures decorate many a lavish coffee-table book, and the Kama Sutra has been treated as if it were pornographic. It was attributed to the Brahmin priest Vatsayana in the third or fourth century AD, the Brahmin being the most elevated of the four Hindu social classes. Parrinder[27] puts all this into proper perspective and his account should be read for further details.

In the modern movements, central to the Hindu religion is the guru. One example is Ramakrishna, who has founded religious, educational and social welfare centres throughout India and elsewhere. Perhaps the most famous Hindu reformer was Gandhi.

Four ideal concepts are basic to Hindu life – duty, gain, love and salvation – and these are worked out in great detail for each class of society. However, one of the clues to attitudes towards abortion and contraception in any religion is how women are viewed and treated, although this is sometimes highly ambivalent. It is of interest to note in this context that a distinctive feature of Hindu cults is that many of the deities worshipped are female. Temple prostitution, on the other hand, along with the suppression of widow-burning (*suttee*), was stopped by the British with the help of Hindu reformers.

Rituals of sexual union can be traced back to the Vedas. The custom of child marriage also goes back to ancient times. The principle seemed to be that the husband should be three times the age of his wife. A woman's hope was to bear children, since the mother was the centre of the family, although in Hindu society it was the man, father or husband, who had complete disposal of the woman, daughter or wife. However, rules of caste hedged round the options open in the choice of a wife. The remarriage of a widow was forbidden from an early date because she must always revere her husband. Sexual intercourse was not only a physical act; it was also given the value of a religious ritual.

In spite of the general positive attitudes towards love and sex, there were other offshoots which led towards asceticism and mysticism, with suppression or denial of sexuality.

In summary it could be said that Hinduism shows a mild tendency to oppose abortion and to promote the continuity of the family, but there has been as much divergence between thought and practice in India as in the West. In any case the classical principles and traditions of Hinduism do not seem to have generated a strong cultural basis for contemporary opposition to more permissive abortion laws.

The Faith of the Sikhs

Sikhs are particularly known for their warrior-like qualities and, in this country, for their distinctive turbans. A Sikh (the word means, literally, a 'Learner') is a follower of Guru Nanak (1469–1539) and his successors, whose movement was founded in 1500.[28] There are now about 14 million believers. Nanak was the first of 10 gurus, or teachers, of the Sikhs. He was married with two sons. Legend has it that he was a poor husband, restless and unhappy and thought to be mad. He eventually left his wife and became a wandering teacher.

Sikhs embrace fundamental Hindu beliefs in *karma* and rebirth, but these are mixed with theistic beliefs in grace and salvation. In the seventeenth century the tenth guru (G. Singh) founded the Khalsa, a militant group, to resist oppression by Muslim leaders. One of the five marks of members was long, uncut hair and a beard. (The wearing of a turban and comb – possibly a symbol of virility – is a cherished tradition rather than a scriptural injunction.) A dagger was formerly worn to defend their faith and community.

It was a brotherhood open to all classes and both sexes, very worldly and strong in defending home and community. Khalsa women could follow duties similar to those of the men. They were neither secluded nor veiled and worshipped with the men in the temples. (In 1985 Britain's first Sikh woman magistrate was appointed.) In spite of his own broken marriage, Nanak praised women and denounced their oppression; some of his followers had more than one wife.

The Rahit or Sikh code of conduct was issued for all those who entered the Khalsa order; an authorized version of it was eventually produced in 1950. This included the obligation to bear the 'five Ks' (uncut hair, dagger or sword, breeches, comb and iron bangle) and to avoid four particular sins – cutting one's hair, eating meat killed in the Muslim manner, adultery and smoking.

In 1945 a general guide to the Sikh way of life was adopted. This has been summarized by Parrinder:[29]

> Sikhs were told now to have nothing to do with caste, ideas of pollution, full-moon ceremonies, wearing sacred threads, or praying at tombs. Infanticide was condemned outright, as was child marriage. Other men's wives should be respected as one's own mother, and their daughters as one's own. A man should enjoy his wife's company, and women should be loyal to their husbands. Women should not be veiled, and caste should have no place in marriage. [Marriages are 'assisted' rather than 'arranged'.]

Islam

The Islamic faith is constantly in the news nowadays and has undergone many upheavals and modifications over the years. It is the more extremist elements which catch the headlines with such practices as cutting the hands off thieves and, at least in Western eyes, excessively harsh punishments for adultery and drinking alcohol. Many countries are nominally Muslim or have a sizeable minority who profess the faith. Islam is often inextricably bound up with the political fortunes of a country, and when a more fundamentalist approach is re-imposed after years of a more liberal interpretation, it seems as if it is often the women who have the most to lose. It has been estimated that there are somewhere between 600 million and 1,100 million believers in the world.

Islam was founded about 1,400 years ago by the Prophet Muhammad (*c.* 570–632). He was born in Mecca and spent his early life as a merchant. In middle life an inner conviction dawned on him that he was the prophet chosen by Allah (God) to convey eternal messages to the Arabs, just as Moses had to the Jews and Jesus to the Christians. These divine revelations continued from around 610, when he was 40, until his death in 632 at the age of 62 and form the Koran (Qur'an). Part of the tradition is that he himself could neither read nor write. He denied being in any way a perfect man and said he was simply a channel for Allah. Eventually his teachings were regarded as having universal applicability and the text is considered sacred. In form it is about the length of the New Testament and is divided into Suras, or chapters. (An English paperback translation is available.[30])

The Qur'an contains many prescriptions on legal and social topics, all embodied in the law of Islam or Shari'a (literally 'clear path'). It includes various Pillars of Islam, the main five being profession of faith, worship, almsgiving, pilgrimage and fasting. These are binding on all sane adult male and female believers who have attained puberty or the age of 15.

Islam means 'submission to God' and the adherent, or Muslim, is one who submits himself to Allah. As the Prophet Muhammad was only the channel for the revelations (regarded as the final unfolding of God's laws, superseding Judaism and Christianity), it is misleading to call the faith 'Muhammadanism'. There is no distinction between the religious sphere and ordinary everyday life, as all facets of human activity are covered by Islamic laws.[31]

There are two broad subdivisions of Islam: Shi'ism and Sunnism. Shi'ism originally referred to the 'partisans' (*shia*) of 'Ali and over the centuries developed its own body of law. This differed in minor ways (e.g. inheritance and the status of women) from that of the majority of Sunnis. Especially important historically was the conversion of Persia (Iran) in the sixteenth century from Sunnism to Shi'ism. Less well known is the fact that one esoteric branch of Shi'ism, known as the Ismailis, became a sub-sect in the eighth century. This is the sect whose forty-ninth Imam (literally, 'exemplar' or leader) is His Highness Prince Karim Aga Khan. It has recently opened a centre in South Kensington in London and has some 15,000 adherents in Britain. *Sunna* means 'custom' or 'code of behaviour', as exemplified by Muhammad's example, which in turn was embodied in the traditional literature. His followers were therefore called 'people of the Sunna and the community', hence Sunnis.

The name 'Ayatullah' – so very familiar in recent years – refers to a high dignitary of the Shi'i religious hierarchy. Ayatullahs are the nearest equivalent in Islam to our clergymen, but they originated as outstanding scholars and interpreters of the faith. Nowadays Ayatullah seems to be used as a name for a charismatic leader. This is seen in the rise of Ayatullah Khumaini, who in the 1960s emerged as the main political opponent of the then Shah of Iran, who after the revolution of 1978–9 became recognized as the supreme temporal representative in Iran of the Hidden Iman ('faith').

It seems to me that classical Islam regarded women as intellectually inferior to men and of subordinate legal status. This can be disputed, and, as so often happens with ancient religious texts, various interpretations are possible. However, women in many nominally Islamic countries have been virtually excluded from public life. Veiling, or covering of the body and head, which was apparently instituted for the protection of the Prophet's wives, was later extended to other free Muslim women, varying in degree from country to country.

Islamic modernism has often attacked veiling as a symbol of women's subjection, with the fundamentalists insisting on its retention. However, when the Shah of Iran outlawed the veil in 1937 it caused great consternation and outcries about Western influence. The movement to give women greater freedom is very much part and parcel of Islamic modernism, which began with Qasim Amin (1865–1908), who advocated a reinterpretation of the Qur'an and tradition as well as appealing to natural justice and individual freedom. In the last two decades secular legislation in many Islamic countries has been assisting this process.

Muslim marriage is essentially a civil contract: partners should be of equal social status, and the bride receives a dowry. Child betrothal is possible, but a minimum age for marriage has been laid down in many countries by secular law. Polygamy was sanctioned by the Qur'an but is now often discouraged. Modern laws have also tried to mitigate unilateral divorce by the husband.

Zina denotes illicit sexual relations and covers both adultery and fornication, so that sexual intercourse is condemned outside marriage and concubinage. Prescribed penalties are flogging or stoning, but guilt can be proved only on the evidence of four eye witnesses. In practice, women considered as erring have often been disposed of by their relatives without recourse to formal law.

Attitudes towards abortion have changed over the centuries. In 1355 the Grand Mufti issued a dictum allowing contraception, but abortion was considered permissible only for such reasons as the interruption of a lactating mother's milk, which would endanger the existing child. After quickening, abortion was prohibited in all circumstances.

A number of predominantly Islamic countries have since liberalized their laws. In 1964 the Grand Mufti of Jordan allowed abortion, provided that the embryo had not achieved human shape, interpreted as occurring at 120 days' gestation. Other countries followed suit: Morocco (1967), Tunisia (1973), Iran (1976, but subject to reversal), Kuwait (1982). Much depends on the relationship with the state, with some Muslim countries permitting termination only to save the life of the mother or not at all.[32]

A case in point is Turkey, where a more pragmatic approach was adopted in view of the fast increasing population. The population was approaching 50 million with a 2.5 per cent rate of increase. In May 1983 legalized abortion was introduced. A previous attempt in 1978 had been thwarted by Muslim opposition. The new law, ratified by the National Security Council, allows abortion until the tenth week of pregnancy. After that time abortion remains illegal unless essential for medical reasons, with jail terms of up to 20 years for transgressions. Sterilization of both men and women is permitted as a means of birth control. These measures are also aimed at radically reducing the number of illegal abortions, often performed under terribly primitive conditions by untrained people and said to number several thousands each year.

In Nigeria there is less likelihood of the liberalization of the abortion laws, as there are both strong Muslim and Roman Catholic factions. One reason given for the success of Islam in spite of its apparent harshness in some spheres is that it treats the lowest groups in society as being just as worth while as the highest.

Secularization and the psychology of belief

The much broader issue of how religion can affect the biological side of our existence has recently been documented by Reynolds and Tanner.[33] They devote a whole chapter to religious influences on infanticide and abortion. They also point out that the famous Hippocratic oath, which, among other things, forbids a doctor to involve himself in an abortion, may be of a much later date than that to which it is usually assigned. There is no record of it being used in the pre-Christian era, even though Hippocrates himself lived in the fifth century BC. It could have been a later reaction to the apparent callousness of the Greek ideal of health. It is still widely believed that, on qualifying, all doctors somehow 'take' the Hippocratic oath, but this is not so, as I can attest from personal experience.

While on the subject of doctors' ethical obligations, it is perhaps not so well known just how many 'oaths', declarations and codes there are, apart from the Hippocratic one. A lot of them have been produced under the aegis of the World Medical Association, and most were revised again in 1983. The main ones are the World Medical Association's International Code of Medical Ethics and the Declarations of Geneva, Helsinki, Lisbon (1981), Sydney, Oslo, Tokyo, Hawaii and Venice. Some have subtly altered the wording of, for example, 'respect for life from conception' to 'from its beginning'. We might ask what the moral and religious standing of these rules is. An underlying assumption might be that medical ethics are bound and justified by some more fundamental moral principles, but that is not so. In practice, ethical rules are relative and not absolute.

Secular alternatives to religion, while they are obviously not religions, must have in common certain commitments, as opposed to religious beliefs, which perform the same function. One definition of religion is 'a system of beliefs and practices by means of which a group of people struggle with the ultimate problems of human life' or, as Kolakowski succinctly puts it, 'the socially established worship of the eternal reality'.[34] However, beliefs or faith can also have secular connotations – for example, positivism with its 'faith' in science, Marxism with its 'faith' in revolution (noting in passing that Karl Marx was descended from a long line of Jewish rabbis) and Freudianism, with its 'faith' in psychoanalysis. Utilitarianism, humanism and other philosophical traditions also have their own versions of the ultimate existentialist problems. What is certain is that human beings have needs which require satisfaction through some system.

Religious beliefs may include such ideas as that life is sacred and that killing and abortion are always wrong. This latter view may appeal to a certain type of personality that likes things cut and dried, sees things in terms of black and white and feels uncomfortable with any grey or relativist stance. How are such beliefs held, especially when minority beliefs often call forth hostility from the majority? One explanation is the 'theory of cognitive dissonance', and its application to religious experience is clearly described by Batson and Ventis.[35]

Dissonance results when a person simultaneously accepts as true two cognitions that are inconsistent with one another, this being an unpleasant state from which we all try to escape. The person can escape dissonance either by changing one of the cognitions or by adding new cognitions consonant with whichever is most resistant to change. Festinger, who first proposed this theory, made the point that dissonance deals with psychological rather than logical inconsistency.

This theory suggests that there are important psychological consequences of holding devout religious and similar beliefs. How is evidence condemning these beliefs dealt with? Are they changed, or modified, or even given up entirely? The theory suggests quite the opposite under the following conditions:

(1) there must be a firm conviction;
(2) there must be public commitment to this conviction;
(3) the conviction must be amenable to unequivocal disconfirmation;
(4) such disconfirmation must occur;
(5) social support must be available to the believer subsequent to the disconfirmation.

This implies, and the implication is borne out by experience, that devout religious beliefs are highly resistant to change. It is suggested there are three basic reasons for this. First, the beliefs provide important personal benefits to the believer; second, they are more resistant to change because they involve public commitment; and, third, the devout believer typically does not pursue his faith in isolation.

On a more speculative note, the possibility of a dissonance interpretation has been mooted for the origin of Christianity. Employing the four strategies available to reduce inconsistency between existing beliefs and disconfirming information – denial, bolstering, differentiation and transcendence – it has been argued that these strategies underlay the development of a number of key beliefs among the early Christians. Such beliefs, which could be products of dissonance reduction, are:

(1) Jesus was not only a great teacher but the Messiah predicted by the prophets;
(2) Jesus had an extraordinary and prodigious birth and childhood;
(3) Jesus was endorsed as Saviour by God, holy men and himself;
(4) Jesus' death was transitory and for a purpose;
(5) Jesus knew about, predicted and chose his own death.

It is contended that these and similar beliefs served to rationalize the dashed hopes of Jesus' followers and that out of this intensification and rationalization Christianity was born.

As is well known, religion was viewed by Marx as 'the opium of the people' and by Freud as a universal obsessional neurosis. As the former, it diverts attention from here-and-now social and material needs. Promises of eternal happiness may mitigate fear of death and make it more acceptable, but they divert attention from poor living conditions and encourage passive acceptance of the *status quo.*

The decline of religious beliefs has been more marked in the twentieth century than at any other time in history, with a rapid advance in 'secularization' – although this term itself has various meanings.[36] It means, for instance, the decline in power and prestige of religious teachers and the ending of State support for religious bodies, religious teaching in national schools and religious tests for public office or civil rights. It also entails the end of legislative protection for religious doctrines such as the prohibition of contraceptives, the censorship or control of literature and other intellectual activities designed to safeguard religion. In the USA Church and State are strictly separate, although most Americans are personally attached to one or other of the Christian Churches; the Republic of India is officially secular, although many are devout Hindus.

The term can also mean the decline of widespread interest in religious traditions, leading to fewer adherents. In communist countries there have been systematic official attempts to suppress religion as being antisocial, offering instead elements shared by religion such as rallies, music and ritual, idealism, uniformity of dogma and hero worship. Albania is the only communist country formally to have abolished religion, although the majority of its citizens were Muslims.

Religion is by its very nature divisive, engendering prejudice and sometimes fanaticism by creating a dichotomy between believers and non-believers. Much depends on how rigorously or literally received religious truths are accepted and acted upon. At one extreme this can give rise to fundamentalism, as seen in the recent rise in Islamic fundamentalism. At the other end of the spectrum are attempts at 'demythologization' – for instance, attempts to point out the myths and legends in the Bible and to try to transcribe the biblical message in a way that is compatible with modern science and philosophy.

How the State can and does overrule some traditional religious beliefs and practices by passing secular laws is illustrated in chapter 6, where I have reviewed abortion legislation in various countries.

3

Laying Down the Law

Early history

In Anglo-Saxon times both the ecclesiastical and the secular laws dealt with abortion, the former being concerned with spiritual sanctions and the latter with compensation. The Leges Henrici was a compilation of Anglo-Saxon laws attributed to the time of Henry I, which decreed:

> Women who have illicit intercourse and destroy their unborn children, and those who help them to expel the fetus from the womb, are expelled from the Church for their lives by an old ruling, but now it is more leniently laid down that they should do penance for ten years. If a woman deliberately got rid of her fetus within forty days, she must do penance for four years; if it was done after it was alive, because it amounts to homicide, she must do penance for seven years.

The situation in later years is summarized by B. M. Dickens[1] as follows:

> The advent of the Norman Conquest had consequences for the law relating to abortion, notwithstanding the fact that both Edward the Confessor and William the Conqueror were kings instilled in the Christian ethic. Before the Conquest, the system of courts blended

> secular and ecclesiastical personnel, law and administration. Although William decreed that the law of England was to be maintained as in former times, he separated the secular and ecclesiastical courts, and each developed a distinctive, even if occasionally competing jurisdiction. By the twelfth century the ecclesiastical courts claimed a wide jurisdiction, including a criminal jurisdiction over religious and moral matters, and a corrective jurisdiction over clergy and laity alike. Abortion was regarded primarily as an ecclesiastical offence, the crime consisting in denying the prospect of eternal life to the soul of the unborn, and so unbaptized child. The ecclesiastical courts became more severe in their treatment of abortion and throughout the Middle Ages in Western Europe, guilty women were condemned on a capital charge, as the Sixth Ecumenical Council had ordained.

The protection common law afforded to human life certainly extended to the unborn child but whether abortion after quickening amounted to homicide or a lesser offence is not clear beyond doubt from the authorities cited, and views on this issue possibly altered at different periods. Common law was, of course, much influenced by the state of medical knowledge at the time. Bracton (early thirteenth century) claimed that abortion after animation (i.e. when the fetus was alive) was homicide, but later authorities do not follow this view. Coke, in his *Institutes of the Laws of England* (1628–44), denied homicide and reduced the crime to 'a great misprision' committed when a woman was 'quick with child', but the consequences are not described. There is a certain amount of controversy as to what Coke intended. One reading of his judgment was 'a great misprision and so murder', while others have said it should have been 'no murder', with misprision being equivalent to misdemeanour. This is discussed by Means,[2] who thinks he also got the common law wrong, so that even after quickening abortion was still not a misprision. However, Blackstone (1765), in his commentaries on the laws of England, treated abortion as a common law misdemeanour and suggested that manslaughter was a possible interpretation of Bracton's characterization of abortion. He did not adopt the modern division of crimes into felonies and misdemeanours, but by then, according to common usage, misdemeanours were 'smaller faults and omissions of lesser consequence'.

Even accepting that during the sixteenth and early seventeenth centuries abortion was an offence bordering on the capital, it would probably have been prosecuted not in the common law courts but in the ecclesiastical. During the course of the civil wars (1642–9), however, the higher ecclesiastical courts were abolished and, in spite of the Restoration (1660), never regained their former authority. Also the growing practice of making ecclesiastical offences statutory felonies, which took them into common law, further assisted their demise.

The nineteenth century

It appears that before 1803 the crime of abortion was a common law misdemeanour capable of commission by the pregnant woman herself and by other persons, but in either case only provided that the stage of quickening (that is, about mid-term) had been reached. Lord Ellenborough's Act of 1803 made the procuring of an abortion a statutory felony, punishable by death if done after quickening. It did not, however, explicitly refer to a woman aborting herself. Section 2 was the great innovation, in that abortion before quickening also became a crime for the first time, with punishment varying from a fine, through imprisonment and whipping, to transportation for up to 14 years. Thus the Act perpetuated the original ecclesiastical distinction, reserving the death penalty for abortion of the *embryo formatus*.

The Act was also noteworthy for the terminology used, as this is the only occasion when a statute had actually used the word 'abortion' as well as 'miscarriage', perhaps considering 'abortion' the proper term for termination before quickening and 'procuring a miscarriage' for afterwards, although some commentators see their use here as synonymous. In the actual debate on Section 1, which employs only the word 'miscarriage', Lord Ellenborough himself consistently used the word 'abortion' to identify the forbidden act.

The first prosecution under the 1803 Act was in 1811, when a man was accused of giving savin oil of juniper (a popular abortifacient of the early nineteenth century) to his girlfriend. He was acquitted. By 1853, according to the *Lancet*, abortion was common. The British medical profession organized several campaigns against abortion in the period up to 1914. For example, the *British Medical Journal* waged a long-running campaign against 'baby-farming', which included abortion, infanticide and adoption. A second campaign by the *Lancet* attacked abortifacient pills, particularly those containing lead, following the death of a woman in 1893 from lead poisoning. An estimate published in the *Malthusian* in 1914 suggested that 100,000 working-class women took abortifacient pills annually, with possibly 400 or 500 deaths annually between the years 1926 and 1935.[3]

Lord Lansdowne's Act of 1828 did not persist with this linguistic distinction: it repealed the 1803 Act but maintained the 'ecclesiastical' distinction. It introduced slightly more lenient penalties for abortion before quickening but was no more explicit on the question of whether an unaided woman procuring or attempting to procure her own abortion was covered by the Act.

The Offences Against the Person Act 1837 finally abandoned the distinction of before and after quickening and at the same time abolished the death penalty. The actual time of quickening, or being 'quick with child', has always been an arbitrary one, but it is usually taken to be when the mother herself first feels or thinks she feels movements (this can vary from the sixteenth to the twentieth week) or when somebody examining her can feel or see some movement.

The Offences Against the Person Act 1861 is the most important of the nineteenth-century legislation, as it remains in force to this day and is still used to prosecute those carrying out illegal abortions. It is worth pointing out, however, as this seems to have been forgotten by present-day commentators, that this Act was passed primarily to protect the mother and not the fetus, as at this time termination of pregnancy was a hazardous procedure with a substantial mortality rate.

The main provisions of the 1861 Act come under Sections 58–9. For the first time it was clearly laid down that a woman procuring her own abortion was also guilty of a felony. Section 58 declares:

> Every woman, being with child, who, with Intent to procure her own Miscarriage, shall unlawfully administer to herself any Poison or other noxious Thing, or shall unlawfully use any Instrument or other Means whatsoever with the like Intent and whatsoever, with the Intent to procure the Miscarriage of any Woman whether she be or be not with Child, shall unlawfully administer to her or cause to be taken by her any Poison of other noxious Thing, or shall unlawfully use any Instrument or other means whatsoever with the like Intent, shall be guilty of Felony.

The maximum penalty was life imprisonment. Section 59 created a new offence, with a maximum penalty of five years' imprisonment, by providing that

> whosoever shall unlawfully supply or procure any Poison or other noxious Thing, or any Instrument or Thing whatsoever, knowing that the same is intended to be unlawfully used or employed with Intent to procure the Miscarriage of any Woman, whether she be or be not with Child, shall be guilty of a Misdemeanour.

The Act made no special provisions for therapeutic abortion to save the mother's life. There was also a gap in the law in respect of the child who was destroyed in the process of being born.

The twentieth century

The Infant Life (Preservation) Act 1929 introduced the offence of 'child destruction', from the time when an embryo is 'viable' at 28 weeks onwards, this being permissible only to save the mother's life. The maximum penalty is life imprisonment. At first sight this Act may seem rather recherché, but it has subsequently turned out to be very important, for a number of reasons. It is still the law today as it was not repealed by the introduction of the 1967 Abortion Act – indeed, it complements the later Act. Anti-abortionists, having been unsuccessful in their attacks on the main Abortion Act 1967, have recently turned their attention to the 1929 Act instead. If this Act could be altered, it would indirectly affect the whole abortion legislation. It is also important as it highlights a vulnerable grey area in the law, once again raising fundamental questions about the nature of death and the law on homicide. Finally, it is concerned with the nature of viability, which in turn focuses attention on the time limits set forth for legal abortions and public concern over neonatal deaths. I can give here only the merest outline of the complex legal issues raised; further, very detailed discussion can be found in Skegg.[4] Also this section should be read in conjunction with others in this book dealing with infanticide (chapter 5) and the legal limits to abortion (chapter 7).

The actual wording of the Act is crucial, as it was intended to plug the gap between abortion and murder. Its full title is 'An Act to amend the law with regard to the destruction of children at or before birth.' Section 1(1) states:

> Subject as hereinafter in this subsection provided, any person who, with intent to destroy the life of a child capable of being born alive, by any wilful act causes a child to die before it has an existence independent of it mother, shall be guilty of an offence, to wit, of child destruction, and shall be liable on conviction thereof or indictment to imprisonment for life: Provided that no person shall be found guilty of an offence under this section unless it is proved that the act which caused the death of the child was not done in good faith for the purpose only of preserving the life of the mother.

Section 1(2) states:

> For the purposes of this Act, evidence that a woman had at any

> material time been pregnant for a period of twenty-eight weeks or more shall be prima-facie proof that she was at that time pregnant of a child capable of being born alive.

In this last context it is important to note that 'capable of being born alive' is not synonymous with 'capable of survival', nor does the Act state that a live child is incapable of being born before the completion of 28 weeks' pregnancy.

There are some circumstances in which an abortion would be lawful for the purposes of the law relating to abortion, yet still constitute the offence of child destruction. The difficulty lies in determining the extent of the protection afforded to fetal life by the 1929 Act. Before 1929 it was widely believed that it was possible to avoid prosecution by killing a child in the course of a normal birth but before it was fully born. As such conduct did not amount to an attempt to procure a miscarriage, it did not amount to the offence of abortion. As the child was not fully born, the deed was not murder either. Earlier attempts to close this loophole had been unsuccessful.

If a charge of homicide is to be brought, this in turn depends on the legal definition of when life begins, and the child must have existed independently of its mother – it must have been '*in rerum natura*'. However, as there is no means to determine at what instant the circulation of the fetus and the mother become so dissociated as to allow the child to exist independently, there is considerable uncertainty about the precise moment at which a child comes under the protection of the law.

According to some experts, the child is a living being when it has an existence independent of the mother or has been wholly expelled from the mother's body, although apparently the afterbirth and cord need not also have been expelled. Other legal authorities suggest that breathing is the main criterion for life, while others again maintain that life can exist before the child starts to breathe.

The confusion was exemplified by the case in 1983 in which a child survived an abortion operation, but the doctor concerned, Mr Anthony Hamilton, apparently did not actively intervene to keep it alive, although the child did eventually receive treatment, survived and was subsequently adopted. The charge brought against Mr Hamilton was 'attempting to murder' the child, while it was widely believed in legal circles that had the child died, his action would have constituted child destruction and nothing more. He was eventually found not guilty.

It has been argued that a great many abortions are, indeed, performed 'with intent to destroy the life of a child capable of being born alive' and that very few of these are 'for the purpose of preserving the life of the mother'. If this were so, some doctors could unwittingly be committing the offence of child destruction. Legally the controversy revolves, in large measure, around the interpretation of the words 'a child capable of being born alive' and 'preserving the life of the mother'.

Disagreement arises over whether an unborn child which is *not* capable of surviving independently outside its mother's body is a 'child capable of being born alive' for the purposes of the offence of child destruction. Skegg[5] concludes that Section 1(1) should be construed as protecting the lives of viable but not of non-viable fetuses. There is still, however, a theoretical gap. If a non-viable fetus miscarries spontaneously or is being born prematurely, it would not be an offence to kill it intentionally during the course of birth, even though it would be murder to kill it intentionally once it was fully extruded from its mother's body. Nevertheless, this gap is of little practical importance. The serious gap in English law prior to 1929 was that it was not an offence to kill a viable child during the course of birth. The 1929 Act supplements the law of murder by making it an offence to kill such a child before it has an existence independent of its mother, unless it is done in good faith to preserve her life. Section 1(2) was included to assist in the problem of proof, as it is sometimes difficult to establish viability. The 1967 Abortion Act was enacted on the assumption that the 1929 Act would provide continuing protection for viable but not for non-viable fetuses.

As will be seen later in this chapter, the reasonable assumption that to 'preserve the life of the mother' meant preventing her death was extended to a broader assumption of danger to life, and then danger to health, so that there are very few circumstances nowadays in which preservation of the health of the mother – much less her life – would require a doctor to kill a viable fetus intentionally.

However, it has long been accepted that if something were done to a child *before* it was born which caused the child to die *after* it was born (for instance, procuring an abortion after the first three months, or causing the death of the child after removal or expulsion from the mother's body by such procedures as hysterectomy or induction of a mini-labour), this could constitute murder. So, could a doctor be guilty of murder if an abortion were carried out legally under Section 1 of the 1967 Abortion Act if the child did not die until after it was fully born? The 1967 Act would provide a defence to the charge of murder but could also involve external elements and fault elements. After lengthy legal arguments Skegg[6] concludes: 'it is only by ensuring that the child is not born alive, following an abortion, that a doctor can be certain that his conduct could not under any circumstances amount to the offence of murder'.

To recapitulate briefly, and to continue my chronological account of the development of abortion legislation, the offences of child destruction and of procuring a miscarriage were closely allied and could overlap, in that the latter also covered the case of destroying the life of a viable child before independent existence. The position was regularized by Section 2(2) and 2(3) of the 1929 Act, which allowed a jury to find an accused person not guilty of the alternative offence of child destruction and vice versa. Otherwise it left previous legislation untouched, so that there were still no exceptions in favour of termination at a time when the fetus was regarded in law as not capable of being born alive.

That individual judges were not happy with the existing laws is shown by the well publicized cases tried by Mr Justice McCardie in the 1930s. He was convinced that the 1861 Act was out of touch with the realities of life, so in November 1931 he spoke out. He had before him two women defendants, both of whom had aborted themselves. Theoretically they could have been given life sentences, but instead he bound them over. He said: 'In my opinion the law in regard to illegal operations should be substantially amended. It is out of keeping with the conditions that prevail in the world around us.'

In the background to this legislation was mounting public concern at the apparent increase in criminal abortions, although accurate statistics have always been difficult to obtain. At the same time therapeutic abortions were becoming more acceptable and medically safer, and the whole topic was more freely discussed. Certain social and cultural movements were beginning to exert some influence, along with a more liberal and permissive attitude in society at large – the coming of the welfare state, the spread of secularization and the gathering momentum of the feminist movement being notable examples.

In fact, certain women's organizations provided the final impetus for the founding, on 17 February 1936, of the Abortion Law Reform Association (ALRA). It was at first organized and dominated by women, although men were encouraged to join. Two years after its formation it had 274 members. In that same year the British Medical Association set up a special committee to consider the medical aspects of abortion. It recommended a revision of the law to allow some exceptions to be made for therapeutic abortion.

The matter was brought to a head in 1938 by the case of *R.* v. *Bourne.* Mr Aleck Bourne, a consultant obstetrician at St Mary's Hospital, London, terminated the pregnancy of a 14-year-old girl who had been brutally raped by four soldiers. (He had both her and her parents' consent.) He reported his action to the authorities in order to make a test case. It was tried by Mr Justice MacNaghton, whose summing up presented a liberal interpretation of the 1861 and 1929 Acts.

He argued that repeated use of the word 'unlawful' indicated that Parliament had conceived of some circumstances in which abortion might be lawful (legal): for example, if it was performed in good faith to protect the life of the mother. He further argued that no clear distinction could be made between a threat to life and a threat to health. He ruled: 'If the doctor is of the opinion ... that the probable consequences ... will be to make the woman a physical or mental wreck, the jury is quite entitled to take the view that the doctor ... is operating for the purpose of preserving the life of the mother.' The *Bourne* case thus established when an abortion may be lawfully procured and also outlined the proper rights, practices and duties of the medical profession. (Although this case is well documented and rightly famous, what is not so well known is that Bourne later opposed the law being extended too far and in the 1960s he joined the Society for the Protection of Unborn Children and worked against further liberalization of the law.)

The *Bourne* case was further assessed by the Inter-departmental Committee set up in 1937 under the chairmanship of Norman Birkett. It reported in 1939 but rejected proposals for widening the grounds for legal abortion with particular regard for the population level at that time. The intervention of the Second World War prevented an adequate debate on the Report or any further progress.

After the Second World War two further cases, not so well known and not officially reported, further influenced the trend towards liberalizing the law. In *R.* v. *Bergman and Ferguson* (1948) it was indicated that if the termination were carried out in good faith to preserve the *health* of the mother, the court would not look too closely into the extent of the danger to the *life* of the mother. In *R.* v. *Newton and Stungo* (1958) it was made clear that in preserving the life or health of a woman, 'health' included mental health.

Case law is never as satisfactory as statute law, and there were further pressures for change. Also, legal abortions were still relatively few in number, illegal ones common and both legal and medical opinion unsure of the law.[7] It was not surprising, therefore, that six attempts were made at abortion law reform, largely in the form of Private Members' Bills, before the definitive legislation of 1967 was enacted. These Bills were in 1952–3 (Joseph Reeves), 1954 (Lord Amulree), 1961 (Kenneth Robinson), 1965 (Renée Short), 1965–6 (Lord Silkin), 1966 (S. W. Digby) and 1966 (David Steel). This last one became the Abortion Act 1967, which I will now briefly describe, leaving detailed considerations to the next chapter.

The main provisions of the Abortion Act 1967

The Act came into operation on 27 April 1968 and applies to England, Wales and Scotland. It is essentially permissive; that is, abortion is permitted (but not obligatory) and prosecution will not follow if certain conditions are fulfilled. As already noted, the previous legislation of 1861 and 1929 remain in force. The Abortion Act is concerned with abortion up to viability, previously legally defined by the 1929 Act as 28 weeks. The full title of the Act summarizes its main intention: 'An Act to amend and clarify the law relating to the termination of pregnancy by a registered medical practitioner'.

The main provisions are contained in Section 1:

1 Subject to the provisions of this Section, a person shall not be guilty of an offence under the law relating to abortion when a pregnancy is terminated by a registered medical practitioner if two registered medical practitioners are of the opinion, formed in good faith –
   (a) that the continuance of pregnancy would involve risk to the life of the pregnant woman, or injury to the physical or mental health of the pregnant woman or any existing children of her family, greater than if the pregnancy were terminated; or
   (b) that there is a substantial risk if the child were born that it would suffer from such physical or mental abnormalities as to be seriously handicapped.

2 In determining whether continuance of pregnancy would involve

> risk of injury to health, as is mentioned in paragraph (a) of subsection 1 of this section, account may be taken of the pregnant woman's actual or reasonably foreseeable environment.

Other provisions of the Act are that termination must be carried out in a National Health Service hospital or other place approved by the Ministry of Health. In a case of dire emergency when 'termination is immediately necessary to save the life or to prevent grave injury to the physical or mental health of the pregnant women' this may be done by one medical practitioner.

The Regulations (1968) provide special forms which have to be completed in all cases. Schedule 1 covers Certificates A and B. Certificate A is completed by the two doctors recommending the termination. Neither of these doctors needs to be a specialist or consultant. The four clauses of the Act are printed on Certificate A, one or more of which must be ringed, thus giving the reason for recommending termination (as outlined in Section 1 above). Apart from the name and address of the patient, no other details are included. Certificate B is to be completed for an emergency operation and signed by the doctor carrying it out, stating that it is either to save the woman's life or to prevent grave permanent injury to her health. It has also to be recorded whether the form was completed before the operation was carried out; if this was not reasonably practicable, then it should be done within twenty-four hours. These certificates are not to be destroyed for three years afterwards.

Schedule 2 concerns the form (HSA3) to be completed by the doctor who actually does the operation. It has to be completed within a week and sent in a sealed envelope to the Chief Medical Officer at the Ministry of Health. As originally constituted (a new form has recently been introduced), it contained further details about the place where the operation was carried out, certain social and medical details about the patient, as well as the following grounds for termination of pregnancy: (a) medical condition of woman, (b) suspected medical condition of fetus, (c) non-medical grounds. The type of operation, and whether it was performed with or without sterilization and with any immediate complications or death, is also recorded.

This form of treatment is unique in that there is an escape clause, on grounds of conscience, for those not wishing to participate. Section 4 covers this but puts the burden of proof on to the person claiming it. As an exception to this general provision Section 4(2) provides that such conscientious objection cannot relieve a person from 'any duty to participate in treatment which is necessary to save the life or to prevent grave permanent injury to the physical or mental health of a pregnant woman', which is the position under existing law. This, unfortunately, makes termination of pregnancy divisive and unique, as there is no other form of treatment for which doctors and nurses can claim this type of exemption. It therefore makes it even more emotive and 'special'.

Section 2 of the Abortion Act has been dubbed the 'social clause' and has caused a great deal of misunderstanding. It is not a 'let-out', as is so commonly thought, as any adverse social circumstances cannot *by themselves* be grounds for recommending termination. The wording is quite clear on this; in assessing the risk to health such factors *may* be taken into consideration, which is standard medical practice anyway.

As with all legislation, there have been difficulties over interpreting the precise meaning of certain words and phrases but very few actual test cases. The Act has also been criticized for what is left out – for instance, there is nothing in it about suicide, the age of consent, rape or incest. As regards rape, by the time the case had been tried the woman could be in such an advanced state of pregnancy that termination would be inadvisable. However, immediate advice on postcoital contraception can be made available to any woman who complains that she has been sexually assaulted or raped. Many cases of pregnancies resulting from incest are terminated anyway on criteria already laid down by the Act, although not all the victims want this, and other arrangements can sometimes be made.

A detailed discussion of how the Act works in practice is given in the next chapter.

Scottish law

Scottish law has always been rather more liberal in its attitude towards abortion and less tied down by statutes. Neither the 1861 nor the 1929 Act applied. The famous *Bourne* case would probably never have taken place in Scotland because prosecutions were unlikely against reputable medical practitioners carrying out therapeutic operations.

Scottish law has now been brought into line with English law, as the Abortion Act 1967 applies but with special Regulations (1968). Before that various authorities took the view that abortion was not criminal if carried out as a 'necessary medical operation', although there was no case law to support this. Criminal intent was the crux of any prosecution.

The first recorded charge of abortion in Scotland was in 1763. It was considered to be criminal to cause or procure an abortion with felonious intent, and the accused could be the woman herself, but there are no modern cases in which the mother herself was charged, and there has always been the difficulty of convicting an abortionist without the mother's evidence. It was also a crime for her to take drugs to procure her own abortion, even if the attempt was unsuccessful. Abortion could be committed at any stage between conception and birth. However, in bringing such charges it had to be proved that the woman was actually pregnant at the time: it was no crime, for instance, to supply a non-pregnant woman with an abortifacient.

Ireland

The Abortion Act 1967 does not apply to Northern Ireland: in both North and South the 1861 Act is still in operation. The North was specifically excluded from much of the British liberalizing legislation of the 1960s (for example, the law permitting male homosexuality in certain circumstances), so the only legal amendments have been the 1929 Act and the *Bourne* case.

A survey in 1973–4 found that in Eire 54 per cent thought that divorce should never be allowed and seven out of 10 regarded premarital sex as always wrong. On abortion, 74 per cent regarded it as always wrong and 21 per cent as generally wrong. Attitudes towards artificial birth control were more liberal.

A 1980 Gallup Poll showed that four out of five in Eire thought that abortion should be illegal in all circumstances. Catholics in the North seemed to be more liberal than those in the South, as 35 per cent would allow abortions in certain circumstances. In spite of this (apparent) lack of public support for abortion, increasing numbers of Irish women come to England for this purpose.

Nevertheless, there has been some progress towards liberalization. An Ulster pregnancy advisory service was started in 1971 and in 1978 was vigorously campaigning for better sex education. The proportion of Catholics applying to the Ulster service for abortions increased to nearly 30 per cent in 1978. Roughly 35 per cent of women of childbearing age are Catholics, and there may now be a merging of fertility rates between Roman Catholics and non-Catholics.

A Northern Ireland Abortion Campaign (NIAC) was started in 1980 following the death of a girl after a back-street abortion, and it began to inform Westminster MPs about the facts, but 11 out of 12 Northern Irish MPs opposed the extension of abortion rights, and the Minister of State for Northern Ireland noted (in 1981) that since direct rule in 1972 the Government felt it should not change the law unless it could be shown that this would have broad support among the people. However, in 1981 1,441 women from Northern Ireland had abortions in England; by 1982 this figure had risen to 1,510.

That changes are taking place in Eire is shown by the Supreme Court decision in 1974 which ruled that a law forbidding importation of contraceptives was unconstitutional. Polls showed a vast majority in favour. An attempt was made in 1974 to legalize birth control, but this ended in chaos. In 1979 Charles Haughey introduced another Bill, which came into operation (the Health Family Planning Act 1979) in 1980. This allowed, for the first time, the legal sale of contraceptives but with restrictions. These included the fact that non-medical birth control was allowable only on a doctor's prescription and then had to be purchased at a chemist. In February 1980 the Women's Right to Choose Campaign was set up, and later an Irish branch of the Society for the Protection of Unborn Children (SPUC) was launched.

In 1981 the EEC Parliament debated women's rights on a document produced by its Women's Group. It accepted the need for safe legal abortion as a last resort. Thirteen out of 15 Eire members voted against, and two abstained. However, these moves alarmed the Irish Church hierarchy, and in April 1981 another campaign was launched to insert an anti-abortion amendment into the Constitution. To the outsider this campaign seemed rather extraordinary, as abortion was already prohibited by the 1861 Act. The law against abortion in the Republic permits no exceptions, statutory or judge-made, although a so-called 'secondary' abortion is sanctioned when this is an incidental and inevitable consequence of some major medical emergency.

The Pro-Life Amendment Campaign (PLAC) had to amend its original proposal for 'the absolute right to life of every unborn child', as this did not allow for ectopic pregnancy, when abortion was allowed by the Church. Perhaps the reason for trying to alter the Constitution was to prevent any future liberalization, especially in the light of what had recently happened in other Catholic countries like Italy. However, the amendment was opposed by all the major Protestant Churches in the Republic, as well as by the Chief Rabbi. Tying the law to Catholic doctrine could damage any future détente with the Protestants of the North. They were also mindful of the American experience, when the courts had used the Constitution to set aside laws enforcing an unconditional ban to abortion (fully described in chapter 6). There was, finally, the possibility of the intervention of the European Court of Human Rights.

In practice this leads to the hypocritical situation of Irish women coming over to England for their abortions, often giving fake addresses so that official statistics are almost certainly an underestimate. In 1981 the number was 3,600; in 1983 it was 3,700. Three-quarters of the women had been using no form of contraception, and most were single, middle-class and living in Dublin.

Latest figures (*The Times*, 10 April 1985) show an 8 per cent increase to 3,026 during the first nine months of 1984. If that trend continues, it will mean that more than 4,000 women will have crossed the Irish Sea for an abortion here, an all-time record. Other figures (released by the Dublin Health Department) show that almost 8 per cent of all registered births in the Republic during the third quarter of 1984 were illegitimate. In the under-20 age group almost 60 per cent were to unmarried mothers. The 8 per cent increase in the number of women having abortions in England compares with a 5 per cent rise during the same period among women from Northern Ireland who came to England for abortions.

4

A Guide to Legal Abortion Today

The 1967 Act

All legal abortions in England are now governed by the provisions of the 1967 Act. As previously noted, it sets out four principal conditions under which abortions may be carried out: risks to life; risks to physical or mental health; for the sake of others; and risks of having a handicapped child.

Risks to Life

To take in turn the main clauses of the Act, the first one is particularly unfortunately worded. That the risk to life of the pregnant woman is 'greater than if the pregnancy were terminated' can be shown to be true anyway: the risk to life is greater in childbirth than in early termination, or, putting it the other way round, it is now safer to have an early termination than it is to give birth – not that termination is entirely without risk (far from it).

We can draw such conclusions from official statistics published periodically by the DHSS under the rather cumbersome title of *Report on Confidential Enquiries into Maternal Deaths in England and Wales.*[1] For example, during the years 1967–75 there were 1,045 maternal deaths due to purely obstetrical complications. Taking the year 1971, calculations show that comparable death rates for abortion were 3.4 deaths per 100,000, with 18.0 per 100,000 for maternal mortality. By 1980 the maternal mortality rate – defined as the number of deaths due to pregnancy and childbirth per 1,000 total births (live and stillborn) per year – was 0.12 for England and Wales.

Perhaps the pendulum has swung too far in the opposite direction, with abortion now being regarded as a trivial procedure, like having a tooth out, with no serious risks. It is true that by and large it is a remarkably safe procedure when done in proper surroundings on a fit woman in the first trimester of pregnancy. Possible physical and emotional complications are described in the next chapter; here I am concerned solely with deaths, which can still occur.

For the years 1968–71 there were 48 deaths from termination – an average of 14 a year. In 1976–8 there were 15 deaths from legal abortions; in 1978, 6 deaths in 111,851 legal abortions. Taking the whole period from April 1968 to the end of 1982 there were 88 deaths after abortion operations carried out in the NHS, giving an overall rate of 11.44 per 100,000 cases; this was nine times the rate in the private sector. Between 1978 and 1982 inclusive there were 488,860 abortions done privately, and for these five years the death rate in the private sector was 0.4 per 100,000 abortions, one-eleventh of the NHS rate. From these statistics the message seems to be, at least in terms of risk of death, that it is safer to have an abortion done privately.

Why this should be so is a difficult question to answer, as there are many possible variables involved. One suggestion put forward was that NHS operations were more often done by less experienced junior doctors, but there is little proper epidemiological evidence to support this simplistic claim.[2] However, it is worth emphasizing that NHS abortions are still very safe and that some 2 million were carried out between

1968 and 1982. (Further discussion on NHS/private differences can be found in the next chapter.)

One of the hoped-for benefits of the new legislation was to stop the trade in illegal operations, with their terrible toll on health and life. During the years 1943–62 London coroners recorded 276 deaths due to self-induced or illegal abortions. Of these 90 were caused by the woman herself, 75 by others and the other 111 left 'open' or undetermined. The fall in numbers in the second decade was probably due to the introduction of antibiotics.[3]

To return to our main theme, Clause 1 of the Abortion Act, there are now very few physical conditions that occur during pregnancy which could be regarded as being a threat to the mother's life – that is, apart from the risk of suicide, which could, however, be brought under Clause 2 as affecting mental health. This first clause would seem to be largely redundant or could be used to justify any early abortion.

The question of suicide is an important one, as there is a common belief, often promulgated by those who are really anti-abortion, to the effect that pregnant women never commit suicide. This is quite untrue, although, fortunately, it is a relatively rare occurrence.

We know from a vast amount of research that there are two overlapping populations – those who threaten, attempt or make 'suicidal gestures' and those who succeed and do kill themselves. It is sometimes difficult even for the very experienced psychiatrist to assess the risk that a particular woman will actually kill herself. Most suicides should be preventable. In terms of psychiatric disorder, the most commonly associated condition is a depressive illness, which is eminently treatable in most cases. There are two contrasting general statistical trends here: the incidence of depression in women is twice that in men; and although more men commit suicide, more women make attempts.

However, statistical trends are not necessarily helpful in assessing the risk in a particular woman. Much depends on socio-cultural factors, and suicide statistics are anyway notoriously unreliable and subject to many influences, no more so than when it comes to suicide in pregnancy (better considered as suicide *and* pregnancy to take account of some of the more complicated associations so often ignored or missed by researchers). Pregnancy-related suicides can occur in a variety of settings.

(1) A woman may actually not be pregnant but thought or feared she might be.
(2) A woman may incidentally be found to be pregnant (at an autopsy) but she may not necessarily have known this.
(3) The suicide may be part of a desperate attempt at a self-induced abortion, regardless of possible consequences to the woman herself.
(4) A woman with a vulnerable personality may be driven to suicide by an unwelcome pregnancy, perhaps the last straw in a chain of misfortunes.
(5) A suicide attempt may be part of a depressive or other illness following pregnancy (postnatal or puerperal).
(6) 'Symptoms' of pregnancy (e.g. feeling ill with persistent vomiting) may contribute to despair.
(7) A woman may suffer from a morbid fear that the fetus may be damaged or malformed in some way. This may occur after a failed suicide attempt by an overdose.
(8) Pregnancy in early teens may contribute to a later suicide.
(9) A woman, either rightly or wrongly, may believe herself to be infertile.
(10) Going to have, or threatening to have, an illegal abortion may be seen as equivalent to suicide.

The whole subject of suicide in pregnancy has recently been extensively reviewed in a published symposium, with contributions from the USA, Australia, Sweden and England.[4] There were both more suicide attempts (which usually run at anything from 5–20 times the number of completed suicides, although some people die even when suicide was not intended) and more actual suicides in the 1960s than in the 1980s, and that is certainly my own experience. Of a series of 65 patients seen by myself during the first full year after the Abortion Act became law, I considered that 28 per cent were in grave danger of making a serious attempt at suicide.[5]

Why such cases should now be much rarer is well summarized by one of the contributors to the symposium just mentioned:[6]

> Perhaps it is possible to explain these differences by considering that family planning, legalization and availability of abortion, and improvement in education and the standard of living, have become almost universal for the countries reported. It is generally recognized that there has also been a concomitant relaxation of religious and moral scruples and greater sexual awareness and freedoms. These have, perhaps, resulted in a better self-image by the woman and lessened her internal frustrations in association with pregnancy.

Two of the best sources of reliable statistics that we have are the 'Confidential Reports on Maternal Deaths' already mentioned and coroners' reports. From these it can be proved definitively that some pregnant women do kill themselves. Although numbers are small, every case is a preventable tragedy. During the years 1967–75, out of the 1,045 maternal deaths in England and Wales 53 were suicides during pregnancy, labour, delivery and the first year after childbirth. This is one suicide for every maternal death due to obstetrical causes (5 per cent). If women who killed themselves after pregnancy are excluded, 18 women committed suicide during pregnancy, or there was one suicide for every 58 maternal deaths (1.7 per cent). Put another way, this is roughly 0.5 suicides per 100,000. This is actually below the 'usual' or expected suicide rate for women in the age group 15–45, so the overall conclusion would be that between 1 and 7 per cent of women aged 15–45 years who take their own lives are pregnant at the time.

Looking carefully at coroners' reports for the London Administrative County during the 20 years between 1943 and 1962 (i.e. before the present Abortion Act became law), Dr Weir[7] found there were 1,696 completed suicides out of a population of about 3.25 million, with a mean annual number of live births of some 55,000. There were 1,444 cases in which a verdict of suicide was recorded, and 53 of these were pregnant; 252 cases were probably suicide, although another verdict was recorded, and 13 of these were pregnant. Out of the total of 1,696 cases, 66 (4 per cent) were pregnant at the time of death.

Of course, the opposite situation can also occur: pregnancy can be a protective factor which prevents women from attempting suicide. There is some evidence that age may be a crucial factor in this. The protective effect is much stronger when the woman is over 25. By then she is more likely to be married and wanting to have children or at least is prepared to have them.

One interesting finding came out of an American follow-up study connecting teenage pregnancy with later suicide. This concerned 105 New Haven residents who were 17 or under when they gave birth. Of these 14 subsequently attempted or threatened suicide, a much higher rate than would be expected. The risk was higher among single girls, Catholics and those not from poverty areas. Suicidal behaviour was also associated with pregnancy complications and sexually transmitted disease. This excess in suicidal attempts could be due to the stresses of the pregnancy, or both the pregnancy and the suicide attempt could be forms of disturbed adolescent behaviour.[8]

In the late 1960s and 1970s attempted suicides (sometimes called parasuicides or deliberate self-harm) began to assume almost epidemic proportions and constituted a sizeable proportion of all medical emergencies admitted to general hospitals. Cutting wrists or taking an overdose were favourite methods. To some doctors, perhaps lacking adequate psychiatric training, these patients were a nuisance, and one reads reports about 'manipulative young women' or 'immature, attention-seeking young girls'. In slightly less judgemental terminology it became fashionable to talk of the 'cry for help', and this may indeed be an apt label. None the less, such attempts are usually symptomatic of genuine despair and desperation. These women deserve serious assessment and sympathetic hearing, with supportive follow-up arrangements. Once a suicide attempt has been made, the chances of another attempt are greatly increased, as well as a possible future fatal outcome.

Miss C was a 21-year-old Muslim girl who was working in this country as an *au pair* girl. I was asked to see her following her admission to the local general hospital after she had taken an overdose of aspirins. She also complained of abdominal pain. Her story was that she had been seduced by the father of the child she was looking after. She had been in Britain for only eight months and had come to this country to improve her English. Coincidentally the family to whom she was *au pair* was well known to the psychiatric service. The father was an unstable psychopath of 45, and his wife also had a long psychiatric history. When he realized the girl was pregnant he tried a knitting needle on her; this not only caused her abdominal pain but also made her feel even more desperate. She had no friends here and did not dare go home, so she swallowed half a bottle of aspirins in the hope that she might kill herself. Both her parents were Muslims, in their late forties, and her father ran a restaurant in her native country. He had always been very strict with his two daughters (he had six sons as well) and was not keen on her going abroad, although she had read English at university and wanted to be an interpreter. She had had no serious boyfriends at home and was a rather serious, studious girl, still professing to the family religion. She maintained she was trapped in this unsuitable home, persistently bullied and then seduced by her employer, apparently with the knowledge of his wife. He had threatened to write to her parents unless she continued to have sex with him, but when I interviewed him he tried to put the blame on her, implying she had only taken the overdose to frighten him. I arranged a termination for her, and shortly afterwards she returned to her own country. She sent me a postcard some months later to say she was well, very grateful and was just starting a new job as an interpreter.

However, the precise risk to life is often a problem to estimate and quantify and peculiarly difficult to put into meaningful legislation. The major concern is usually with the risks to health ('morbidity') rather than fatal consequences ('mortality'), and this is where the second clause of the 1967 Act is so important and, in practice, the one most commonly used.

An unusual risk to life is when the pregnant girl is threatened by somebody else (e.g. an outraged father) or, because of cultural pressures, is forced into a suicide attempt.

Miss K was a single, 20-year-old Indian girl who worked in a factory but spoke no English. Her parents were strict Sikhs and knew nothing of her referral. (She was accompanied by a friend who also acted as an interpreter.) Miss K herself was extremely agitated, tearful and depressed. She complained of sickness, giddiness and poor appetite. She said that she dare not tell her parents, as either her father would kill her or she would be forced to commit suicide. Her interpreter assured me that she was not exaggerating. It was difficult to get a detailed history from her. She had one sister and two brothers. Her father was described as very strict. He worked on a farm. All she would say about her mother was that she was always ill. She had never felt close to her parents, had had an unhappy childhood and the only trade she had learnt was tailoring. She was now 10 weeks pregnant, the result of a secret liaison over the previous six months with a 30-year-old Englishman who, she thought, was probably married. She had had intercourse with him on three or four occasions without any contraceptive precautions. She had no previous psychiatric history, in the sense that she had never been referred to a psychiatrist, but she did complain of many non-specific symptoms which could be interpreted as neurotic. I thought that termination was indicated but was going to be difficult to accomplish without her parents knowing. I finally arranged with her GP and a gynaecologist that the parents should be told that the girl had menstrual problems which required immediate hospital investigation and that this would include a minor diagnostic procedure. This was as near to the truth as I could make it. She did have a menstrual upset (amenorrhoea or lack of periods!), and the standard investigation for this is a dilatation and curettage (D and C) which can also be used for terminating a pregnancy. This was eventually carried out, along with some discreet advice on contraception.

Risks to Physical or Mental Health

Criticisms have been made of the rather vague wording of the Act ('injury to physical or mental health'), particularly as no definition is given of just how great this risk should be. Technically, the doctor is really being asked for a prognosis, that is, an opinion as to what might happen to a woman's health in the future if a certain course of action is or is not taken. This is often very difficult to be certain about, especially with mental health, as very rarely is physical health involved. In other words, if the pregnancy is allowed to continue, what effect *might* this have on her health? If an abortion is performed, what effect *might* this have on her health? However, the clause may also be interpreted as permitting an abortion now, even though her mental and physical health is good, in order to prevent possible illness in the future if something is not done about her pregnancy.

In calculating just how often the four clauses have been used, either singly or in combination, since the Abortion Act became law, the figure is a fairly constant one at around 70–80 per cent (88 per cent in 1982) for this (second) clause, so that in practice the vast majority of legal abortions carried out in this country are for the sake of the mental health of the mother, on the assumption that if the pregnancy were allowed to continue, it would injure her mental health more than if the pregnancy were terminated. It is also noteworthy that a decreasing proportion of these women are seen by a psychiatrist, so that most operations now done ostensibly on mental health grounds are arranged between a GP or other doctor and a gynaecologist.

There are no guidelines as to the *degree* of danger to health that should be invoked, nor to what is actually meant by 'mental health' in this context. This allows for the widest possible interpretation, from the view of hardliners who say there are no psychiatric indications at all (taking risk to mental health to refer to psychosis, maintaining there is no particular danger of deterioration either during or after pregnancy) to the opposite extreme, that of abortion virtually on demand, when minor worries, unhappiness at not being able to cope, are taken to mean injury to mental health.

An attempt to define health was made by the World Health Organization (WHO), but it produced an impossibly idealistic definition of little use in the real world: 'A state of complete physical, mental and social well-being and not merely the absence of disease or infirmity'. The semantic confusion becomes even worse when considering mental health. Some community surveys in the USA, using a variety of techniques designed to assess mental health from unstructured interviews to rating scales and questionnaires, have found alarmingly high percentages of neurosis and other symptoms of mental illness among the general population. Some of these investigations have reached the rather ludicrous conclusion that it is normal (in the statistical sense) to be mentally ill, so that estimates of the incidence of mental illness vary from claims that some form of psychiatric ill-health is almost universal to the assertion that it is practically non-existent. Indeed, the main thrust of anti-psychiatry movements, from the 1950s onwards, has been that mental illness is a myth, a product of social, political and cultural factors, 'invented' by psychiatrists and other interested parties so that they may exercise power, authority and control.

Trying to define mental illness has defeated some of the best brains in the country. For example, in the Mental Health Acts of 1959 and 1983 mental illness was left undefined. Under the new Mental Health Act 1983 there are (legally) four categories of mental disorder: mental illness, mental impairment, severe mental impairment and psychopathic disorder, the last three being defined. The definition of 'mental illness' is left to the clinical judgement of doctors. However, there is some clarification of the question of who should *not* be considered mentally disordered. Section 1(3) of the Act states that a person may not be dealt with under the Act as suffering from mental disorder 'by reason only of promiscuity or other immoral conduct, sexual deviancy, or dependence on alcohol or drugs'.

Admittedly, the classical 'medical model' – i.e. a specific collection of signs and symptoms which regularly occur together (syndrome) with a demonstrable pathology, causation, course and prognosis – is not always applicable to mental disorders as currently understood. Taking a wider view, are 'health' and 'disease' descriptive or evaluative concepts, and what is the relationship between illness and disease? A philosopher might further ask: If health and disease are evaluative concepts, what is their relationship to other evaluative concepts, such as moral ones? Or is the distinction between descriptive and evaluative concepts itself untenable? Or can the evaluative conclusion that a woman is ill be derived logically from the descriptive premise that she displays certain symptoms?

Concepts of health and disease would seem to me to be both descriptive and evaluative; certainly, in the latter case we have to think that something is bad or undesirable about a condition before classifying it as a disease. A statement describing symptoms does not entail the statement that a patient has a disease unless it is coupled with a definition of the disease, which states that to have such symptoms is to have the disease. However, this definition, besides bordering on the tautological, encapsulates an evaluation and is more than a mere definition of a word. A norm has to be supplied (via the definition) before the conclusion can be drawn.

Mental disorders tend to have vaguer definitions than physical disorders, but there is no logical difficulty in giving more precise definitions, which will encapsulate the value judgement that such conditions are bad and also determine more precisely what treatments will remove these conditions. If that is done and the value judgements in the definition are accepted, then psychiatric treatment can be justified. The difference between mental disorder and moral, social or political deviation lies not in the fact that the former is less evaluative but rather in the source of the norms of value judgements. With diseases the patient may be expected to agree to the norms (the notion that the condition is bad); therefore if she believes that the treatment will remove the condition, she will accept it. In the cases of moral, social or political deviation this is not so – hence compulsory 'treatment' for such conditions will be in many cases an infringement of liberty unless done by due process of law.

The difference between an illness and a disease can be illustrated by the fact that a patient complains of feeling ill but not of being diseased, but the wider concept of disease can be portrayed as 'dis-ease'. To some there can never be any disease unless there is some tangible disorder of the anatomy or physiology. In the case of many 'functional' psychiatric disorders this cannot (as yet) be demonstrated, although some rather more subtle biochemical lesions may yet be found.

Looking at illness from another, rather more pragmatic perspective, it has three general characteristics: distress, disability and disadvantage. These criteria can certainly be applied to mental disorder. By distress is meant pain or suffering, which can manifest itself as anxiety, guilt feelings, depression, paranoid ideas and obsessional doubts, to name just a few possibilities. Disability can be impaired efficiency, either general or more specific, like poor concentration, loss of memory and loss of interest or the will to live. Anxiety is a good example. We all have our own optimal level. Anxiety alerts the organism, keeps us on our toes, has survival value and actually increases efficiency. Above a certain level it does just the opposite, so that neurotic disorders generally can be seen to be based on feelings and reactions experienced by everyone (hence the truism 'We are all potentially neurotic') but are grossly exaggerated, last for an excessively long time or are inappropriate responses to particular stimuli or situations. Disadvantages may be personal and practical (as a result, for example, of impaired efficiency) or perhaps biological (as may be seen by the very low fertility of schizophrenics as well as their low marriage rates).

Certainly, my own experience and that of others who have published their results is that women seen for termination of pregnancy on mental health grounds are mostly suffering from neurotic conditions with or without minor personality disorders, often with social problems as well but rarely with psychotic conditions. Some of these states may be difficult to classify precisely, especially using the diagnostic criteria of the Ninth Revision of the International Classification of Diseases,[9] the official system used in the UK and the one on which our national statistics are based. Some doctors simply put 'anxiety' as the diagnosis on the form completed for legal abortions. (For the emotional complications of abortion see chapter 5.)

For the Sake of Others

The third clause of the Abortion Act, allowing termination for the sake of any existing child or children of the pregnant woman, causes me most concern, as it goes against the accepted tradition that it is the maternal and fetal health which are the crucial and central issue. Under this clause it is possible to terminate the pregnancy of a perfectly healthy woman with a perfectly healthy fetus. In my view this widens the conditions unnecessarily and opens the way for termination for the sake of all sorts of other people, for example, husband, grandparents, parents-in-law, for all of whose sake I have been asked to arrange terminations.

Theoretically it is clear for which sort of case this was originally intended: the overburdened woman who is already only just coping with several children and who could not manage another one. But in this instance the other children would suffer only because their mother could not cope, a matter which could be covered by the second clause as adversely affecting her health. Another hypothetical case would be a woman who already had a mentally handicapped child at home and would not be able to manage with another baby unless the handicapped one was institutionalized, but again I feel this sort of situation could be covered by the second clause.

The rights of the husband have recently been decided in a test case, *Paton* v. *Trustees of the British Pregnancy Advisory Service* (1978). Mrs Paton, pregnant and separated from her husband, wanted an abortion, but he tried to stop it, claiming his consent had not been obtained. He failed for two reasons: first, there is nothing in the Abortion Act which states that the consent of the putative father is necessary; secondly, the judge decided there was no right invested in the unborn child which someone else could champion on his own or the child's behalf.

Mr Paton then took the case to the European Commission on Human Rights in the case *Paton* v. *United Kingdom* (1980).

The father of the child had advanced two separate arguments: first, he had personal rights in connection with his child; secondly, he had standing as a parent or guardian to bring proceedings on behalf of the child for its protection. However, the Commission affirmed the UK decision as being consistent with the European Convention on Human Rights. The situation in the USA is similar as the law does not allow the husband to veto his wife's decision to have an abortion (but see section on Japan, page 250, for a different view).

This does not mean to say that there are no difficulties surrounding this matter, as a recent case of my own will illustrate.

A 34-year-old married woman became pregnant for the third time as a result of a contraceptive failure. Her husband came with her to the consultation. He was obviously in a very depressed and agitated state and told me that unless I recommended an abortion for his wife, *he* would commit suicide. His wife, although distressed, did not really want an abortion. She had had one some nine years previously and was still feeling extremely guilty about it. As already outlined, strictly an abortion cannot be recommended under the Act for the sake of the husband's health, and I felt that if the abortion were carried out, it could lead to prolonged resentment and hostility on the part of the wife towards her husband and so endanger the marriage. She was physically and mentally healthy and had no special social problems. It is also against my own practice to recommend termination for a woman who (in my view) is fundamentally against it and additionally, in this case, had reacted badly to a previous abortion. In the end I managed to persuade the husband to enter a psychiatric hospital for treatment and let the pregnancy continue.

Risks of Having a Handicapped Child

The fourth clause was obviously influenced by the thalidomide tragedies and the known effects of rubella (German measles) in producing congenital abnormalities. It is invoked in about 1–2 per cent of cases. As far as I am aware, the interpretation of the actual wording of this part of the Act (i.e. the precise meaning of 'substantial risk' and 'seriously handicapped') has never been tested in court. The latter could be, and has been, interpreted as meaning 'incapable of leading an independent existence when of an age to do so' or something similar. Some genetically determined conditions may also qualify, like Huntington's chorea, which is inherited as a non-sex-linked dominant condition, meaning that a particular fetus has a 50 per cent chance of inheriting the condition, although the disease itself is not usually manifest until after about the age of 35. In sex-linked inherited conditions like haemophilia it is necessary to know the sex of the fetus, and this can be determined. It affects one in two boy babies born to women carrying the disease.

It is much more difficult to be precise about the genetic risk for the major psychotic conditions, such as schizophrenia, apart from stating some rather general figures such as an increased risk to the child of the order of about 10–15 per cent above chance expectation if one of the parents is schizophrenic. Of course, if the mother herself is schizophrenic, termination could be considered for the sake of her own health under Clause 2.

One of the practical difficulties is trying to be sure that a particular fetus is affected. For instance, the mother may say she has been in contact with a case of German measles.

Mrs P was aged 28 and had been married for eight years. She already had five children and said she 'carried' badly, could not go through with another pregnancy and, in any case, had just had German measles. Also, her nerves were in a bad state. She complained of dizzy spells, cystitis and bad headaches. She felt, too, that they could not afford another child. She was about 11 weeks pregnant. Her parents were still alive, but she didn't get on very well with either of them. She had five brothers and one sister. She had a poor work record of unskilled jobs. At the age of 15 she had been raped and became pregnant but, with the help of her mother, kept the child. She eventually married a bus conductor one year older than herself, being pregnant at the time. The pregnancy ended in a spontaneous miscarriage. In spite of the regular use of a cap for contraception, she managed to have four more children: at the time she was seen they were aged 12, 7, 5, 3 and 2. The present pregnancy was unwanted; she did not know how it could have happened; and she was very depressed at having 'fallen' again. After the pregnancy was terminated, she was sterilized.

A further difficulty lies in estimating just how *severely* affected the fetus may be. Some authorities have tried to argue that nature herself decides, in that the fetuses most severely affected will either die *in utero* and/or spontaneously abort. However, such an experience can be traumatic and may induce the fear of having a second deformed child which can seriously damage a woman's mental health, as the following case demonstrates.

Mrs M was a 27-year-old married woman who was ten weeks pregnant and terrified in case the baby might be born with a congenital defect and die like her last one. Since the death of that baby a few hours after birth, she had been tense, irritable and depressed and had suffered from bad headaches. She had, in fact, been attending her GP regularly over the previous four years with symptoms of phobic anxiety and had received a number of minor tranquillizers and anti-depressants. She described her mother as a worrying type; her father had recurrent headaches; her brother also had headaches and 'bad nerves'; and her only sister was described as shy and nervous. She left school at 16 and had a good work record. She married a policeman, slightly older than herself, when she was aged 20. The marriage was a happy one, and there were no sexual problems. Contraception was usually with a sheath except just before a period. She had suffered one spontaneous miscarriage, the deformed baby which had died 18 months previously, and had one girl aged 6. There were no particular financial worries. She was fond of children and a good mother. She had suffered from recurrent migraine since the age of 16. Termination was recommended, with advice about a contraceptive pill, along with genetic counselling.

Since the thalidomide case both the medical profession and the general public have become much more aware of possible risks in taking any sort of drug during early pregnancy. Because of the legal and financial (compensation) implications most pharmaceutical companies try and cover themselves when they produce a new drug by issuing a warning about possible harmful effects during pregnancy. Of course, any new drug has to go through very rigorous testing procedures, both in animals and humans, before being released for general medical use. But what about the case of a woman who inadvertently takes some medication either not realizing she was pregnant at the time or not realizing the medicine could be harmful? There have been some campaigns mounted with the aim of having everything which can be bought from the chemist labelled with a warning notice about pregnancy. Some even want the pharmacist to ask every woman he serves if she might be pregnant. These do not seem to be very realistic expectations and perhaps those demanding such impractical measures would also like to consider the effects of alcohol and smoking on pregnancy.

Diagnosing handicap before birth

Without going into too many technical details, I want at this point briefly to summarize the ways we now have at our disposal for obtaining direct information about the presence or absence of abnormality in the unborn fetus, bearing in mind that 2 per cent of babies in England and Wales are born with a congenital abnormality. Some of these techniques are very recent and may not be available all over the country.[10]

(1) Clinical examination and tests on the mother, e.g. alphafetoprotein (AFP) levels in her serum. An increase usually indicates spina bifida or similar defect. The test is done at 14 weeks but needs confirming by amniocentesis (see point 4 below). Hopefully, tests on the mother's blood may some day render amniocentesis obsolete.

(2) Ultrasound examination: sound waves at high frequency (over 20,000 vibrations per second) are passed through the body (painlessly) and reveal the size and shape of the fetus. With today's high-resolution ultrasound equipment and growing operator expertise many congenital abnormalities can be diagnosed prenatally, giving an early option for abortion. In late

pregnancy, when abortion is no longer feasible, the detection of an anomaly may significantly affect further management (e.g. planning a delivery where paediatric surgery is available). However, the detection of some conditions, like hydrocephalus, may not be possible until 24–26 weeks.

Diagnosis by ultrasound is now made in one of three ways: (a) by direct visualization of the defect, (b) by demonstrating disproportionate growth of a particular fetal part, (c) by recognizing the effect of the anomaly on adjacent structures.

The main controversy surrounding the use of ultrasound scans in pregnancy is whether they should be used routinely in all pregnancies because there might be some undesirable side-effects. An early scan at about 16 weeks can establish gestational age accurately, localize the placenta and detect multiple pregnancy and some congenital abnormalities. It may also help psychological bonding with the fetus. The consensus of modern opinion is that any possible hazards from the procedure have not become apparent over the 25 years it has been in use but none the less the case for *routine* use remains unproven.

(3) Examination of the non-cellular constituents of amniotic fluid.

(4) Examination of cultures derived from cells in the amniotic fluid. The cells and fluid are obtained by amniocentesis, which is still the main way to diagnose Down's syndrome (mongolism). This is done by passing a hypodermic needle through the mother's abdomen (near the navel) into the womb and then sucking up some of the fluid which surrounds the fetus. Getting the fluid out is quickly done and does not usually require a local anaesthetic.

The relevant risks involved depend very much on the mother's age. An amniocentesis can be done on the NHS for all women aged 37 or over (in the USA it is

35 for routine testing), but any anxious mother in this country can have the test done privately. At age 35 the overall risk of finding a fetal abnormality is of the order of 1 in 300, with a 1 in 50 chance of precipitating a miscarriage by the procedure itself. At age 40 the incidence of fetal abnormalities jumps to 1 in 100, and by age 46 it is as high as 1 in 20 for Down's syndrome.

Other possible dangers of amniocentesis are the introduction of infection or, more rarely, damage to a fetal limb, but the procedure cannot be done until about 16–19 weeks of pregnancy, and then the tests take about four weeks to complete.

(5) Inspection of the fetus by fetoscopy. This was first introduced into clinical practice in 1973. Under local anaesthesia and sedation a small tube with a telescopic end is inserted through the abdominal wall into the amniotic cavity. Apart from direct inspection, samples of fetal blood and other tissues can also be obtained. Experts now claim that fetoscopy has become an effective procedure for the diagnosis of at least 50 congenital abnormalities and can also be used as an aid to treating the fetus while it is still in the womb. The optimal time for fetoscopy is 15–18 weeks, but fetal blood sampling is usually delayed until 18–20 weeks' gestation.

(6) Examination of fetal blood obtained from placental (afterbirth) vessels at fetoscopy.

(7) Examination of fetal tissues (e.g. skin) obtained at fetoscopy.

(8) Examination of material obtained by taking what is called 'chorionic villus sampling'. This means obtaining a tiny sample from the processes, rich in blood vessels, which grow out from the outermost layer of the envelope surrounding the fertilized ovum. This procedure makes it possible to diagnose genetic disorders before the end of the first trimester of pregnancy. The technique is to place a cannula, or special forceps, into

> an area rich in chorionic villi at 8–11 weeks' gestation and to obtain a sample either by aspiration or by directly cutting a small piece. This has to be done by the safest possible technique without puncturing the amniotic sac, precipitating a miscarriage, causing fetal death or introducing infection. The technique is being used increasingly to detect such hereditary disorders as muscular dystrophy and the blood diseases thalassaemia, sickle-cell anaemia and haemophilia. All this is possible because the tissue sampled carries the same genetic configuration as the fetus.

These procedures offer prospects for selective abortion but also bring with them a great deal of mental anguish, particularly during the wait for results.[11] They also need to be taken into consideration before rushing too hastily into reducing the time limit (from 28 weeks) for legal abortions. These improved methods for prenatal diagnosis again highlight a number of ethical issues, recently discussed in the *British Medical Journal.*[12]

There are four interrelated issues: the moral justification for selective abortion; the rights of parents as against the rights of society; problems of consent and duress; and questions of risk and benefit inherent in the development of new techniques.

As regards the first, it can already be seen that the 1967 Abortion Act supports a liberal policy of abortion of abnormal fetuses especially if pregnant women feel unable to cope with the upbringing of a handicapped child. Some see better information as a clear moral gain allowing the avoidance of suffering, the weeding out of conditions which natural selection would in any case discard, the earlier termination of pregnancies where the outcome for the fetus is inevitably fatal and the continuation of those clearly established as normal. Others fear the appearance of a eugenic philosophy which would regard all less-than-perfect human beings as inferior and would promote what some have called 'ante-natal euthanasia'. Inevitably, the spectre of the 'master race' and all that happened in Nazi Germany is advanced as an awful warning of possible consequences. It is a truism that modern scientific advances can be used for good or evil purposes, yet this should not hinder progress or education of the public, so 'informed consent' continues to have real meaning. It seems to me that, with the exceptions mentioned in this book, our present legislation is an acceptable compromise between totally opposed views.

These tests can, of course, readily detect the sex of the fetus. The question then arises: Should parents be able to terminate a pregnancy simply because the child is of the 'wrong' sex? With present legislation this can be done only for sex-linked hereditary disorders, and most people would, I think, want it to stay that way. In other words, mere preference for either a boy or a girl should not be grounds for abortion. There have been recent allegations that some groups in Britain, such as Asians, are abusing this facility. If it is shown that the fetus is female an abortion is sought on any convincing pretext when the real reason is that a girl is not wanted as this would mean extra expense in finding her a dowry in a traditional marriage (*The Times*, 25 June 1985).

What about the opposite case, when a mother is not willing to have an abortion even though tests have shown the fetus to be severely handicapped or the carrier of a pathological gene? Should she be required by law to have an abortion in order to save the fetus from becoming a handicapped child or society from an economic burden? This would clearly trespass across present boundaries, which deal only with requests for termination and are in no sense coercive or obligatory. A move in this direction might herald the eugenic programme so feared by some.

However, it is also tempting to suggest that mass screening, to be fully effective, should be compulsory for groups clearly identified as at risk, and that terminations should be carried out if the tests are positive even though the tests themselves are not compulsory. The answer seems to be that there can be no moral obligation, far less a legal one, to undergo prenatal diagnosis when there is no moral consensus on the justifiability of abortion.

Finally, there are the familiar problems of risk versus benefit. An earlier prenatal test (e.g. chorionic sampling) is desirable in order to avoid the risk and trauma of later termination, but though the risks to the mother appear negligible, the risks to the fetus cannot be measured accurately. How much should mothers be subjected to new and sometimes experimental techniques, and how much should they be told? The complication in prenatal diagnosis is that not one but two individuals are affected. It has been suggested that a handicapped person may later sue for 'wrongful life'. As yet no court has upheld such a claim, nor does it seem likely that such a legal obligation to terminate another's life could be established. This matter is further discussed in the next section.

The legal rights of a fetus

It might be as well to pause here for a moment to summarize the legal, as opposed to the moral, rights of a fetus. In fact, the legal status of the unborn child, and the rights of others to make decisions affecting it, are problematic areas. In February 1982 Mary McKay, aged 6, was told by the Court of Appeal that it was not possible in law to sue her GP for failing to recommend an abortion. Her mother had had German measles during pregnancy, and Mary was born seriously handicapped. There may still be further hearings among the doctors and the Area Health Authority involved as to whether there was any negligence involved. One question is whether a doctor is negligent if he fails to advise a mother to have an abortion, but the judiciary has already decided that there is no legal right not to be born. Following the thalidomide disaster, legislation was passed – the Congenital Disabilities (Civil Liabilities) Act 1976 – barring any further 'wrongful life' claims.[13]

It seems, then, that the fetus has no legal rights: these do not arise until the child is born and born alive. What never seems to have been tested is a situation in which under succession law the fetus may have been bequeathed inherited property. If there were a threat to this property, could some third party intervene to protect the unborn child's interest, perhaps to prevent the fetus from being aborted?

In civil litigation there must be some element of personal interest involved. For instance, an individual anti-abortionist cannot prosecute a particular gynaecologist simply because he or she finds abortion offensive. Nor can the criminal law be enforced by an individual acting in a private capacity, except in very special circumstances and with the permission of the Director of Public Prosecutions or the Attorney-General. The legal options open to those who oppose abortion are limited. In other words, an action cannot be brought on behalf of an unborn child to prevent it from being aborted. Nor can anyone seek an injunction to prevent that abortion on the grounds that it infringes his or her own rights. It is still theoretically possible to have a test case if an abortion were to be performed when there were apparently no valid grounds for doing so and the putative father made specific allegations about this.

Numbers of legal and illegal abortions

One of the virtues of the present Abortion Act is that for the first time we are able to compile reliable statistics, so that trends can be monitored. These are collected for the Department of Health and Social Security (DHSS) by the Office of Population Censuses and Surveys (OPCS) and published by Her Majesty's Stationery Office (HMSO) for all to see.[14] This puts us in the position of being able to confirm or refute, for instance, the allegation that the Act is opening the floodgates of abortion, although while we can be fairly confident that the absolute numbers are correct, some of the other information collected may be distorted – for example, women may lie about their ages or their country of origin.

However, official figures can now be quoted to counter such emotive allegations (beloved of certain journalists) as that London has become the 'abortion capital' of the world, or that numbers of abortions are ever-increasing, or that the Abortion Act 1967 is a 'charter for promiscuity', mainly for young, single working-class girls who use it as a form of contraception. Further adverse comment has been made about foreigners flocking to this country on special charter flights, giving rise to a rather sordid commercial picture. There is some truth in this last allegation, although the majority of foreign women do not overburden the NHS, as they go to the private sector.

So what do the actual statistics show? Absolute numbers are not as helpful as relative or proportional ones. For example, one reason for an increase in the number of abortions may be an increase in the number of women in the population of childbearing age. Figures can also be expressed as a proportion of live births, or as a percentage of all conceptions.

The absolute numbers have fluctuated rather, for 1980 it was 128,927. By 1982 the figure was 163,045, but by 1983 this had dropped to 127,375. There is some evidence that figures for 1984–5 may again have increased. (Figures for teenagers and under-age girls are discussed in the next section.) Putting these statistics in another way and dealing only with women resident in Britain, numbers have now evened out to around 11–12 per 1,000 women in the age group 15–44. A GP with an average list of 2,500 patients might expect to have between 7 and 10 women presenting each year with an abortion problem. As a percentage of live births, the figure for abortions works out at around 18 per cent.

From figures I calculated over the first five years of the Act the proportion of 'ever-marrieds' (i.e. those who had been married at some time in their lives) to single women remained remarkably constant at around 53 per cent (44 per cent married, 9 per cent widowed, separated or divorced) and 47 per cent single. Breaking down the figures by age groups, the highest percentage of women having abortions was in the age group of 20–34. The higher proportion of single women in the last few years may reflect a later age for marriage, more divorces or more couples living together. Certainly, the earlier figures did not support the popular stereotype of the predominance of the very young, single girl.

If the numbers are beginning to creep up again, there are four main reasons which might explain this:[15]

(1) disenchantment with 'safe' methods of contraception – for instance, the pill – after the publication of unfavourable reports (every time there is a 'cancer scare' this is likely to happen, although there is no convincing evidence to show that long-term use of the pill is associated in any simple way with cancer of either the breast or the cervix);
(2) pressure on health authorities to reduce regional variations in abortion availability;
(3) reluctance to cope with unplanned children because of the economic recession;
(4) reduction in family planning services due to financial constraints on the NHS.

The number of foreign women coming here for abortions has fluctuated a great deal, much depending on the abortion laws and the availability of abortion in various European countries. (For more details see chapter 6.) By 1983 nearly 35,000 foreign women were coming to Britain for abortions, including 500 girls under the age of 16. Should we be acquiescing in this? I suppose the answer largely depends on feelings and attitudes rather than other factors. Looked at more objectively, it could be said that we have a long tradition in this country of providing expert medical treatment for people from all over the world and that this is merely an extension of that tradition. If it were not abortions but something like cardiac surgery or kidney transplants that

Britain was providing, such additional factors as national pride and prestige, with perhaps economic advantages, might also be mentioned.

One of the hoped-for benefits of the Act was that it would put a stop to back-street illegal abortions, with all their attendant hazards. For obvious reasons, and as noted earlier, statistics for illegal operations are difficult to obtain and to verify and therefore remain contentious. Anti-abortionists maintained that liberalizing the law would increase rather than decrease the numbers of illegal abortions, but to settle this argument one has to agree on the figures, especially on how they are obtained. Some ways of measuring illegal abortions are to consult the 'Confidential Reports on Maternal Deaths', to calculate admissions to hospital for incomplete and septic abortions and to review the number of prosecutions. Certainly, in the last there has been a very marked drop: in 1975 only two cases were recorded of procuring illegal abortions.

One author, Cavadino,[16] argued that the only reliable index was the number of hospital discharges after treatment for incomplete abortions, and even then there were difficulties over the interpretation of the figures. However, from these figures he sought to show that there had been an increase in illegal operations. This was refuted by Francome,[17] who showed that Cavadino had tried to discount all indices for measuring illegal abortions except the one that suited his purpose and that even in the statistics he did use there were several errors. The conclusion was that the index used was highly unreliable and that there had, in fact, been a significant fall in the number of illegal abortions. Francome further considered that the number of illegal abortions had fallen from 100,000 (80,000 illegal and 20,000 quasi-legal) annually before the introduction of the 1967 Act to around 8,000 a year. This much quoted figure of 100,000 illegal abortions annually derives from an estimate published in 1940[18] from figures provided by the British Medical Association for both spontaneous and induced abortions. Of course, this is only an estimate and has been disputed, not only by those with an axe to grind but also by the medical establishment: a report by the Royal College of Obstetricians and Gynaecologists in 1966 suggested a figure of 14,600 a year.

Even if it could be shown that legalizing abortion did not reduce the total numbers of abortions there could still be a considerable advantage in that there would be a marked reduction in both deaths and general morbidity.

Teenage pregnancies and abortions

In 1976 there were 20,000 illegitimate births to girls under 20. In 1977 there were 27,990 abortions (27 per cent of the total) performed on girls aged 16–19 and 3,592 (3.5 per cent) on girls under the age of 16. In 1980 the figures were 32,270 (24.7 per cent) and 3,648 (2.8 per cent) respectively. By 1983 over a quarter of all abortions were done on girls under 20. The figure for the 16–19 age group was 31,000.

Taking the years 1971–80, the live birth rate in girls aged 15–19 dropped from 51 to 31 per 1,000, a greater rate of fall than in any other age group except that of women aged 40–44. Less than a third of this fall can be accounted for by an increase in the abortion rate. From 1970 to 1977 the birth rate in the 15–19 age group fell by 20.4 per 1,000, while the abortion rate rose by only 6 per thousand. Since 1977 there have been slight increases in both birth and abortion rates, perhaps because fears about the safety of the contraceptive pill have led to changes to less reliable methods. There has also been an increase in the number of girls at risk, with a decreasing age for the onset of puberty (menarche).[19]

What is most worrying, perhaps, is the number of pregnancies and abortions in girls under the age of consent (16), although some 15-year-olds can be surprisingly mature and can make good mothers if given adequate support. Over the five-year period 1974–8 there were 18,851 pregnancies in schoolgirls aged 15. Of these 12,873 were terminated. There has, however, been an increase in the number of 15-year-old girls in England and Wales over these years, but the increase in the number of pregnancies is out of proportion to this.[20] Since 1950 there has been a sevenfold true increase in the number of pregnant 15-year-olds in England and Wales, so that now, on average, somewhere between 3,000 and 4,000 abortions a year are carried out in this age group. The actual figure for 1983 was 4,100.

Apart from increased medical risks to both mother and baby, there are also psychological complications to consider, especially as very young girls often present relatively late in pregnancy, and important ethical and legal issues as well. I (and, I'm sure, many other doctors) have had the experience of being confronted by very angry parents, accompanied by their pregnant under-age daughters, who have demanded that she have an abortion forthwith. No mention is made of the girl's own wishes. In such circumstances I always insist on interviewing the girl first, on her own, before seeing the parents.

Two cases will illustrate some of the problems encountered with very young teenage pregnancies.

Alice was a 15-year-old schoolgirl who had been adopted at an early age. Her parents, who came with her, demanded she be aborted at once. They were both schoolteachers in their mid-fifties and were extremely rigid, puritanical, over-protective and over-anxious. Alice was 13 weeks pregnant. When seen by her GP she had denied ever having had intercourse. Her GP described her in his letter to me as 'sexually mature, wilful and untruthful'. When I saw her on her own she admitted being pregnant but was unsure what, if anything, she wanted to do about it. When asked whether she could foresee any particular consequences if she went on with the pregnancy, she mentioned two things: the effect locally on her father's reputation and the fact that she herself would have to leave school. She started menstruating at 10½ and was informed about the physiological facts of life by her mother. Her periods were always regular. Her (to me) not very convincing story was that over the past year she had been seeing a boy of 21 who was engaged to somebody else but had said that he found the patient 'incredibly attractive'. On one occasion only they had sexual intercourse, and he withdrew before ejaculating (coitus interruptus). She was a willing partner, did not claim she had been raped or coerced in any way and was not drunk at the time. She was of average intelligence, looked older than her years and was doing reasonably well at school. She said she got on fairly well with her father but could not stand her mother. She denied any other troubles, but at the age of 10 she had indulged in a lot of petty theft, which had gone on for a whole year. After further counselling she decided it would be in everybody's best interest if she had an abortion.

Joy was another 15-year-old schoolgirl who presented with both her parents, who insisted on an abortion as she was below the age of consent. She was nine weeks pregnant, and at first, after telling her parents, she had said that she wanted to have the baby, as she wanted someone of her very own to love and look after. She had now changed her mind, however, or so the parents alleged. When I saw her on her own she said that she did want an abortion, although this was due not to parental pressure but to the realization of what would be entailed if she had a baby and the fact that she was beginning to feel quite ill: she was vomiting a lot, was irritable and had backache. Other significant facts emerged later in the interview. Six months previously her best friend had been killed in a road accident. Joy was extremely upset by this, frequently visited her grave and felt very guilty about a row they had had the last time she saw her friend. Also, she was very keen to stay on at school – she wanted to be a vet – but her parents were insisting that she leave at the earliest opportunity to help run their shop. Her parents were both over-protective yet rejecting and could not understand why she was so 'wilful'. Her mother was attending her GP with symptoms of anxiety and was receiving tranquillizers. Joy was their eldest child, the others being boys aged 14, 12 and 8. Her boyfriend was a local lad of 17 whom she'd known for about four months. Her parents strongly disapproved of him and said he was not good enough for her. He was very fond of her and wanted to marry her. According to Joy, intercourse had occurred on three occasions only, twice using a sheath and once with him withdrawing. Her parents wished to prosecute the young man, but they had intimated in a roundabout way that if she had an abortion, if the whole thing was hushed up and if she did not see him again, then no further action would be taken. Termination was duly carried out, and Joy was seen later, when she had resumed secret meetings with the same boy but was on the pill and was still hoping to marry him.

This type of situation, more than any other, raises the fundamental issues of the rights of parents versus the rights of their children. Nor is the legal situation always entirely clear if a gynaecologist terminates simply with the parents' permission or, indeed, against their wishes. A further complication, which must always be considered with very young pregnant girls, is the possibility of incest.

In 1981 (re P(minor) FD, 26 October 1981, Butler-Sloss J.) an important legal precedent was set concerning an under-age girl who first became pregnant aged 14.[21] The girl was taken into care and, in November 1980, gave birth to a boy. She was subsequently transferred to a mother-and-baby unit for minors. In August 1981 she was again found to be pregnant and requested an abortion, but this was firmly opposed on religious grounds by her parents, who were Seventh Day Adventists. The local authority made her a ward of court and invited the court to make an order directing her pregnancy to be terminated. Both social worker and medical opinions favoured termination on the grounds that she was at risk from developing postnatal depression and further psychiatric disorder later. The girl understood about abortion and its possible undesirable effects, including guilt feelings. In fact, the girl herself had wanted the first pregnancy terminated, but this was opposed by her parents, and as she was already 18 weeks pregnant when first examined, it was allowed to continue.

Judgment was made in favour of the girl and termination recommended under the Abortion Act on the grounds that there would be a risk to her mental health if the pregnancy were allowed to continue. It was also recommended that she be fitted with an IUD.[22]

A number of legal points were raised by this case, namely, the interpretation of Section 1 of the Abortion Act, the overriding of her parents' authority and the provision of contraception to a girl under the age of consent, which could amount to connivance in unlawful sexual intercourse. The girl herself committed no offence under Sections 5 and 6 of the Sexual Offences Act 1956, though she was the one at risk and must be protected by contraception. This pragmatism calls the consent laws into question, together with the issue of public morality.

Girls under 16 may in exceptional circumstances give consent to treatment, especially if it is informed consent and they understand the full implications of the treatment. In 1974, as guidance for doctors, the Medical Defence Union stated:

> When the girl is under 16 her parents should always be consulted unless she forbids the practitioner to do so. The written consent of the parents should be obtained but their refusal should not be allowed to prevent a lawful termination to which the patient herself consents and which is considered to be clinically necessary. Conversely a termination should never be carried out in opposition to the girl's wishes even if the parents demand it.

Similar guidelines had been issued by the General Medical Council to help GPs placed in such a situation; they should try first to persuade the girl to confide in her parents and seek their advice and guidance, but if she was unwilling to do this, her wishes should be respected.

It must be remembered that if a girl has enough sense to come for medical advice on her own, then by and large she is probably well able to make up her own mind and give informed consent. Also, some parents are inadequate, unhelpful and positively harmful in their influence, and in these cases it would be doing the girl a disservice to try to make her confide in them. The mere fact that she has come to consult her GP without their knowledge may be symptomatic of this. Last, there is the fundamental principle of medical confidentiality, which should apply to any patient, of whatever age, unless there are extremely compelling reasons for breaking this.

The *Gillick* case

This was the position until 1984, when the *Gillick* case caused a change in the guidelines issued to doctors. Mrs Gillick is a Roman Catholic mother of 10 children who was affronted by the prospect of one of her under-age daughters being prescribed the contraceptive pill without her mother's consent. Technically Mrs Gillick claimed that a DHSS memorandum of guidance, issued in 1980, allowing doctors to use discretion over parental consent was unlawful. She maintained that it invited doctors to contravene Sections 6 and 28 of the Sexual Offences Act 1956. Section 28 forbids the causing or encouraging of sexual intercourse with a girl under 16, and Section 6 makes it an offence to be an accessory. She further claimed that under Section 8(1) of the Family Law Reform Act 1969 patients under 16 cannot consent to medical treatment.

Initially her claim was dismissed: in law the claim was against two defendants, the West Norfolk and Wisbech Area Health Authority and the DHSS, and was heard by Mr Justice Woolf. He issued his judgment on 26 July 1983. However, the matter did not rest there, as the case was taken to the Court of Appeal, which overruled the earlier decision (*The Times*, Law Report, 21 December 1984). The judges declared that in essence there were two matters to be investigated: (a) the extent of a parent's rights and duties with respect to the medical treatment of a girl under 16, and (b) the extent to which, if at all, the provision of the criminal law assisted in the determination of the extent of the parent's rights and duties in relation specifically to contraception or abortion advice treatment. They then considered the case law in these areas, and in the end the Court of Appeal granted two declarations:

(1) that the Health Service Notice HN(80)46, issued by the DHSS in December 1980, had no authority in law and gave advice which was unlawful and wrong;
(2) that no doctor or other person employed by the Health Authority, either in the family planning service or otherwise, might give any contraceptive or abortion advice to any child of Mrs Gillick's under the age of 16 without the prior knowledge and consent of the child's parent or guardian save in cases of emergency or with leave of the court.

As is usual in such rulings, there was no attempt to define an 'emergency', so this still left a loophole for doctors to use their clinical judgement, but leave was given for appeal to the House of Lords. In the meantime the General Medical Council (GMC) revised its advice on confidentiality in this context (paragraph 4, p. 21, in the pamphlet *Professional Conduct and Discipline: Fitness to Practise* (1985)):

> Where a child below the age of 16 requests treatment concerning a pregnancy or contraceptive advice, the doctor must particularly have in mind the need to avoid impairing parental responsibility or family stability. The doctor should withhold advice on treatment except in an emergency or with the leave of a competent court, but in any event he should observe the rules of professional secrecy.

Note that once again there is no attempt to define an emergency.

Earlier guidance by the British Medical Association, as given in a press statement on 21 December 1984, was rather different. It stated that the Court of Appeal had not suggested that it would be a criminal offence for a doctor to prescribe the pill for a girl under 16 for the purpose of safeguarding her health without consulting her parents. This is correct, but Lord Justice Parker had pointed out other pitfalls under Section 14 of the Sexual Offences Act 1956, whereby a doctor doing a vaginal examination on such a girl as a preliminary to contraceptive advice, without her parents' consent, at least risked prosecution for indecent assault. Also, it had always been the law that for a plain civil trespass to a child a parent had the right to sue in certain circumstances. The British Medical Association also posed the sort of situation I have already alluded to: a 15-year-old girl thrown out or abandoned by her family, or even sexually abused by them, who was then at risk of becoming pregnant. The Medical Defence Union's cautious answer to this sort of problem is that in such a case the child should be taken into care by the local authority, which can then, with suitable court backing, assume parental rights. The 'emergency' will last only for the relatively short time needed to make a care order.

The whole medico-legal position was again reviewed by the Legal Correspondent of the *British Medical Journal* in January 1985,[23] when it was pointed out that there are much wider issues involved, namely, all medical treatment to all young people, boys and girls. But it warns:

> Clearly in some cases doctors will form the view that the parents have forfeited any right to be consulted, but while doctors are entitled to form such a view they have no right in law to act upon such a view. If they do so they will abrogate to themselves the entitlement to affect other people's rights. Doctors have no right in law to follow such a course, and if they do go along that road they will attract the odium that falls on those who seek to control the lives of the people without their consent.

Nevertheless, many doctors and agencies that specialize in helping young people in trouble are very worried that the Court of Appeal decision will give rise to more illegitimate pregnancies, more illegal abortions and more misery, with an increase in physical and mental morbidity among young girls.

Already there are allegations that two girls committed suicide as a result of this ruling (*The Times*, 8 February 1985), although no proof was ever forthcoming.

It is not only we who have these problems over teenage pregnancies and abortions. A recently published report by a research and educational organization called the Alan Guttmacher Institute (*The Times*, 16 March 1985) stated that American teenagers have more pregnancies, births and abortions than adolescents of any other industrialized nation in the world. The pregnancy rate for Americans aged 15–19 was 96 per 1,000, compared with 14 for the Netherlands, 35 for Sweden, 43 for France, 44 for Canada and 45 for England and Wales. The teenage abortion rate for the USA was far ahead of the rates in any of the 37 countries studied. Black American teenagers had a higher percentage rate than white, 163 per 1,000 compared with 83 per 1,000. Taking white teenagers alone, American adolescents still top the rates for all other developed countries for pregnancies and abortions.

This study concluded that the lowest rates of teenage pregnancies were in countries with liberal attitudes towards sex, which provided easy access to contraceptives at low cost and *without* parental approval and which had comprehensive sex education programmes. It also found that ready access to abortion services did not lead teenagers to have more abortions. Other interesting comparisons were that 60 out of every 1,000 American women had had an abortion by the age of 18. Comparable figures were the Netherlands 7, England and Wales 20, France 30, Canada 24 and Sweden 30. One reason suggested for the high American teenage pregnancy rate was fears about the association of the pill with ill-health.

Again, I think, there is confusion between moral and medical issues, especially in Britain. Latest medical research has shown that there are no special risks for young girls who take a low-oestrogen pill after two or three years' use. Nor is there any convincing statistical evidence that prescribing contraceptives for this age group results in any increase in pregnancies and abortions. Most doctors would like to make a distinction between age of consent to sexual intercourse, which few would like to see lowered,[24] and age of consent to medical treatment, which many would like to leave as it was before the *Gillick* case.

The British Medical Association (BMA), after seeking legal guidance and having extensive discussions within the medical profession, issued a further statement on the subject in May 1985 (*The Times*, 4 May 1985). It was held to be very unlikely for any doctor to face prosecution if he did prescribe a contraceptive pill to an under-age girl. This would mean bringing a civil action against the doctor. The rule that parental consent should be sought before prescribing the pill or abortion applied only to those two areas. Doctors could still, for instance, treat sexually transmitted diseases, as well as other conditions, on a confidential basis without informing the parents; they could provide sex education, advise about personal relationships and even advise about the mechanics of birth-control methods without fear of breaking the law.

It was emphasized that the Court of Appeal's ruling was unclear and was subject to review by the House of Lords, but because the judgment was based in common law rather than statute there was little prospect that criminal charges would ensue. Under civil law a parent would have to find a form of action to bring, and it was very difficult to see what form of action could be brought. There was still the further loophole of what constituted an emergency. None the less, doctors must obey the law as it stood.

Following the Court of Appeal judgment there has been at least one case where a court has intervened against the wishes of the girl's mother. A pregnant 15-year-old girl had gone to an Advisory Centre, lied about her age but asked for a pregnancy test. It was positive. She returned three weeks later, admitted she was only 15 and asked for help. Her mother would not agree to termination so the Advisory Centre helped the girl apply to the court. She did so and was made a ward of court. The judge then allowed the abortion to go ahead and also agreed that the girl should be prescribed contraceptives (*The Times*, 21 May 1985).

The Law Lords finally issued their judgment on 17 October 1985 with a 3 to 2 ruling against Mrs Gillick and in favour of the original DHSS guidelines to doctors (Law Report, *The Times*, 18 October 1985).

Lord Fraser stated that the three strands of argument raised in the appeal were:

(1) whether a girl under the age of 16 had the legal capacity to give valid consent to contraceptive advice and treatment including medical examination;
(2) whether giving such advice and treatment to a girl under 16 without her parents' consent infringed the parents' rights; and
(3) whether a doctor who gave such advice or treatment to a girl under 16 without her parents' consent incurred criminal liability.

After a careful consideration of the relevant statutes he concluded that there was no provision to hold that a girl under 16 lacked the legal capacity to consent to contraceptive advice, examination and treatment, provided that she had sufficient understanding and intelligence to know what they involved.

However, it was agreed by all concerned that it would still be 'most unusual' for a doctor to give such advice and treatment without the knowledge and consent of the parents. In such a situation where the girl refused either to tell her parents herself or permit the doctor to do so, the doctor would be justified in proceeding without the parents' consent or even knowledge provided he was satisfied that:

(1) the girl would understand his advice;
(2) he could not persuade her to inform her parents or to allow him to do so;
(3) she was very likely to have sexual intercourse with or without contraceptive treatment;

(4) unless she received contraceptive advice or treatment her physical or mental health or both were likely to suffer; and
(5) her best interests required him to give her contraceptive advice, treatment or both without parental consent.

Lord Scarman in concurring pointed out that there were three features of today's society which were unknown to our predecessors: (a) contraception as a subject for medical advice and treatment; (b) the increasing independence of young people; and (c) the changed status of women. Unless and until Parliament thought fit to intervene, the courts should establish a principle flexible enough to enable justice to be achieved by its application to particular circumstances placed before them.

Lord Bridge delivered an opinion concurring to the extent of setting aside the declaration made by the Court of Appeal that the DHSS memorandum was contrary to law.

Lord Brandon in dissenting stated that sexual intercourse between a man and a girl under age was a serious criminal offence so far as the man was concerned. It followed that for any person to promote, encourage or facilitate the commission of such an act might itself be a criminal offence, and in any event be contrary to public policy. That applied equally to a parent, doctor or social worker. It had been open to Parliament to alter the 'age of consent' but it had not done so and in his view it would not be right for the House of Lords, by holding that girls under 16 could lawfully be provided with contraceptive facilities, to undermine or circumvent the criminal law which Parliament had enacted. The criminal law and civil law should march hand in hand on all issues, including that raised in the present case, and to allow inconsistency or contradiction between them would serve only to discredit the rule of law as a whole.

Lord Templeman also dissenting said that an unmarried girl under 16 did not possess the power in law to decide for herself to practise contraception. It was doubtful whether a girl under 16 was capable of a balanced judgment to embark on sexual intercourse, fortified by the illusion that medical science would protect her in mind and body and ignoring the danger of leaping from childhood to adulthood without the difficult formative transitional experiences of adolescence. 'There are many things which a girl under 16 needed to practise, but sex was not one of them.' He had three specific objections to the doctor acting without parental consent. In the first place his clinical judgment could not be complete without further information from her parents, otherwise he would be relying solely on whatever the girl chose to tell him. Secondly, when a parent did eventually find out this could lead to a serious rupture of good relations between members of the family and between the family and the doctor. Thirdly, secret provision of contraception would encourage the girl to indulge in sexual intercourse and that offended basic principles of morality and religion which ought not to be sabotaged in stealth by kind permission of the National Health Service.

After hearing the ruling Mrs Gillick said she would not attempt to take the case to the European Court of Human Rights as that would be attempting to impose foreign law on Britain. But she would monitor the effects of the ruling and encourage others to do likewise. She also wanted to press parents who discover that their children have been prescribed contraceptives without their consent to take the doctors concerned to the General Medical Council.

The Minister of Health announced that he would reinstate immediately the DHSS guidelines and would then institute a full review of the whole matter taking into account the Law Lords' judgment as well as the wide range of views expressed on the issues involved.

As already noted, in the months between the Court of Appeal's ruling and the judgment of the Law Lords there had been much uncertainty about how best to help girls under the age of 16 in need of contraceptive advice. According to an article on 'teenage mothers' (*The Times*, 18 October 1985) in 1984 some 17,000 girls under the age of 16 were taking the pill and about one-third of these did not have their parents' consent to do so. For them, during these months of uncertainty, unless they got their mothers' written consent, supplies were stopped. Also, birth control leaflets put out by the Family Planning Association (FPA) were withdrawn for fear of prosecution. Further case studies are given in this article pointing to the need to allow doctors the necessary discretion now happily returned to them by the Law Lords' ruling.

Involvement of the young men concerned

Talk of public morality in this context highlights very clearly society's hypocrisy and the 'double standard'. What about the young men who get these girls pregnant? They are actually committing a serious offence too, but rarely in practice do they get punished for it.[25] For example, in 1977 over 5,000 pregnancies were recorded in Britain among girls below the age of 16, but only 3,681 'offences' came to the notice of the police.

In *R.* v. *Taylor* (1977, WLR 112) the Court of Appeal described the 'wide spectrum of guilt' which is covered by the offence of unlawful sexual intercourse with a girl under 16 and provided some guidance over sentencing. At present there are two offences: sexual intercourse with a girl under the age of 13, for which the maximum penalty is life imprisonment, and sexual intercourse with a girl under the age of 16, which carries a maximum penalty of two years' imprisonment (Sexual Offences Act 1956). Then there is the so-called 'young man's defence' (Section 6(3) of the 1956 Act): a man can be found not guilty if he was under 24 at the time, had not previously been charged with a like offence and believed the girl to be aged 16 or over.

However, there are very few actual prosecutions, whatever the age of the man or the girl, although prosecution becomes more likely the greater the disparity in their ages. For every adult prosecuted in the years 1967–77 two were cautioned; for juveniles the ratio was 1 to 10. In 1980 the Criminal Law Revision Committee recommended[26] that the two offences should continue and that it would be a defence if the defendant believed he was lawfully married to the girl and also if he believed her to be aged 16 or over. They rejected the suggestion that a man should not be guilty of unlawful sexual intercourse unless there were some fixed age difference between the parties, nor should it be material to liability that the girl took the initiative.

Unplanned pregnancies

The phrase 'unplanned pregnancies' rather begs the question. Perhaps some 40 per cent of pregnancies among married women are unplanned – it often seems there is no really convenient time for having a baby! However, many women, once they realize they are pregnant, accept it, so that 'unplanned' and 'unwanted' are by no means synonymous.[27] Others will hesitate or vacillate, at first inclined to regret it and feel angry, especially if they also feel ill and are troubled by persistent nausea or vomiting. By the time the middle three months of pregnancy are reached they may never have felt better in their lives and not only begin to accept the pregnancy but are also pleased about it.

Others will, of course, never accept a particular pregnancy but for various reasons do not approve of abortion either, so reluctantly go on with it. Once the child is born many 'succumb' to the baby and become happy again. Others still cannot accept the situation, suffer from marked feelings of regret and may (albeit without fully realizing it) 'take it out' on the baby or its father. This fact may come to light only later on, when the child presents with a behavioural or developmental problem and perhaps ends up at a child guidance clinic. Alternatively, it manifests as a marital or sexual problem with the parents, requiring further expert counselling or other treatment. So there is a whole continuum of unplanned, resented, unwanted, regretted and rejected pregnancies.

In order to understand better the often complicated emotions, situations and motives which lie behind a referral for termination, a thorough understanding of the woman's background is necessary. Obviously, too, the more one can understand these factors, the better the advice and help that can be given for the future. As already noted, the vast majority of abortions carried out today are done for what can best be described as psycho-social reasons and not because of 'straightforward' physical or mental illness. When the Abortion Act 1967 first became law psychiatrists were fairly frequently involved in these decisions. Now they are much less involved, although the problems have remained much the same.

There are a large number of possible reasons – some conscious, others unconscious or at best mixed ('ambivalent') – why a woman will seek termination of her pregnancy.[28] Only some of the more commonly encountered ones will be mentioned here and those particularly impinging on mental health issues which come within my own professional experience. I shall avoid, too, much speculation along psychoanalytical lines about possible deep-seated unconscious factors. There may not always be agreement between the woman and her professional advisers as to what are the major motives involved, and sometimes these must remain at a conjectural or anecdotal level, but whatever they are, they must be seen in the context of her social and cultural background.

A young girl may become pregnant because of carelessness, curiosity or in rebellion against her parents and the establishment. Family problems are often part of the background. She may come from a loveless family, feel lonely and rejected and want someone of her own to possess and love, or she may be out to prove something – perhaps that she is a 'real' woman or has power over men. Occasionally she will be trying to force a reluctant boy into marriage. For the very young, pregnancy can sometimes be the equivalent of a suicidal gesture with a complicated mixture of underlying emotions such as despair, a desire for help, hostility, resentment and feelings of alienation. Such a girl may leave home and drift anonymously around a big city, trying to hide her pregnancy and perhaps almost convincing herself that it has not really happened. This can mean presenting for abortion relatively late on in pregnancy, thus increasing the risks.

Sheer ignorance, or at least reported failure of contraception, is a common finding. In some girls who indulge in what psychologists are pleased to call 'risk-taking behaviour' there is no excitement in sexual intercourse if it is made 'safe' by contraception. The overall risk has been calculated: the chance of becoming pregnant from any one act of intercourse is only 20 per cent, so most girls who take the risk get away with it. Others can be caught out on the spur of the moment, or in special circumstances like at a party, having been plied with too many drinks, or on holiday abroad. It is here that the 'good' girl may well get caught, as she is not the sort who would dream of carrying a packet of condoms around in her handbag or be on the pill. Still others leave 'that sort of thing' to the boy.

A few girls are simply feckless and seem to learn nothing from experience, even though they are of average intelligence. They drift from man to man without ever forming a lasting or committed relationship. This sort of girl may well have been pregnant before, may perhaps have had previous abortions (as well as sexually transmitted disease) and may come to expect abortion every time she 'gets into trouble'.

At the time of becoming pregnant a girl may have convinced herself that she is 'in love' and nothing else matters, but when her lover decides to leave her on learning she is pregnant, she not unnaturally becomes despondent and bitter. Certain families may try to get together over this sort of situation and may perhaps persuade the couple to marry, which can sometimes have disastrous consequences for all concerned.

More difficult is the woman who feels trapped, angry and frustrated and demands an abortion as of right. An immature girl who has married too young in order to get away from an unsatisfactory home and is not yet really capable of coping with the responsibilities of marriage may panic when she becomes pregnant, not only because of her own feelings of inadequacy but also because of the changes and restrictions in her life which having a child will bring – 'confinement' in all senses of the word. She may also worry unduly about the effects of pregnancy on her figure and looks and may wonder whether her husband or other men will stop finding her attractive. The more deeply disturbed find it very difficult to come to terms with the biological consequences of being a woman and refer to 'this thing growing inside me' or describe pregnancy as 'animal', 'disgusting' or 'obscene', or they may be terrified of the birth process itself and the anticipated pain.

One of the most important general principles, to my mind, is that no woman should have an abortion against her will and that some women may need help in resisting undue pressure. This can come from the putative father, who may say, in effect, that he will have her back only if she gets rid of the baby. Others in authority may unwittingly adopt very moralistic attitudes and may try to make a girl go on with her pregnancy in the hope that it will 'teach her a lesson' and so prevent the situation from arising again.

As with the single girl, the married woman may also emphasize her economic difficulties or poor social circumstances. She may say she cannot afford it, will have to move or will lose her job. An older married woman with several children may be just coping, though she is always tired and feeling worn out. If she gets pregnant again, particularly after being very careful over contraception, this can shatter her morale and cause a deep depression. There may be a long gap since the last child, and she may have got used to the idea of having completed her family.

Mrs K was a 43-year-old married Roman Catholic who was 9 weeks pregnant and 'at the end of her tether', as she could not face coping with another child. She felt she could not give it the same love and care as she had given to her other children, due to her poor health. She had a long history of menstrual troubles, anaemia and difficult births. She complained specifically of feeling utterly miserable and chronically tired; she suffered from headaches and slept badly. Both her parents were still alive, but her mother had in the past had in-patient psychiatric treatment for depression. She had four sisters and three brothers. She herself had worked part-time as a nursing auxiliary and was married to a 53-year-old hospital porter. Although the marriage was generally happy, the sexual side had been difficult. She had tried to keep to the 'rhythm method' of contraception. They had five children aged 19, 17, 14, 11 and 9. The last birth had been a particularly difficult one, and she had suffered from a severe haemorrhage which had required a blood transfusion. For some months afterwards she had felt quite depressed and had not wanted to go out. Two years before, she had started seeing her GP with vague aches and pains and general nervousness. After further discussion with her and her husband, and in consultation with the gynaecologist, it was finally decided that a hysterectomy was the best way of dealing with the patient's medical problems.

A woman may also feel too old and may even think that she is menopausal and could not conceive again.

Mrs M-S was a 46-year-old widow and 20 weeks pregnant. Her second husband had died 18 months previously, and she had found it very hard to adjust without him. The marriage had been a very happy one, sexually active and fulfilling, and she had five children ranging in age from 18 to 7. Her first husband had been tragically killed in a car accident only six weeks after they were married. During the past year she had felt depressed and sexually frustrated, but as her periods had practically ceased, she also thought she was menopausal. She had been left with a large house and garden to cope with, although there was a very reliable and trustworthy gardener, whom she had known for many years, to help her. He was aged 50 and separated from his wife. He had befriended her during her bereavement and would spend a lot of time talking to her over cups of tea. Much to her later shame and regret, she had sexual intercourse with him on two occasions but did not take any contraceptive precautions, as she thought she could not possibly conceive at her time of life. Unfortunately she did and became abjectly depressed and racked with guilt feelings while still really suffering from a morbid grief reaction following her husband's death. She was very grateful to be offered a termination as well as the opportunity to talk through her misery and guilt.

Another situation arises when an apparently stable, happily married woman, with no financial or social problems, appears acutely distressed at another pregnancy. Eventually she reluctantly admits that there is a 'possibility' that her husband may not be the father. Does a pregnancy resulting from an extramarital affair qualify for an abortion? It all depends, although it is easy to fall into the trap of making a value judgement. Two patients whom I saw will illustrate what I mean.

Mrs A was a 31-year-old married woman who came on her own without her husband's knowledge. She requested termination and was 8 weeks pregnant as the result of an extramarital affair. She had no specific complaints about her health, either mental or physical, but did say she was distressed as she was pregnant by another man and did not wish to upset her husband. There was nothing of note in her family history. She had gone to university, followed by teacher training college. She had been married for eight years to a highly qualified engineer who was away from home a lot on business and seemed (to her) to live only for his work. She described him as distant and undemonstrative. Sexual adjustment had been poor; she rarely enjoyed sex and, in fact, there had been no intercourse with her husband over the past two years. They had three children aged 6, 4 and 2. Her lover was a 40-year-old single man whom she had known for three years and with whom she had regular sexual intercourse when her husband was away. He knew she was pregnant, had never said he wanted to marry her and had urged her 'to get rid of it'. They had never used any contraceptives, only coitus interruptus and the safe period. I found it very difficult to interpret the Abortion Act to include this woman and did not recommend an abortion.

Mrs O was a 35-year-old married woman who had also become pregnant as the result of an extramarital affair. She was 12 weeks pregnant when I first saw her and was quite depressed. She had been vomiting a lot, was feeling ill, was sleeping badly and was off her food. A year before her father had died. She was very upset over this, as she had always been very close to him. Her only sexual experience prior to marriage at the age of 20 was with her future husband. He was a farm worker and described as a good husband and father. They had two children, aged 12 and 8, and practised coitus interruptus. One night, as her husband was not feeling like it, she went to a party on her own. She got very drunk and had intercourse with a Pakistani in his car as he was taking her home after the party. She did not claim that she was raped, only befuddled with drink. She had no idea whether or not he had used any contraceptive precautions. She knew nothing about him, could not even remember his name and had never seen or heard from him since. It had been a great strain trying to keep the pregnancy from her husband, especially as she felt so ill. In her previous psychiatric history she had become depressed when they had been threatened with eviction from their tied cottage and had been treated as an out-patient. She had tried to abort herself by taking large doses of Epsom salts, but nothing had happened. After consulting her GP and a gynaecologist I finally decided that in this case the pregnancy should be terminated. (I remember another such case where the possible father was an eminent black diplomat, the woman and her husband both being white.)

Also encountered is the situation where a marriage is already breaking down but the partners come together again for a final attempt at a reconciliation, during which the wife becomes pregnant. The husband then decides, after all, to leave his wife literally holding the baby.

While a great deal of research has been devoted to the problems of pregnant women wanting abortions, surprisingly little research has been done on the fathers. One reason for this is the persistence, in many guises, of the 'double standard'. However, in some cases the father may not be known or has disappeared from the scene, or it may be that the girl is rather simple and could easily be exploited by unscrupulous men.

Anna was an 18-year-old factory worker, unmarried and, at the time of referral, 12 weeks pregnant. She was said to be rather backward and slow-witted. She came to the consultation with her mother, a 46-year-old shop assistant. Anna complained of feeling cold, sick, tired and moody and was off her food. She said that she did not want the baby. She was the eldest of three children, had had an unhappy childhood and did not get on well with her father. She had left school at 15 and could barely read or write. Her periods started at 12 and were irregular, painful and often heavy. She had been given some pills for this condition. She first had sexual intercourse at 17 with the young lad who had got her pregnant. He was now 21, out of work and described by the patient's mother as 'vicious and temperamental'. When I tried to find out from Anna whether they had used any contraceptive precautions she did not seem to understand what I meant. She simply told me that her boyfriend had said, 'You'll be all right.' On more formal testing she came out as borderline subnormal in intelligence. An abortion was arranged and a coil fitted.

A husband's rights in the matter of his wife's abortion have already been alluded to, but his attitude may be crucial in reaching the right decision. He may be coercing her into having an abortion or, at the opposite extreme, insisting on repeated pregnancies perhaps to provide proof of his own virility. Some men resent the prospect of a baby and feel jealous and worried in case they receive less love and attention themselves. On the other hand, a husband may find himself in an awful quandary, unwilling to sacrifice his own child, yet wanting to do the best for his distraught wife who cannot face another pregnancy.

In still other instances a man may want to keep his wife tied down with children and may be unable to accept her as an equal or even a rival. Dislike of the contraceptive pill may mask hidden fears, such as that she may be unfaithful (perhaps he himself would like to be unfaithful but dare not, so he 'projects' his desire on to her) or that he dislikes losing control of the situation. On the other hand, he may have been tricked into a pregnancy by his wife's 'forgetting' to take her pill.

Difficulties and delays in obtaining abortions

There have been many comparisons made between patients having abortions on the NHS with those done privately without always realizing that there are really three groups involved: the NHS; those done at 'cost price' by the various charitable organisations like the British Pregnancy Advisory Service; and, thirdly, those done for profit by commercial agencies. However, most comparisons are given as just NHS versus private. Many criticisms have been made of the NHS provisions and I will outline some of these in this section, but it is only fair to point out that there are far fewer criticisms published of the 'private sector'.

With a free, comprehensive health service and the law applying equally to all, it should not matter where you live or who you are, but unfortunately it does. Some women are penalized simply because they live in an area where NHS abortions are difficult to obtain, although in all other respects they 'qualify' for termination. Generally speaking, the new legislation got off to a bad start, as no extra finance or facilities were forthcoming after the introduction of the 1967 Act. The expectation was that the extra work generated would be slotted into existing facilities. In 1979 a kind of league table was drawn up showing the proportion of abortions carried out in 1977 under the NHS by different regional health authorities.[29] For the whole country the average was 48 per cent NHS abortions but with wide variations, from a low of 22 per cent in Birmingham to a high of 90 per cent in Newcastle-upon-Tyne. In East Anglia the proportion was 53 per cent and in Oxford 56 per cent. In 1979 the overall proportion of NHS abortions had dropped to 47 per cent.

Some reasons which have been suggested to account for these regional variations are, first, that the DHSS may not have allocated sufficient funds to allow particular regions to expand their abortion services; secondly, that health authorities may not have endeavoured to provide more facilities for abortion; thirdly, that GPs may not be prepared to refer more women for NHS abortions and that NHS gynaecologists may not wish, or be available, to perform more abortions (a survey in 1981 showed that only one-third of NHS advertisements for consultant posts in obstetrics and gynaecology specified the provision of an abortion service in the job description); fourthly, that the number of women demanding NHS abortions may not have increased (unlikely, as patients often have to travel considerable distances and have to pay for private-sector abortions). The report 'Abortion and the NHS: the first decade'[30] concluded: 'At all levels in the NHS pressure from anti-abortionists, fear of becoming entangled in emotional and political issues, unwillingness to commit more resources for abortion, and the apparent success of the private sector have probably combined to maintain the *status quo*.'

It is also noteworthy that women who are single and have no children are less likely than other women to have an abortion under the NHS. It is not clear whether the NHS in effect discriminates against women or whether the private sector provides a more acceptable service for them.

Overall a smaller percentage of abortions are carried out among the unskilled, and it has been shown that the NHS abortion rate was one-third higher, the non-NHS abortion rate ten times higher and the total abortion rate more than twice as high in professional and middle-class women as it was among the unskilled.

A survey of 180 women living in the London Borough of Camden was carried out by the British Pregnancy Advisory Service in 1982 to find out why there was a relatively low use of the NHS services.[31] Half those interviewed opted to use private and charitable clinics. Women who consulted an NHS doctor had to wait longer for their operation, and there was a 66 per cent chance of having an early abortion through private treatment as compared with 50 per cent on the NHS. Only 35 per cent had an abortion within two weeks of seeing an NHS doctor, compared with 73 per cent in the private sector. Given a choice, 32 per cent of the women said they would prefer private treatment mainly because of the slow referral procedures in the NHS and their anticipation of hostility or poor treatment and lack of day-care facilities. Although 91 per cent were registered with a GP, only two-thirds consulted their doctors about their pregnancy. The attitude of GPs is crucial in helping women with such problems, but many women, rightly or wrongly, fear contempt, censure, rejection or hostility from their doctor.

That it is much safer to have an abortion done privately than under the NHS has been convincingly shown in the latest collaborative study of the two Royal Colleges (GPs and Obstetricians).[32] Delays were much longer in the NHS, especially with women over 13 weeks pregnant. Sometimes this was for administrative and bureaucratic reasons, but in other cases it was deliberate because at this stage of pregnancy instillation of prostaglandins was most commonly used in the NHS but not privately (56 and 10 per cent respectively). This procedure increases the risk of infection. The reasons suggested for the all-round lower rate of complications in the private sector were that abortions were done earlier in pregnancy; that less use was made of prostaglandin instillation and concurrent sterilization; that more operations were done on out-patients; and that for those who were hospitalized their length of stay was shorter. Even when these differences were simultaneously controlled, the NHS remained a significant independent risk factor, especially for those with more advanced pregnancies (over 13 weeks). It was likely, too, that doctors in the private sector were more senior and more experienced. (The actual complications are further discussed in a later section.)

Suggestions about practical ways of improving the situation include the following:

(1) GPs to be encouraged to provide prompt pregnancy testing by providing NHS payment for this.
(2) Pregnancy testing, information and counselling could be provided at NHS community family planning clinics for direct access by women who considered their GPs were unhelpful.
(3) Hospital gynaecologists should accept referral from family planning clinics as well as from GPs.
(4) Health authorities should try and predict the abortion load for their district and encourage the gynaecologists to suggest ways of coping with the work. The creation of day-care units and use of sessional doctors for first trimester abortions could divert up to 80 per cent of abortion patients from the in-patient service.
(5) More health authorities should use the charitable organizations by paying them as agents for the provision of abortion for NHS patients.[33]

Late abortions

Not all causes of delay are the fault of 'the system'. For instance, having irregular periods can cause genuine delay in recognition of pregnancy. On the other hand, some women may go a long time 'pretending', both to themselves and to others, that they are not really pregnant or run away from home and seek medical attention when in a relatively advanced stage of pregnancy. Studies of reasons for delay in seeking advice among a group of 300 women in the Wessex Region were published in 1980.[34] Of these 75 per cent suspected they were pregnant within six weeks of their last period; 41 per cent had by that time decided they would want an abortion if pregnant, but only 29 per cent had talked to a doctor within the six weeks, and only 13 per cent had obtained confirmation of pregnancy by that time.

Important variables here were age, in that 81 per cent of women aged 35 and over suspected they were pregnant by six weeks, while only 64 per cent of those aged 17–19 did so. Of the older women 94 per cent had decided on abortion within 10 weeks, by which time only 70 per cent of the younger ones had done so. This is reflected in the stage of pregnancy at abortion: 63 per cent of the older women had an abortion before 10 weeks, but only 27 per cent of the younger ones did. Younger women discussed their situation with a larger number of other people, had more difficulty in obtaining neutral counselling and were more likely to be confused and to have doubts about what to do. Most frequently consulted were boyfriends, girlfriends and GPs. In this study 78 per cent of those obtaining an abortion had initially consulted a GP, but about 7 per cent of GPs had refused to refer the women for abortion.

These factors are put into perspective by the report entitled 'Late Abortions', issued by the Royal College of Obstetricians and Gynaecologists (1984), where 'needless delays' in many cases are blamed on inefficient NHS administration. Statistics are quoted to show that thousands of women medically referred for abortions had to wait for up to 12 weeks before having their operations. One in five women referred before the twelfth week of pregnancy did not have the abortion until between the twentieth and twenty-third weeks. These delays increased the risks of both physical and emotional complications, and as young women formed a large proportion of those having delayed abortions, there was an urgent need to provide more help for them.

Most of the late abortions were carried out in the private sector. Young women (aged less than 20) were major users – they constituted more than 40 per cent of cases treated on grounds other than fetal risk. Among the very late abortions they constituted more than half of all such cases notified.

A number of factors were reported to account for the operation being done at a late stage. These included failure to recognize the pregnancy because of unexpected failure of contraception or irregular menstruation, and prolonged indecision, apprehension and changes in personal relationships, principally with the father. The abortion services also contributed to avoidable delays, particularly in the NHS. Over half of the women whose abortions were done outside the NHS did not go to their family doctors in the first instance. In the very late abortions married women aged 20–39 and older women appeared to require self-referral less often than the young and the unmarried. Even though some under-reporting of early medical complications was found, it was concluded that such complications did not appear to constitute a major hazard to the health or life of the women, even in late abortions.

Most of the abortions for suspected or confirmed fetal abnormality had to be delayed until the second trimester and often to beyond 20 weeks' gestation. A large proportion of second-trimester abortions performed in England and Wales were carried out on foreign women. Most of these were done in private clinics in the London area. Also, a large proportion of late second-trimester abortions were performed by a relatively small number of doctors. Second-trimester abortions were rarely done as day cases in the NHS, largely because methods chosen make day care inappropriate. The techniques chosen in the NHS were those that demanded greater intensity and duration of care.

As a result of these and previous findings, certain recommendations were made – for instance, better education and counselling services, especially to minimize delay. Since young women formed a large proportion of these late abortions, and since there was often hesitation or reluctance in seeking help from GPs, many more Youth Advisory Centres should be established, and they should be well advertised and easily accessible for informal advice.

5

Abortion and Afterwards: Dilemmas and Decisions

Mental health issues in decisions

The contributions of scientific psychology to understanding the decision process concerning abortion are relatively few and often remote from real-life situations. Psychologists might itemize four elements in the situation: the clinical and social data about the patient ('stimulus' material); the participants in the decision-making; the social context of the decision; and the form which the decision takes ('response'). The best way of trying to order all possible variables is to devise a hierarchy of preferred reasons for advising termination, but the conversion of a mixture of facts and values – basically a social-ethical discussion – into a psychological-medical one can run into difficulties. It inevitably gets confused with questions of authority, responsibility and power.[1]

Previously, the psychiatrist particularly was frequently put in a difficult position by an emotionally disturbed and demanding patient whom he had never met before, often with no other history available and with great pressure being brought to bear on him for a quick decision. The decision was very much concerned with prognosis (the prediction of future consequences), acknowledged as one of the most difficult aspects of psychiatry.[2] Sometimes the GP was helpful, especially when he had extensive knowledge of the patient and her background. At other times the patient was also relatively unknown to the referring GP, or he was unsympathetic towards her plight or to the Abortion Act. Just what criteria were used by individual doctors in selecting patients for psychiatric referral are difficult to identify and make generalizations about, but implicit in these referrals were certain assumptions and expectations about the psychiatrist.

Sometimes the psychiatrist seemed to be seen as the patient's advocate, who would marshall all the relevant information and then put her case to the gynaecologist. It was this type of function which was sought more often than the more traditional one of expert diagnosis or assessment of mental state, and this is probably one of the reasons for the decline in the search for psychiatric opinions.[3]

In the end the psychiatrist must make his own assessment of the patient's current state, in the light of her previous history and present situation, and then relate this to her pregnancy and future in terms of different possible methods of management, one of the options being termination.

It is still unfortunately true that the 'termination patients', out of all proportion to their actual numbers, can cause more dissent and ill-feeling among professional colleagues than almost any other type of patient. It does not help, for instance, when one is called upon to clear up somebody else's 'mistake', as in the case of a patient referred for psychiatric treatment because she has reacted badly to termination, when the abortion was not carried out on one's own recommendation and was perhaps done in a different part of the country. As a result of all the emotive issues involved, the doctor, the patient or sometimes both may become society's scapegoat. If it is the patient, this can only increase her conflict and guilt feelings (hence the importance of the attitude of doctors and nurses).

When a psychiatric opinion is sought before abortion there are certain technical problems associated with assessment which I will mention very briefly. A thorough history is essential, as well as, ideally, a detailed history from the husband, a relative, a friend or her sexual partner as well. My own practice has always been to insist on interviewing the patient first, on her own, however young she is, and then to see only whoever has come with her, either by myself or in conjunction with my social worker. It is vital to allow enough time to assess the patient and her situation properly. A decision should be made as soon as possible, especially if there are doubts about the duration of the pregnancy.

The stage of pregnancy reached is important both physically and psychologically. After about 12 weeks the technical difficulties and risks of abortion become greater. Following quickening it is less easy for a woman to think about the fetus as a 'lump of jelly', as after she has felt it move inside her it is bound to assume a more individual existence.

As stated earlier, the majority of patients seen by a psychiatrist suffer from mixed neurotic states, sometimes the consequence of longstanding personality problems. The main presenting symptoms are usually anxiety or depression or a mixture of the two. The abortion may be just another crisis in a personal history marked by many such episodes.

Mrs B was 35 and had been married three times. Over the past 17 years or so she had been going to doctors about various nervous symptoms, chiefly a fear of going out (agoraphobia), over-sensitivity to noise, irritability and periods of depression. She had once attended a psychiatric outpatient clinic and had felt better for about a year, but this did not last. She was an only child of elderly parents, both of whom had suffered from 'bad nerves' and who eventually separated. She had had an unhappy childhood, had left school at 15 and had then done various secretarial jobs. Her first two marriages ended in divorce. Her third husband was an accountant one year older than herself. She described their marriage as unhappy, with poor sexual adjustment and the use of the 'safe period' as the only method of contraception. In the past she had had one spontaneous miscarriage and four children, aged 12, 9, 7 and 4. She was eight weeks pregnant and said she could go through with it if her husband would support her and love her more. When I saw her husband he expressed genuine concern for his wife and said he would do anything to help and was very much against termination. It was decided to let the pregnancy continue, and it went successfully to term. Her husband had a vasectomy and after a few joint counselling sessions they seemed much happier together.

The commonest sort of personality disorder encountered is that of the anxious, insecure and dependent woman, sometimes with hysterical traits as well.

Eileen was a single Irish Roman Catholic girl of 18, some 10 weeks pregnant when first seen, on her own. She was in quite a state, shaking and crying, wetting her bed at night and unable to concentrate on her work. She had already had one illegitimate child, and that had been a very traumatic experience for her, as she was only 16 at the time. The baby was subsequently adopted. It turned out she had been enuretic (bed-wetting) since she was 12 and a year before had had pills from her doctor to calm her nerves. She also stuttered when she got anxious. Her parents were in their forties, and she had an older sister who was engaged. Her father worked in a car factory, had a violent temper and spent most of his spare time drinking. Eileen had always been afraid of him, as he used to beat her as a child. Her mother seemed to fade into the background, had 'bad nerves' and a chronic cough. Eileen first had sexual intercourse when she was 15 but with only two boys since then. Her current boyfriend was aged 18 and she said they were officially engaged. They had been having regular intercourse without any contraceptive precautions, and he knew she was pregnant but had not come with her. She was so distressed when she found herself pregnant again that she tried to abort herself, first by taking some pills supplied to her by a girlfriend and then by using a knitting needle on herself. This had produced a little bleeding on two separate occasions. A further appointment was made to see her and her fiancé, but they never turned up.

Occasionally the psychopathic type is met. She shows a pattern of almost lifelong problems in most areas of her life, with marked antisocial trends to the fore.

Miss T was 27 years old, unmarried, living in a homeless families' unit with her two young children. She complained of being irritable and depressed and could not stand another pregnancy. She had had a miserable childhood. Her father sexually assaulted her and was eventually sent to prison for having intercourse with her both anally and vaginally. She had three brothers and three sisters and had lived in some poverty. At the age of 13 she was referred to a child-guidance clinic and then to a special school. Later she was sent to an approved school, then Borstal, finally landing in prison for being involved in a robbery with violence. She was of limited intelligence and only semi-literate. She started menstruating at 11 and had intercourse at 15. She thought she had had intercourse with about a dozen different men since then. This was her fifth pregnancy: out of the four children (all by different fathers) she had kept two, her mother had taken one and the other one had been adopted. The latest pregnancy was by a 25-year-old single Irishman whom she had met in a pub. They lived together for a few weeks, but he started to get violent and she left him. She thought he had used a sheath but was not sure. Termination was agreed, along with further contraceptive advice.

I particularly remember another patient, who put me in the unusual position of very much wanting to recommend an abortion but who adamantly refused. She said she was, in fact, looking forward to having her baby, as she was going to torture and maltreat it to make up for all the bad times she had had in her life and to show how much she hated men and especially the father of this particular child.

Those with sexual problems may get pregnant in an effort to 'cure' themselves or on the advice of well-meaning friends or doctors. I have seen a number of lesbian and bisexual women, for instance, who were unsure of their sexual identity but had become pregnant and had then developed panic attacks with suicidal depression. It is hoped that such advice as 'Get yourself a man' or 'Get married and have a baby' is no longer handed out to such women.

Women already suffering from a mental illness may become pregnant as a result of their illness, which in turn could lead to a further exacerbation of the illness, either during the course of the pregnancy or in the months afterwards. There is, too, a possible added genetic risk to the child. Those suffering from what used to be called manic-depressive psychosis but is now more fashionably known as bi-polar affective illness (i.e. with marked 'highs' and 'lows', excitement and depression) may get pregnant in either phase of the illness. One of the symptoms of mania (the excited phase) can be increased libido and sexually uninhibited behaviour (one variety of so-called 'nymphomania') which is quite out of character with a woman's normal self. In a depressive phase it is more usual for such a patient to lose all interest in sex (and perhaps to stop taking the contraceptive pill), but occasionally she may prostitute herself or not care what happens to her as she feels useless, hopeless and bad.

Angela was a single 20-year-old student and eight weeks pregnant. She requested termination on the grounds that pregnancy could ruin her career and aggravate her family problems. Also, she was living on her own, was suffering from insomnia and was feeling very depressed. She was studying for further A-levels and business studies at a technical college. Her parents had been very unhappily married. Two years before she was referred to me her father had committed suicide by shooting himself. She had found his body. Her mother, who had a long history of paranoid schizophrenia, blamed Angela for her father's suicide and totally rejected her. She had one sister who had 'dropped out' from university, had been on drugs and had also had psychiatric treatment. Angela first had sexual intercourse when she was 18 and with two different men in all. The present pregnancy had resulted from a single act of intercourse with a man she had known only slightly for about a year. One night when they were out together she got a little drunk and that was when it happened. When he learned that she was pregnant he said he did not want anything more to do with her. Angela had first seen a psychiatrist when she was taking O-levels. At this time her parents were quarrelling a lot, and she found it very difficult to cope with her mother's aggressive and derogatory attitude towards her. I recommended a termination and saw her again three weeks afterwards to assess her condition. She said she was grateful and relieved and could now face life again and get on with her studies.

It is relatively unusual for a schizophrenic woman to become pregnant, but if she does, this can raise all the issues previously outlined. Also, nowadays there is the added complication that women suffering from these types of illness may be on long-term, continuous medication, either lithium in the case of bipolar illness or a depot preparation of one of the major tranquillizers in the case of schizophrenia. These drugs may harm the fetus in early pregnancy or cause complications at the time of delivery, yet if they were stopped, there would be a strong possibility of an acute relapse of the underlying illness. To a much lesser degree the same sort of situation can arise in an epileptic.

It has been established that one of the most vulnerable times in a woman's life for succumbing to mental illness is following childbirth (called variously puerperal, postpartum or postnatal illness), although comparative statistics are not always reliable due to difficulties in defining the length of the puerperium (the time taken for the body to return to its original, non-pregnant state), which can vary with different researchers from six weeks to three months or even longer. The law 'allows' a woman a whole year to recover from the possible mental effects of childbirth and lactation (Infanticide Act 1938).

In fact, puerperal mental illness was first clinically described by Hippocrates in the fourth century BC in his *Third Book of Epidemics*. He described a woman who gave birth to twins and on the sixth day after the birth suffered from insomnia and restlessness. By the eleventh day she was delirious and by the seventeenth dead. This was probably what would now be classified as a toxic-confusional psychosis, and she could have been saved by modern treatment, which would include careful nursing, tranquillizers and antibiotics.

Still one of the most outstanding books on the subject, as far as I know never translated into English, was written by a Frenchman in the nineteenth century. He was L. V. Marcé and the book, *Traité de la Folie des Femmes Enceintes, des Nouvelles Accouchées et des Nourrices*, was published in Paris in 1858. When, in 1980, it was decided to try to form a group of doctors and other professional workers interested in the psychosomatic problems of childbirth and its aftermath, the Marcé Society was named after him in his honour. He died at the tragically early age of 36.

Another landmark was the publication in 1962 of Hamilton's book on postpartum psychiatric problems.[4] (He has recently updated his views.) Since then there has been a vast amount of research to try to discover just why this is such a vulnerable time in a woman's life. The results of all this research have just been authoritatively summarized, with the following conclusions.[5] We still know little about the precise causation. The few risk factors known suggest that emotional and physical elements are both associated with psychotic and depressive illnesses at this time. A constitutional predisposition to developing a depressive disorder or its opposite is of major importance, but it is still unclear what it is about childbirth that acts as a trigger. Marital disharmony, mixed feelings about motherhood and other psychological stresses of understandable kinds appear to play a major role in causing puerperal depressions, but these are the kinds of stress which lead to depression at other times of life, and we still do not understand why depression should be so common in the puerperium.

An American survey[6] investigated the number of women admitted to a psychiatric hospital who were either pregnant or within nine months after delivery. These were compared with expected rates, on the assumption there was no relationship between admission and childbearing. There was an actual deficit in admissions during pregnancy and almost all the excess occurred during the first three months after delivery, with a high proportion suffering from some form of depression, so that the risk of mental breakdown was between three and five times greater in the first three months following childbirth. The actual risk of a woman being admitted to a psychiatric hospital in this country is of the order of one per 500 births within six months after childbirth but less than this taking three months as the puerperium.[7]

This puerperal vulnerability is relevant to abortion in several ways. First, if mental illness can follow childbirth, it can also follow abortion, so what are the chances of this happening? Secondly, if a pregnancy is allowed to continue, what is the likelihood of a puerperal mental illness occurring? Thirdly, if a woman has a history of a puerperal mental illness with her last pregnancy, what is the likelihood of this happening again with any subsequent pregnancy? Although different types of mental disorder are associated with the puerperium, there are no unique ones which do not occur at other times as well.[8]

In practice, the most common disorder is a depressive one. There are basically three sorts. First, there is the 'maternity blues', a self-limiting minor condition which is so common (around 60–80 per cent) and transient that it can be regarded as normal and so can be left out of the abortion debate. Secondly, there is a fluctuating neurotic type, 'postnatal depression', which occurs in 10–20 per cent of cases (the risk is five to seven times greater) and can cause much unhappiness and non-specific ill-health, especially when unrecognized and untreated. In one study of such cases half the women remained persistently depressed after one year.[9] The third one is a more serious type of psychotic depression, which occurs in about one in 1,000 births.

One of the main hazards associated with a depressive illness is suicide, with the added risk of infanticide during the puerperium. With modern methods of treatment the prognosis for postnatal depression is that about 60 per cent of patients recover fully within a year; others have residual symptoms. For psychotic depression, provided suicide can be avoided, the short-term prognosis is good, but half suffer relapses later. There is about a one in five chance of puerperal depression recurring again with a further pregnancy, whereas the risk for a woman who has had a previous depressive illness not associated with childbearing is about one in 10.

Mrs J was a 30-year-old divorcée who was living with a divorced man, Bill, who wanted to marry her, but she was still unsure about this, especially as he had recently been declared bankrupt. Her own parents were unhappily married, and their frequent quarrelling often ended in violent scenes. Because of this she was brought up largely by her grandparents. She was an only child. She did well at school, was always enterprising and ran a secondhand clothes shop. She was never particularly interested in boys and was a virgin when she married at the age of 21. Sexual adjustment was poor. She was against any form of artificial birth control and so relied on the 'safe period'. There were two children of her former marriage. Eighteen months before she consulted me, she was divorced: her husband said he had found a more 'suitable' woman and wanted custody of their children. Before the divorce was finalized, she had gone to live with Bill and shortly afterwards became pregnant by him. Her previous pregnancies had been difficult, and after the last one she had become depressed. Her depression became so bad that she had to attend a psychiatric clinic for postnatal depression, where she was given anti-depressant pills. The child was now 16 months old and she was nine weeks pregnant, having again relied on the 'safe period'. She said she was still feeling depressed, was worried about the possible effects on the fetus of the pills she had been taking, was anxious about the future generally and about gaining access to her children. She had to keep going to bed and felt very sick most of the time. She asked for termination, and I agreed. She was strongly advised to adopt a safer method of contraception. I offered further out-patient support until she felt really well again.

Termination of pregnancy is less likely to be followed by a depressive illness or other mental disorder than childbirth.[10] Psychiatric admissions (taken as some measure of severity) following abortions are only one-fifth of those following childbirth. This big difference may incidentally give some support to the view that organic factors (biochemical/hormonal) are of major importance in puerperal psychosis, so that post-abortion psychosis could be rarer simply because the biochemical changes following abortion are presumably much less marked than those after childbirth.

In a major new study from Denmark involving large numbers, a comparison was made between women requiring admission to a psychiatric hospital within three months following childbirth with those requiring admission following the same time limit after abortion.[11] In fact elective first trimester legal abortions were compared with normal deliveries. The major findings were for the never married and currently married, and the post-pregnancy risk of admission was the same for the two groups at around 12 per 10,000 abortions or births. Higher psychiatric admission rates were noted for separated, divorced and widowed women having abortions or going through with childbirth.

These are the basic statistical facts to be gleaned from recent research findings on which to base advice and counselling when considering therapeutic abortion.

Special consideration must be given to women who present relatively late in pregnancy, bearing in mind that calculations concerning the stage of pregnancy reached can be several weeks out. Common sense would seem to dictate that the more advanced the pregnancy, the more pressing and serious must be the reasons for advising termination. There are two theories as to why late terminations may cause severe emotional reactions. One is summed up by the aphorism 'The bigger the fetus, the bigger the guilt', and the second theory is that those who present late may do so because they are already emotionally disturbed. The methods of termination also differ in late pregnancy, and all will have experienced quickening.

However, the only British investigation of the subject[12] did not substantiate these gloomy predictions. This reported a follow-up study on a group of 40 women having abortions between the twentieth and the twenty-fourth weeks of pregnancy, when no serious mental after-effects were found.

A case of my own was Chris, a 17-year-old secretary referred to me by a gynaecologist, as she was 17 weeks pregnant, and termination would need to be done by a hysterotomy (a procedure similar to a caesarean section) at this late stage. She was given an urgent appointment to see me but turned up a week later, saying she was so distressed and confused that she had got the date wrong. She told me she had taken a mixture of gin and quinine earlier in the pregnancy in the hope of inducing an abortion, but nothing had happened. Although she had few complaints about her health, she was terribly upset because the man responsible for her pregnancy was Indian. Her parents had refused permission for her to marry and were very prejudiced about coloured people. Her father was a 50-year-old factory worker who, Chris said, had always got it in for her and seemed to prefer her sister. Her mother was aged 40, did not now work and was much more approachable and sympathetic. Chris was the eldest, with one brother and one sister. She had had sexual intercourse with only this one man, a 35-year-old whom she had known for about a year. Another reason for her family's opposition to her marriage was the age difference. She had never had unprotected intercourse, using foaming pessaries on every occasion. She came across as a rather immature girl, of average intelligence, rather shy and anxious. She had never been in any sort of trouble and did not smoke or drink. Her ambivalence towards her pregnancy was shown by the late stage it had reached before she sought help, her gesture towards trying to get rid of it and her failure to keep the appointment on time. She had no previous psychiatric history, was physically fit and not seriously depressed. Weighing up all these factors, I did not think that termination of pregnancy was indicated, but further counselling and help with the family was offered.

Methods of inducing abortions

As part of the counselling process and decision-making, account should be taken of such medical issues as the proposed method of abortion, along with its possible risks and complications. The various ways of inducing an abortion not only vary with the individual gynaecologist and available local facilities but also with the woman's age, her mental and physical health and the stage of her pregnancy. As already emphasized, the sooner it is done, the better.

Methods available are medical, surgical or a mixture of these.[13] The majority of abortions are done under a general anaesthetic, which in itself always carries a slight risk, although on occasions a local anaesthetic only can be used. The object is to evacuate the entire contents of the uterus as completely and as painlessly as possible, under the most hygienic conditions and with the least amount of damage caused to surrounding tissues.

The uterus is pear-shaped and comes to a bottleneck at the outlet, or cervix. This has somehow to be made wider to let out the contents, and it is important that it is stretched as gently as possible, otherwise it may never be as efficient again and may cause trouble later on with wanted pregnancies.

The medical induction of an abortion may involve giving one of the prostaglandins or a similar preparation to aid both the dilatation of the cervix and contractions of the uterus. Some preparations can be given as a vaginal pessary; others can be given intravenously (by a drip into a vein) or inserted into the uterus itself, either into the space occupied by the fetus or between its surrounding membranes and the wall of the uterus. By far the most common way of aborting an early pregnancy (before 12 weeks) is by suction or vacuum aspiration. Something like a small vacuum cleaner, attached to a cannula, is passed through the dilatated cervix and the whole contents of the uterus sucked out.

Up until about 18 weeks of pregnancy the stage of pregnancy is gauged by clinical means, but after this time a special type of ultrasound scanning machine can be used to give an accurate picture of the fetus and its age.[14] The bigger the fetus and the later the pregnancy, the more difficult it is to terminate.

Another way of aborting a more advanced pregnancy is by a hysterotomy. This is like a caesarean section, the fetus being brought out via an incision into the abdominal wall and uterus, which will leave an operation scar. This method was used in 721 cases in 1980 in England and Wales, with quite marked regional variations in its usage. Very occasionally a hysterectomy, removing the whole uterus but leaving the ovaries behind, is used. In surveying the usage of these different methods further discrepancies between the NHS and the private sector have been found. It was alleged in 1982 that hysterotomy was used ten times more often in the NHS in spite of the greater risks involved. About 80 per cent of NHS and 62 per cent of non-NHS hysterotomies were carried out at 16 weeks or even earlier, when other safer techniques were available.[15]

One new technique recently introduced is the possibility of aborting one twin – so-called 'selective fetocide'. The dead twin ceases to grow and is left in the uterus until full term is reached, when it can be expelled along with the live one.

New techniques also bring new problems, especially over the question of medical responsibility. If a nurse could give, or at least supervise, a medical procedure for terminating a pregnancy, would this be in accordance with the Abortion Act, which specifies the attendance of a medical practitioner? When the Act first became law, broadly only surgical procedures were available, so this automatically meant that abortion was carried out by a doctor. The Royal College of Nursing instituted an action on this very point in order to test the legality of nurses' participation.[16] In 1981 the House of Lords, in a split decision (five against to nine for), allowed an appeal made by the DHSS against the decision given by the Court of Appeal in the case brought by the nurses. The DHSS guidelines were that a doctor need not be present throughout the procedure provided that he or she had made the decision to terminate and remained responsible, so this view was upheld.

An abortion may be carried out on an out-patient, day-patient or in-patient basis. Provided the right facilities exist locally, the sort of criteria used for day-care abortions would be that a patient is less than 12 weeks pregnant on clinical assessment, has no serious health problems, has someone to take her home afterwards and is not living alone, and that a doctor is available by telephone if she is at all worried.

From an emotional point of view it is probably best to have a general anaesthetic and a quick surgical procedure, such as vacuum aspiration, if all the conditions are right. A local anaesthetic is rarely used, and it does make the whole process much longer. The usual system is to have an operating list, when something like eight abortions can be done in roughly one and a half hours of operating time. This time factor is what some gynaecologists resent, especially if the abortions seem to be done for what may appear to be relatively trivial reasons.

Physical complications of abortion

All operations carry certain risks, both physical and psychological. Terminations at or after 21 weeks' gestation would normally be done only to save the woman's life or for some other very serious reason. When done on a physically fit woman, before 12 weeks, the risks are very slight. The mortality rate has already been mentioned earlier in this book (see p. 112). The complications can be divided into those occurring at or shortly after the operation and the longer-term ones. The possible emotional complications are discussed in a later section.

Apart from the anaesthetic hazards, the two most serious physical complications are perforating the uterus and splitting or otherwise damaging the cervix. If the end of the cannula or other instrument perforates the uterine wall, this could lead to peritonitis, possibly to an abdominal operation and, in some cases, to removal of the whole of the uterus. Other hazards are infection and bleeding.

The possibility of introducing infection (remote) or of stirring up an existing but symptomless infection like gonorrhoea can be a serious matter. It could lead to the infection spreading to the Fallopian tubes, with consequent (permanent) sterility. Some gynaecologists, for this reason, recommend doing the operation under an antibiotic 'umbrella', with the object of neutralizing any pathological bacteria, but it is difficult to decide just which antibiotic to use, as no single one will be able to deal with all possible bacteria. Others will take swabs beforehand to try to make sure there is no lurking infection to start with. However, a slight rise in temperature after an abortion is not uncommon and not necessarily a sign of infection.

Prolonged bleeding may also be a problem. Both this and the signs of an infection may be due to incomplete evacuation of the uterus. Some bits may be left behind, and this may require doing the operation all over again to get rid of them. On the other hand, it is quite usual for some bleeding to occur for up to about a week after an abortion, but this is usually not serious and the woman can return to work, although she must not use an internal tampon for fear of introducing infection. Some abdominal pain may also occur afterwards but is severe only when there has been incomplete evacuation.

Further possible long-term complications are difficulty in conceiving, sterility, spontaneous abortion, premature labour (putting the baby at risk) and ectopic pregnancies.[17] Apart from factors already mentioned, other general health matters, such as smoking, drinking and diet, need to be taken into account when studying the complications by following up large groups of women after abortions. Infection, excessive dilatation of the cervix and repeated terminations are especially hazardous to those women who have never had children.

It is difficult to put precise figures on these risks as there are so many variables involved and poor standardization (what exactly is meant by a 'severe' haemorrhage?), but official statistics give some indication. The reported rates for infection and bleeding in 1978 were 91 cases (0.83 per 1,000 abortions) and 152 cases (1.39 per 1,000 abortions) respectively.

We now have much more accurate figures to go on, as well as the comparative risks of NHS and private abortions. These were published in 1985[18] and concerned 6,105 women who were carefully monitored and followed up after abortion by both general practitioners and obstetricians. All complications (generally referred to as 'morbidity') were defined and charted for up to three weeks after abortion, thus giving a much better coverage than the 'officially' recorded ones, which related only to one week afterwards or for as long as the patient stayed in hospital. Seventy-two per cent were NHS patients; the private patients had a higher proportion of single women who had never had children, were less likely to smoke and were better educated.

Overall, 85 per cent had abortions during the first trimester, but 36 per cent of private patients had their operations before nine weeks, compared with 20 per cent of the NHS patients. Types of operation were also different, especially for later pregnancies; the NHS favoured uterine instillation with prostaglandins and the private sector suction evacuation with or without forceps.

There were no deaths, but there was some new morbidity in 1,031 cases (16.9 per cent). Of these 612 (10 per cent) were due directly to the abortion procedures. There were major complications in 127 cases (2 per cent). Concurrent sterilization increased the risks. Overall, private patients were at 42 per cent less risk than NHS patients, and smokers were 25 per cent more at risk than non-smokers. When considering only women over 13 weeks pregnant the place of operation was even more important: private patients faced only 30 per cent of the risk of related morbidity found in NHS patients.

Considered in a little more detail, the actual complications and their incidence were put into the following categories.

(1) Haemorrhage occurred in 4 per cent of cases, transfusion or further evacuation of the uterus in 2 per cent.
(2) Infection occurred in 218, or 3.6 per cent, of cases.
(3) Operative trauma in 37 cases (0.6 per cent) consisted of perforation of the uterus in 22 and cervical lacerations in 11; the remainder had anaesthetic complications (local anaesthetic was used in only 3.8 per cent of cases).
(4) Blood-clotting complications (thrombo-embolic) arose in 20 cases (0.5 per cent).
(5) Psychiatric morbidity occurred in 140 cases (2.4 per cent); this is discussed further in the next section.

These results compare favourably with other international surveys, which reported morbidity rates of around 14–16 per cent. Although increasing gestation was a factor, it was not a highly significant one. No evidence was adduced to suggest that the use of prostaglandins had any advantage over suction in respect of morbidity. Their use with instillation, so popular in the NHS, can be an unpleasant experience for the patient: it prolongs hospital stay and costs more but can be done by less experienced staff and is often more acceptable to professional staff than the more difficult and sometimes destructive use of forceps and suction.

These results could be summarized briefly as showing a 10 per cent morbidity, which is reduced to 2 per cent for rather more serious complications directly attributable to the abortion procedure. The main factors which independently affected the morbidity were place of operation (private/NHS), gestation time, method of operation, sterilization at time of abortion and smoking habits. Morbidity was higher in the NHS.

Put another way, as a rough guide about one woman in 50 has major problems afterwards, with remoter risks to later wanted pregnancies of about one in 20. These physical complications must also be put into perspective by comparison with what is known of the often appalling results of illegal operations carried out by untrained back-street abortionists (now, fortunately, rarely seen) or attempts by a desperate woman to abort herself.

On the positive side, it has been shown that there has been an actual fall in the stillbirth rate. From investigations of the demographical characteristics of women having abortions, it appeared that abortions accounted for at least 26 per cent of the fall in the stillbirth rate from 1969 to 1974.[19]

Emotional complications of abortion

It has already been emphasized that, in advising women about abortion, risks and complications (both mental and physical) must be taken into account. In order to have a firm basis for predicting these risks, it is necessary to provide scientific data to eliminate as much guesswork as possible. This is where so-called follow-up studies come into their own. This means taking comparable groups of women, some of whom have had an abortion and some not (ideally they should be randomly allocated to treatment or no treatment, and those observing them should be 'blind' to the groups to which they belong), and then examining them again at intervals for several years afterwards to see how both they and any children have fared.

This is fine in theory, but there are a number of practical difficulties in getting the design just right, not the least being matching the two groups in the first place and standardizing the procedures for evaluating them as well as the indications for abortion and the methods used. It will readily be appreciated that it is very easy to criticize such studies and, if results do not suit one, to say that they are invalid for technical reasons. We have to do the best we can, as it is very important to undertake such research, but we must always be aware of the limitations. Sometimes, as a compromise, comparisons have been made between women having abortions for medical reasons (e.g. German measles) and those having them for psychological reasons.

There are also ethical problems to be considered in doing this type of research. When you come to think of it – I have for some time been planning to do such a project on 100 of my own cases – why should a woman who has been refused an abortion co-operate with the doctor in a research project with no direct benefit to herself? Many leave the area and cannot be traced – for instance, foreign *au pair* girls. Some subsequently marry and perhaps choose not to tell their husbands about a previous abortion; others do not wish to be reminded about traumatic events. Ideally they should be interviewed personally in a structured and standardized way, but some studies have relied on postal or telephone contact instead or have used a third person who was not professionally trained.

Nevertheless, a large number of follow-up studies have been published, mainly in the United Kingdom, Scandinavia and the United States of America.[20] They are not all strictly comparable, as they have often been done for different reasons (criteria are not always given in detail), in different countries and under different legal systems, so care is needed in interpreting results. As already made plain, most published follow-up studies can be criticized on technical and methodological grounds and often have a high drop-out rate at the follow-up stage.

Both from personal experience and after reviewing the relevant literature, I came to the following conclusions in 1972:[21]

> A sizeable proportion of those refused termination do not go to term. For those who do eventually give birth the outlook for the children is poor in terms of both psychiatric morbidity and social adjustment . . . Adverse reactions to therapeutic termination are relatively rare in properly selected cases. Short-term guilt feelings and minor depressive reactions occur in 10–20 per cent. Longer-term and more serious reactions (usually depressive) directly attributable to the operation occur in 1–2 per cent . . . Ignorance of or failure to utilize adequate contraceptive precautions is an important potentially preventable cause of a significant proportion of unwanted pregnancies.

I think that, generally speaking, these conclusions are still valid today.

To support this I would like to cite just three of the most comprehensive studies which have been published since then. One major review of the literature in 1982 came to the conclusion that the great majority of patients suffered no emotional ill-effects afterwards.[22] The second one, a general practice survey in 1984, detailed the demands made on GPs by patients having induced abortions. It confirmed the rarity of significant psychiatric or emotional consequences. Only one case of guilt was encountered. Pre-abortion women seemed to make fewer demands than average; although their attendances increased after their abortions, these remained at a fairly average level.[23] The third one, already referred to in the previous section on physical complications, concerns the 6,105 patients followed up by both GPs and obstetricians and was published in 1985.[24] Psychiatric morbidity occurred in 140 cases (2.4 per cent). Of these two required hospital treatment for schizophrenic illnesses. The remainder suffered from a variety of neurotic conditions ranging from neurotic depression and anxiety to persistent insomnia. Patients with a previous history of depression had a two and a half times greater risk of post-abortion depression, compared with those with no such history. Overall 1,507 had 'some' history of previous mental illness.

Occasionally a condition develops that is similar to an abnormal grief or bereavement reaction, which is a type of reactive depression that can develop in some predisposed women following the death of husband or other close relative. This may become manifest in abortion cases as a period of 'mourning' lasting for the same length of time that the pregnancy would have lasted had it not been terminated. This grief can become reactivated at times of anniversaries – for example the expected birth date, subsequent 'birthdays' or the time of the abortion. One investigation into a sample of women having their first babies found an association between feelings of anxiety and depression in early pregnancy and a previous history of an induced abortion, with the suggestion that this represented the reactivation of mourning previously suppressed.[25]

Women who have abortions on grounds other than those of mental health (e.g. because of suspected fetal abnormality after German measles or for 'genetic' reasons)[26] often seem to suffer more in the way of emotional complications afterwards than those who have abortions for mental health reasons. This was confirmed in such a group of women by comparing them with two other groups, one comprising women who had had abortions for medico-social reasons and the other consisting of women who had experienced spontaneous abortions. In the first group 77 per cent had acute grief reactions akin to those seen after stillbirths or neonatal deaths. Six months later 46 per cent still had symptoms, some requiring psychiatric support, compared with no such reactions after spontaneous abortion or termination for medical-social reasons.[27] Of course, waiting for test results is very stressful, as is the period afterwards, if these are found to be positive, when the woman is faced with the further anxiety of knowing that she is carrying a malformed fetus.

The types of adverse reactions illustrated above are extreme and rare ones, so it needs to be emphasized that far from causing a great deal of mental disorder, abortion actually prevents it in the great majority of cases. Looking at it positively, abortion can be said to be an important treatment procedure for promoting good health. As a psychiatrist I am now asked to see relatively few women for 'routine' abortions. I see mostly those with particularly difficult problems, often mixtures of mental, physical and social difficulties, and those whose abortions have gone wrong, with emotional complications. Therefore I tend to see a highly selective group of severe and difficult cases. In rare cases an abortion becomes an obsession with a woman, who proceeds to blame it for all subsequent problems in her life (and, by implication, holds all the professional people involved in the abortion decision to be responsible). Used in this neurotic way, it can become an excuse or defence, which then prevents her from facing the real problems which lie in her own personality and emotional development. I have even seen this sort of case develop a paranoid (persecutory), hostile attitude towards doctors and authority figures, so (unfortunately for me) I do not now often see the good results of abortion, the alleviation of intolerable anxiety and depression.

Can those at risk of developing psychiatric complications after abortion be identified beforehand? Not always, but there are some useful pointers. Not unexpectedly, those with a previous psychiatric history, and those showing marked ambivalence about the abortion decision, failure to involve their male partner and high anxiety levels after the pregnancy is first diagnosed, are particularly at risk. Religious attitudes must also be taken into account, with due allowance for temporary loss of faith as a manifestation of depression.

The personality type most at risk is that of a woman with marked obsessional traits, high moral and religious standards and strong maternal feelings. However, while recognizing the dangers, such a woman may well offer counter-arguments in favour of abortion to the effect that she would feel even more guilty if she could not look after the child properly or give it the same love, care and opportunities as her other children.

In clinical practice it is not (or should not be) a simple either/or decision (whether termination or not), as other methods of management should also be considered. To summarize, these include treatment of current depression or other emotional problems; interviews with relatives or the putative father; subsequent adoption of the child or sterilization at a later date; help over social problems; and continued counselling and psychotherapy throughout the pregnancy and for as long afterwards as may be necessary.

The question of adoption should not be glossed over too lightly, for the conflict and possible prolonged guilt that can be engendered in an unstable woman faced with this dilemma can be very distressing. Occasionally the baby can be fostered temporarily until the woman marries or finds herself in a better position to care for it herself. Sometimes her own parents can help, even, in exceptional circumstances, adopting it themselves. There are, too, various organizations which supply help, support and counselling services for those women who decide against abortion.

Repeated abortions

A very important part of aftercare is advice on contraception, with an immediate warning that it is possible to become pregnant again as soon as 10 days after an abortion. One of the much publicized criticisms of the Abortion Act is that certain women will abuse it, use abortion as a form of contraception and keep coming back for another abortion when it suits them.

The actual rate for repeated abortions in England and Wales works out at around 11 per 1,000 abortions. This is not excessive, taking into account the high failure rate of certain methods of contraception; nor is it always the feckless, inadequate woman of low intelligence who has more than one abortion. A study published in 1977 of 50 women having a third abortion found that the group contained five nurses and three teachers, which seemed disproportionate. There was also a high incidence of the erratic use of contraception, a history of consulting doctors for psychiatric reasons, unsettled relationships and low educational status. Occasionally there was a history of what seemed like inappropriate contraceptive advice, like reluctance to fit an IUD or refusal to carry out sterilization.[28]

However, it is worth remembering that a subsequent pregnancy following a therapeutic termination points to one of three possibilities: restitution for the aborted fetus, continuation of the neurotic or morbid need to become pregnant, or a healthy reaction to changed circumstances.

Feminists, choice and abortion on demand

In describing methods of abortion and possible complications I have gone into some rather gory medical and surgical detail. I have done this not only because I am a doctor but also deliberately, to remind people that abortion is not merely a theoretical subject for debate or a peg on which to hang one's prejudices but very much a practical matter of life and death. My discussion is also intended as a warning to those who advocate a more 'do-it-yourself' approach and want to take such decisions out of medical hands.

Criticisms over abortion policy have come from the more militant and politically conscious elements of the women's liberation movement, which championed, at one time, the aim of 'abortion on demand'. They rightly protest about the (literally) man-made laws, and the predominantly male judiciary, House of Commons and body of gynaecologists (some would also add the male-dominated, anti-feminist Christian tradition as well). For the feminists, social class, economics and sex roles cannot be ignored in any serious discussion of abortion.

However, the women's liberation movement is itself class-biased, being a predominantly middle-class movement which has had little impact among working-class women and the socially and educationally deprived, who are often the ones most in need. Of course, better educated and more articulate women know best how to 'manipulate the system' and obtain an abortion anyway. Looked at historically, the aims of women's liberation seem to have oscillated between personal and legislative liberation. Consciousness-raising, assertiveness training, medical self-help groups and efforts to remove the stigma from lesbianism are some of the manifestations of the first. The availability of abortion, the Equal Rights Amendment and sex discrimination laws are instances of the second.

The key word that keeps cropping up now is 'choice', and it has now been pointed out that although the 1967 Abortion Act has been a big step forward in liberalizing the law, it does not actually give a woman the right to choose an abortion. She must still plead with doctors, and the NHS is under no obligation to provide free abortions.

More specifically, some talk of a woman's 'autonomy' – her right to decide the fate of her own body – and argue that as the fetus has no capacity for independent life in the first three months of pregnancy, it should be regarded as part of the woman's body anyway. This is not strictly accurate, as there is the fetal 'body' as well, which is (genetically) half the father's. Of course, the fetus could not survive or grow without the maternal support system.

There is no doubt that women have successfully got together, both in Britain and in many other countries, to try to persuade their governments, and sometimes religious leaders, either to introduce abortion or to liberalize existing laws. Considerable publicity has surrounded a few prominent women (certain actresses and writers) who have fearlessly and openly declared that they have had abortions. Sometimes they have acted as catalysts when conditions in their countries were ripe for change anyway. In some countries marches and rallies, often nowadays covered by television and the media, may be the only way in which women can make their views known. Elsewhere the slower and more difficult route of evolution rather than revolution is tried; women gain positions of power and influence so that they can directly influence decision-making.

Whether or not such women call themselves feminists or members of the women's liberation movement is sometimes more a matter of semantics than anything else, but the more radical and extreme wings of such movements probably alienate more people than they influence. As regards feminism, one middle-of-the-road opinion is that the essence of any definition of it, regardless of other ideologies or political orientations, would encompass the view that women suffer from systematic social injustice because of their sex.[29]

That this is still so in practice in this country today is undeniable; British women are still legally inferior in relation to taxation, retirement and pension rights as well as to some aspects of social security and unemployment. There is still a gulf between paper rights and actual rights. Despite laws against sexual discrimination at work there has been little progress for women in the field of employment. Sexual harassment still takes place. Although women head one in seven families, they are still regarded as working only for pocket money or out of boredom. Literature, the media and advertisements continue to rely on sexual innuendo and the degradation of women (not that the cause has been greatly helped by the recent tendency for women to write silly and contentious books about men!).

It is only about 15 years since the women's movement got going. The majority of women live in heterosexual relationships. Whereas in the early days the question was how to live in a male world, it is now how to live with a man on an equal basis. Some progress has been made: there is less stridency and name-calling, more reflection and maturity. Although there are many polemical writers (and it is difficult entirely to avoid polemics on such topics as sexual exploitation and the like), one of the best in recent years is Germaine Greer, whose book *Sex and Destiny: The Politics of Human Fertility* gives a very cogent and racy survey of the subject.[30]

'Abortion on demand', an old battle cry, is inclined to raise the hackles of many a medical man, and I must admit that I am also against it. In the first place it is a very aggressive phrase. Would not 'abortion on request' be a better start? More fundamental objections are that the decision should not be left to the mother alone, who would then have to act as judge in her own cause against the interests of the fetus, and that it deprives the doctor of his medical rights and makes him a rubber stamp, a mere technician. The moral argument is also unimpressive, as it deprives prenatal life of any dignity or value, shows a bias exclusively in favour of the woman and sometimes elevates real but relative values to the status of absolutes. A woman may be poorly informed, may perhaps not understand the procedures involved and the possible complications or may not know about other ways in which she might be helped. She may be confused, ambivalent and, possibly, coerced by others.

What is really needed – and I would wholeheartedly support this – is a genuinely compassionate, unbiased and well informed counselling service, freely available to all. This would meet the other slogan which has perhaps replaced that of 'abortion on demand', and that is 'a woman's right to choose', but to be able to choose, one must be well informed.

Sterilization

One other important aspect of treatment, which is not specifically mentioned in the Act, is sterilization. It is not covered by any particular legislation. Although the legal position is not altogether clear, when it is done in good faith and with the written consent of both partners there is little to fear from the law. However, the practice of sterilizing a woman at the time that she has her abortion has been steadily declining, and it is now only rarely encountered. The number of resident women being sterilized concurrently with abortion had already fallen from a high of 23 per cent in 1968 to 8.6 per cent by 1975. One reason for this decline was the fact that doing the two operations together increases the risks of physical complications.

This is well shown in the group of 6,105 patients seen in 1976–7 and carefully followed up after abortion.[31] Sterilization at the time of abortion was carried out on 15 per cent of the NHS patients and on 5 per cent of private ones. It was found that women who had had concurrent sterilization had a 43 per cent increased risk of postoperative infection – and, of course, that also meant staying in hospital longer. However, the conclusion was cautious: it was not known for certain whether an abortion followed by sterilization at a later date was any safer than doing the two together.

Another study did, in fact, compare small groups of women who were followed up for a year after either postpartum sterilization (childbirth, not abortion) or sterilization at a later date. In terms of any emotional disturbances afterwards there were no differences between the two groups, nor with a control group, so that any upsets were no higher than would be expected in the general population.[32]

Another argument against concurrent abortion and sterilization is that the woman may be in such an emotional state that it would not be right to make an irrevocable decision at such a time. In some cases a woman offers herself for sterilization because she is feeling so guilty about an abortion that sterilization is viewed as a form of punishment. What should never be done (in my opinion), but perhaps was done to some extent in the early years of the Abortion Act, is to make sterilization a condition for carrying out an abortion. This condition, both explicit and implicit, was sometimes a great temptation (for instance, in the case of an apparently feckless woman of limited intelligence who repeatedly got pregnant and could not be relied upon to take effective contraceptive precautions). It was already becoming apparent from several studies that women from social classes IV and V (semi-skilled and unskilled) had substantially higher chances than middle-class women of being sterilized at the time of, or shortly after, an abortion.

Relatively uncommon cases clearly favour sterilization. An example would be an older woman, with a number of children, who thought she had completed her family but was still highly fertile and had failed with various contraceptive procedures. She might also have a history of serious menstrual loss and irregularity, and the best overall method of treatment might be a hysterectomy.

As new techniques of sterilization were introduced in the 1970s, the popularity of sterilization for contraceptive reasons increased. The main innovation was a laparoscopic technique. This entails passing a small tube into the abdominal cavity through a cut in the abdominal wall under a general anaesthetic. Through the tube the Fallopian tubes can be identified and then crushed, cut, or clipped. This requires about two days' stay in hospital and should not be done immediately after childbirth. There are many variations of the operation, but all have the same aim: to destroy the Fallopian tubes or to 'gum them up' (e.g. with liquid silicone), so that ova from the ovaries can no longer pass down them and hence never meet any sperm, so preventing fertilization. Menstrual periods continue after the operation, and the ovaries are unaffected, as are sexual feelings and desire.

This and, indeed, all methods of male and female sterilization should be regarded as permanent and irreversible procedures, a point to be stressed in counselling. Some methods of sterilization are said to offer such-and-such a chance of being reversed in later years, but as yet no firm reliance can be put on this. On the other hand, no method is 100 per cent foolproof, and I have come across women who have become pregnant following sterilization, although with improved modern techniques this is less and less likely.

The question of possible damages when a woman does become pregnant following sterilization was reviewed in the Court of Appeal in an unusual case in which the woman concerned had decided not to have an abortion. After reviewing previous cases, judgment was given to the effect that when a sterilization operation had been negligently performed, so that the woman became pregnant, her conscious decision thereafter not to have an abortion did not prevent her from claiming damages against the surgeons for the pregnancy and its consequences.

The case started as *Mrs Kathleen Emeh* v. *Kensington, Chelsea, and Westminster Area Health Authority* (1984). In 1976 Mrs E, who already had three children, became pregnant again and had a termination with sterilization. Later she was seen by a doctor for depression and in January 1977 was found to be 18 to 20 weeks pregnant. She was offered an abortion, but at this relatively late stage she refused, as she was afraid of the risks. In July she gave birth to a child with congenital abnormalities. She was subsequently re-sterilized.

The High Court ruled she was entitled only to £1,500 damages because her refusal to have an abortion was deemed 'so unreasonable as to eclipse the defendant's breach of duty'. This broke what in law is called *novus actus interveniens*, which really means the chain of causation. However, the Court of Appeal thought this judgment was unnecessarily harsh and the plaintiff's conduct not so utterly unreasonable. Lord Justice Slade said that 'As a matter of public policy, if a woman wished to be sterilized, there was no reason why she should not recover damages for the negligent failure to perform the necessary operation, whether or not the child to which she gave birth thereafter was healthy.' Her appeal was allowed, and she was awarded £26,000 damages (Law Report, *The Times*, 26 July 1984).

As with abortion, so with sterilization there are possible complications, both physical and emotional, and in assessing these there are a large number of variables to be taken into account. Apart from anaesthetic hazards and a small risk of infection, there are very few physical hazards. Where emotional complications are concerned much depends on age, parity (number of children), social and marital adjustment, previous psychiatric history and neurotic predisposition, intelligence, expectations, reasons for and type of operation and physical complications.

The main emotional complications are depression, anxiety (with excessive preoccupation over the operation), guilt, regret and an unjustifiable blaming of the operation for subsequent menstrual upsets, sexual or marital problems. Overall there is no convincing evidence that the operation itself causes psychiatric complications in properly selected subjects, although the risks are greater in those who were disturbed at the time of operation or who had a previous psychiatric history. In fact, many women report improvements in their lives, both sexually and generally, when finally freed from worry over unwanted pregnancies. The consensus from some recent research was that dissatisfaction was expressed by about 10 per cent of women, with less than 5 per cent having lasting serious regrets.[33]

In some respects female sterilization has become too popular and now runs at something like 100,000 a year in England and Wales. By this I mean being done too readily particularly in the private sector in young childless women. This was highlighted in the article in *The Times* (4 August 1985) which provided some evidence that same-day sterilization, with little or no counselling, was readily available in certain private clinics. Little time was given for the women to ask questions, seek further advice or to be told possible risks and consequences in any detail. Yet their 'informed consent' was assumed and forms signed to this effect. According to this same report more than a quarter of women who were sterilized 'on the NHS' in 1983 were in their twenties, so there is certainly no grounds for complacency here either. Guidelines issued by the DHSS to NHS doctors on the subject are just that and cannot be enforced as this would encroach on the much prized clinical freedom of doctors.

The ethical and psycho-social issues become most acute over the sterilization of mentally handicapped girls,[34] who, among other considerations, can be especially vulnerable to sexual exploitation. It is here that the question of informed consent is so often raised. Other ways of helping need to be considered first. Some mildly handicapped girls can manage a contraceptive pill or cope with an IUD. More controversial is the use of the contraceptive hormonal preparation given by injection called Depo-Provera.

Depo-Provera is a synthetic progestogen which both inhibits ovulation and makes the uterus unsuitable for implantation. One injection every three months is all that is required. It is acknowledged to be (and is used as) a useful short-term measure – for example, during a period of disturbed and promiscuous behaviour or in the period immediately following a husband's vasectomy – but it is its long-term use which is queried, supposedly because of its potentially harmful side-effects.

It has, in fact, been in use in Britain since 1978 for short-term contraception and has been found to be at least as effective as the pill and more reliable than a cap, IUD or sheath. It is alleged that it has been misused by some doctors, who have given it to women following an abortion without any counselling or explanation of the dangers. One of its side-effects, which is unpredictable, is intermittent, period-like bleeding, which at times can be heavy and distressing. It may also cause temporary sub-fertility. Other side-effects which have occurred are weight gain, decreased sex drive and depression.

What is not known for certain is what might happen after many years of continuous use, especially any possible association with some form of cancer. The only evidence to date points to the opposite conclusion – that it may well protect women from breast cancer. In April 1983 an independent enquiry was set up in London, composed of medical and legal experts, to advise whether or not Depo-Provera should be licensed for long-term use in Britain. A ban imposed on the drug in 1982 was officially lifted in April 1984, and injections are now available.

Underlying these well publicized controversies are other often unexpressed and unrecognized value judgements about the mentally handicapped – for instance, that they are 'breeding like flies', producing further handicapped or deprived children, increasing the cycle of deprivation, using up valuable resources with an increasing burden on us all. Even the right of such people to have a sex life at all is questioned by some: they could behave 'like animals' and be a source of great social embarrassment.

As sterilization is the most serious procedure, it is here that the question of consent is so difficult. Parents of mentally handicapped adolescents sometimes request sterilization, confusing it with castration, in the mistaken belief that it will also remove all sexual interest and drive as well. The opposite sort of argument has also been advanced: that sterilization may increase promiscuity, with the additional risk that the adolescent may acquire some of the sexually transmitted diseases.

In the very young there is always scope and time for further development, some increase in maturity with consequently 'better' behaviour and, more important, later regrets over the sterilization. With improved methods of training, teaching and treatment, some handicapped children can and do develop certain abilities and skills. In Sweden, for example, no one under the age of 18 years can be sterilized. In some instances the girl herself may actually request sterilization and have enough 'intelligence' to realize its implications.

In some tragic cases a perfectly normal girl can be rendered mentally handicapped by an accident later in life. I recall one such case of my own.

A girl of 20 was crossing the road from the bank where she worked and was knocked down by a motor cyclist, receiving severe head injuries. As a result she functioned at a 'subnormal' level, became sexually promiscuous (and was exploited in this by unscrupulous men), wandered off from home, drank too much and could not be relied upon to take a contraceptive pill. This was a complete personality change and was likely to be permanent. Also, she would never be capable of living a completely independent life or of being a competent mother. She herself requested sterilization, and I was satisfied that she understood the implications. Her mother also wanted it, and her social worker, GP and gynaecologist all agreed. On follow-up she never expressed any regrets about it.

However, careful counselling and unhurried planning is essential, especially for those in 'care' or in institutions, particularly those who have no parents or legal guardians to speak for them.[35] Several workers have commented on the bitterness and regret experienced by some patients who have been sterilized as a pre-condition of institutional discharge or without any consultation.

Where people are deficient in their intellectual and reasoning ability there is always the danger that agents of society will assume global decision-making rights. Such patients are usually non-assertive and easily influenced by authority figures, which makes them extremely passive and pliable. The law and informed current opinion now challenge the assumption of the 'It is in their best interests' type of argument, though the question of the validity of consent remains.

It has been suggested in this context that a legally effective (or valid) consent should have the following elements: first, it should be voluntary; secondly, the patient should be adequately informed and should comprehend the procedure, its likely consequences and what alternative procedures are available, with their consequences; thirdly, where relevant, the sexual partner should be informed and his or her consent obtained.[36]

In England there are no set procedures for applying these principles to sterilizing the mentally handicapped. The judgment given in a Sheffield court case (in re D (a minor) (1976) 1 ALL ER 326) reminded doctors of the issues involved, particularly when the handicapped person was a minor.[37] The judge concluded that sterilization would not be in the best interests of this 11-year-old, mildly retarded girl. She rejected the paediatrician's proposition that when there was parental consent the decision to carry out the operation on a minor was solely within the doctor's clinical judgement even when the purpose was non-therapeutic (i.e. not just for the health of the patient).

To conclude this section on sterilization, and to redress the balance so passionately advocated by many feminists, mention must be made of the possibility of the male sexual partner being sterilized by having a vasectomy operation. This should also be regarded as irreversible. It can be done under the NHS (the NHS (Family Planning) Amendment Act 1972 was passed so that local health authorities would provide voluntary vasectomy services), both for the sake of the man's health as well as for his wife's but not solely for contraceptive reasons. Psychiatric assessment and counselling should not be forgotten in this context either.[38]

Infanticide

The special offence of infanticide was originally introduced as mitigation for a woman who killed her child within 12 months of childbirth. This was originally to avoid the death penalty and, later, the mandatory life sentence for murder. It recognized that a woman might be mentally unbalanced by childbirth and lactation, and not only during the time conventionally regarded as the puerperium but for a whole year after childbirth.

The Infanticide Act of 1922 was subsequently amended by the Infanticide Act of 1938. This Act states that infanticide is not murder if 'the balance of [a woman's] mind was disturbed by reason of her not having fully recovered from the effect of giving birth or by reason of the effect of lactation consequent upon the birth of the child . . .' It is not necessary to prove that the mother's mental disturbance was the cause of her actions, it being sufficient to show that she was mentally disturbed.

Many mothers who commit infanticide also commit suicide. In one studyof 113 mothers who had killed their children 62 per cent committed suicide.[39] The most frequent type of mental disorder associated with infanticide is a severe depressive illness, so that, not surprisingly, in most cases of infanticide the mother can be shown to be mentally disturbed. This is reflected by the fact that since 1849 no woman has been executed for the murder of a child of her own who was under a year old. The number of prosecutions under the Infanticide Act in any one year has always been small: in 1975, for instance, eight women were found guilty, all except one receiving a non-custodial sentence.

In the light of current knowledge and practice the offence could now be best regarded as a form of non-accidental injury to children ('baby-battering') and, as a defence of diminished responsibility covers virtually the same ground, the Butler Committee[40] proposal in 1975 that the special offence of infanticide be abolished, seems a sensible one to me, although it has not yet been implemented. Incidentally, the Infanticide Act does not apply to Scotland, where the charge is 'culpable homicide', the age of the child being considered irrelevant. Some cases of 'baby battering' may result from 'bonding failure', itself exacerbated by the birth of an unwanted and rejected child when the preferred course of action would have been an abortion, but many cases are complicated by a number of adverse background associations, none of which alone, or in any simple fashion, could be said to have caused the aggressive behaviour.

Until very recently there was no offence of attempted infanticide. Women who had been prevented from killing their children, or who had failed in their attempts, were charged instead with a variety of offences ranging from attempted murder to concealment of birth. In 1983 a woman was charged with murder and attempted murder but was actually convicted of infanticide and attempted infanticide concerning two births some two years apart. She was given two years' probation with a condition of psychiatric treatment. This is a unique case, by reason of both the repetition of the offence and the recognition in law of the offence of attempted infanticide (brought under the Criminal Attempts Act 1981).

The case was reported in the *Criminal Law Review* of November 1983 as well as being the subject of a psychiatric report.[41] The world literature between 1751 and 1968 on the psychiatric aspects of the murder of the newborn was reviewed in 1970.[42]

The law on murder has always been difficult for the layman to understand, especially when it comes to the matter of 'intent'. This was again exemplified by the House of Lords ruling that foresight is not the same as intention (Law Report, *The Times*, 22 March 1985).

In some situations homicidal impulses towards a baby may represent anger and resentment against the hated father of the child which cannot be expressed directly because of fear of retribution, retaliation or the fact that he has deserted. This situation has been dubbed the Medea Complex.

This is different from the much more frequent neurotic fears, often found in women with obsessional personalities, that they *might* harm or kill their babies, although these fears are never borne out in their actions. Very few perfectly normal woman, if they are absolutely honest, have not at some time thought of throwing their babies out of the window or taking some such action, especially after a succession of sleepless nights with an overactive child who never seems to sleep or to stop crying. But this happens only in imagination and rarely in reality, although simply thinking such a thing causes feelings of guilt.

An interesting sideline on attitudes towards both female offenders and abortion is revealed by a study of the fate of women murderers who were found to be pregnant at the time of their trial. That ancient views about 'animate' and 'inanimate' fetuses were not so absurd after all can be seen by reference to the time when the law did not stay the execution of a pregnant woman until the fourth month of pregnancy, yet was prepared to prosecute for abortion before that time.

A survey of women executed in Britain since 1843 is given in Patrick Wilson's book *Murderess*.[43] Before 1931, when a woman was sentenced to death, she was asked if she had anything to say in stay of execution. If she alleged she was pregnant, a jury of married women was immediately empanelled in court and reported to the judge on whether or not she was pregnant. If she was pregnant, she was respited until the child was born. When death sentences were very numerous, in the eighteenth century, a condemned woman frequently 'pleaded her belly'. As late as 1807 Mary Masson was executed in Edinburgh for poisoning her husband, having been respited long enough to give birth to her child. It became established practice after 1849 to reprieve a pregnant woman immediately.

In 1931, after a poverty-stricken young woman was condemned to death for killing her baby, a public outcry caused the passing of the Sentence of Death (Expectant Mothers) Act. After that date a pregnant woman found guilty of murder was sentenced to life imprisonment.

Four of the women executed between 1843 and 1955 were pregnant when they were arrested, and the trials of two, Nurse Waddington and Mary Ann Cotten, who were respectively seven and four months pregnant, were delayed, the former for five months and the latter for seven months. Neither murdered because of her pregnancy, but it was clear, at least in the case of Mrs Cotten, that the trial was delayed so that it would not be necessary to reprieve her. Six of the nine pregnant women indicted for murder between 1957 and 1962 killed their own children, four of them attempting to gas themselves and their young children. In each case the mother survived, but at least one child died. Three pregnant girls killed their lovers during violent quarrels. Murders committed during pregnancy may well be precipitated by the physical exhaustion of looking after young children as well or by women's attempts to protect themselves. The 1931 Act did not apply to Scotland. The practice there was for the Lord Advocate to 'restrict the pains of law', with the result that the court was precluded from passing a death sentence but could impose any less severe punishment.

The Royal Commission on Capital Punishment reported in 1953 and found no rational argument for differentiating between the sexes – reminding itself of witnesses who had instanced the most atrocious and cold-blooded cases of women involved in baby farming, when exemption from the death sentence could hardly be justified – so long as capital punishment was retained.

To return to the subject of infanticide in the wider sense, what happens when a relatively late abortion (but one still within the legal time limit) produces a premature baby who is showing signs of life? There is really no doubt about what should be done in this situation, and that is that every effort should be made to resuscitate the baby and care for it in an intensive care unit as if it were an 'ordinary' premature delivery, though scare stories to the contrary have been spread by anti-abortion factions to try to whip up further support for their cause. There is, of course, the related problem that, should such an infant survive, it may well be permanently brain-damaged.

In many cases of deaths of neonates it is not so much positive actions which are involved as 'omissions' – the avoidance of interfering or of introducing measures or treatments – but it is established in law that murder can be committed by an omission. Unfortunately, depending on the circumstances, causing death by an omission can also give rise to a charge of manslaughter or prosecution under Section 1 of the Children's and Young Persons' Act 1933.

To confound the legal picture even further a suggestion has been made[44] that a new category of offence, called 'neonaticide', should be introduced. Neonaticide would involve the killing of a child within the first 28 days of extra-uterine life. The authors also advocate what is effectively perinatal euthanasia:

> It will not be an offence if two doctors, one of whom is a consultant paediatrician, acting in good faith and with the consent of both parents if available, arrange within the first 72 hours of life for the termination of the life of an infant because further life would be intolerable by virtue of pain and suffering or because of severe cerebral incompetence and the underlying condition is not amenable to reasonable medical or surgical treatment.

This proposal comes in the wake of publicity in recent years concerning the problem of the mentally handicapped child who survives the neonatal period. Any attempts to kill it thereafter constitute murder. A tragic example was the case of *R.* v. *Arthur* (1981). This concerned a well respected and conscientious paediatrician who allowed a 'mongol' baby (one with Down's syndrome) to die by placing it on a regime of non-intervention after discussion with the parents, who did not want it. One is reminded here of A. H. Clough's couplet from 'The Latest Decalogue':

> Thou shalt not kill; but need'st not strive
> Officiously to keep alive.

This was really a test case in medical ethics. Halfway through the trial the charge was altered to the lesser one of attempted murder. The question at issue was not that of guilt or innocence in any ordinary sense but that of the duty of the doctor, who had in his care a newborn baby with severe and irreversible handicap and whose parents wished him dead. The paediatrician was eventually acquitted. A similar case earlier in the year had also received a lot of publicity. Another Down's syndrome baby had been born with a blocked gastro-intestinal tract and would have died if not operated upon. The surgeon, following the parent's abandonment of the child, refused to operate. The local authority then assumed parental rights and found another surgeon who did (successfully) operate.

We must place these cases in some sort of perspective. About 1,500 handicapped babies are born in the United Kingdom each week, and, as previously noted, about 2 per cent of all pregnancies end in a malformed baby. Also, we still have an unacceptably high rate of neonatal mortality, especially in certain parts of the country. With handicapped infants we are dealing with probabilities which are hard to assess. A strong case could have been made for not allowing any of the thalidomide victims to survive, yet some have adapted so remarkably well that they are a source of pride and happiness to themselves, their parents and others. A great deal depends on parental attitudes. If parents can and want to give their handicapped baby loving care, and do not overestimate their own abilities or underestimate the problems, this is a strong argument in favour of saving lives under threat. If the child is to be condemned to institutional life, in which it will suffer deprivation and be a burden to others, this is a strong argument for abortion. Particular cases should be decided on their merits – but who should be involved in the decision process?

The question is: Should these decisions be left solely to the parents and doctors, or should laymen and others have a say in the proceedings? Should the law be kept out of the issue as well? A *Times* leader of 6 November 1981 made this comment:

> [Keeping out the law] is wrong. It is of course parents and doctors on whom it falls to make these agonizing decisions in the first place, and they deserve the understanding and support of society. But they are decisions of a kind that require to be taken inside a framework of public morality which finds its expression, and sanction, in the law. How that public morality, embodied in law, is to be brought to bear is a difficult practical question. Neither this lengthy criminal trial (*R.* v. *Arthur*), nor the rapid civil proceedings of the earlier case, has provided satisfactory means of doing so.

6

Population Control and Abortion in Other Countries

One of the most contentious matters is the definition of over-population, which is not as simple as may appear at first sight. Statistics can be quoted (and I will give some later) to show that the population is increasing in various parts of the world, but the controversial issue is whether the available resources can sustain the increase. Some would argue that there is plenty of food in the world and that it could be made available with the aid of modern technology – the fault lies in its utilization and distribution.

The neo-Malthusian argument has been introduced into the debate. T. R. Malthus (1766–1834) was a British economist who believed that any attempts to raise the living standards of the poorest sections of the community were bound to be unsuccessful because this would lead to a population increase, which would in turn outrun resources and so set up a vicious circle. His proffered solution was 'moral restraint', like the postponement of marriage, along with premarital chastity, until parents were able to support a family. Later writers have pointed out that the consequences of this theory could be overcome by adopting birth-control measures within marriage.

Improved health care has, paradoxically, also brought its own disadvantages. People are living longer (hence an increase in the geriatric population), and more babies are surviving. In the nineteenth century the population grew rapidly in all European countries except France, Spain and Ireland.

Some interesting statistics for EEC countries were published by the European Commission in 1983. These showed that the illegitimacy and divorce rates in Britian were among the highest in the EEC: for example, out of every 1,000 babies born in Britian 125 were illegitimate, and the divorce rate was 2.8 per 1,000. There was a slow growth in the birth rate in most EEC countries. Britain's, with 13 children per thousand people born each year, was higher than Italy's, where there were, on average, 11 children per thousand. This was attributed to the 1980 law in Italy which allowed abortion, running at 36 per cent of all live births. Ireland, with a birth rate of 20 per thousand, had the fastest growing population.

The latest statistics for Britian show that for 1984 there was an 11.3 per cent increase in illegitimate births over the previous year, taking the total number to 100,500 which is almost double the figure of 10 years ago. There has also been a corresponding decline in the number of legitimate births to 526,000, the second lowest figure in 100 years of records. The previously quoted EEC figures also showed an encouraging drop in the perinatal mortality rate in the United Kingdom over the previous two decades. In 1960 about 33 babies in every thousand died in the months after birth, but this had dropped to about 13. Progress had been better in Ireland, where over the same period of time the death rate had dropped to just 7 per thousand.

National and international statistics for events which have been, or still are, stigmatized (such as suicide and abortion) are highly unreliable but may nevertheless be useful for plotting trends and helpful to Governments in formulating policies and planning services. Yet in spite of technical advances in making such calculations, it still seems surprisingly difficult to come up with reliable forecasts of such things as the birth rate. This obviously has wide social implications, not only in the more obvious areas, such as agricultural policy, but also in relation to estimates of just how many doctors and teachers will be needed in the next decade or so. Some findings are a useful reminder of what we already know or perhaps guess with common sense (for instance, certain fertility statistics show that a woman's income and level of education are inversely related to the size of her family).

One of the conditions that perpetuate poverty is lack of access to birth-control measures and therapeutic abortion. It is often (wrongly) assumed that poor people want large families, but studies have shown the opposite. The higher birth rate of the poor is due largely to ignorance or the unavailability of birth-control methods. Large families prevent poor people from improving their standards of living. Overcrowding and concentration in urban conditions tend to lead to the greater deprivation of the already disadvantaged and, with an increasing cycle of deprivation, to more poverty, crime and other social evils.

Trends in world population

There is no doubt that there is an alarming increase in the world's population. Every 10 seconds there are 39 births in the world and only 16 deaths. If this worked out at a 2 per cent increase per year, then the world population would double in a 40-year period. Put another way, the world population is growing by about 75 million per year, with the highest rates of growth in Latin America, Africa and Asia. Even though the rate of increase declined from 1.9 per cent in 1970–5 to 1.7 per cent in 1975–80, the population will still double every 40 years. To place the abortion part of the debate in perspective, the United Nations, through UNICEF, estimated in 1982 that more than 17 million children (one every two seconds) died from disease and starvation. We have had another reminder of what such unpredictable factors as drought can do with the tragedies in Ethiopia and elsewhere in Africa.

To combat these undesirable trends, various measures have been proposed for regulating population growth, sometimes advocating persuasion or legislation, sometimes education, indoctrination or social sanctions and rewards. There is the further problem of getting the balance right between civil liberties and the rights of the individual versus interference by the state. There is also the need for the recognition of minority rights, as well as the moral and religious views of different sections of the population.

International concern over these matters has been expressed in research funded by the World Bank. Alarming statistics have been produced: for instance, by the end of the century the total world population is expected to reach 6,000 million, with the vast bulk of this increase occurring in the developing world. The World Bank's report[1] devoted much space to direct measures that Governments could take to ameliorate the situation, like the introduction of family planning programmes, but in many countries married couples still want four or more children, and it will take extensive economic and social changes to change their views. Perhaps the most significant gains (according to the report) have been made by improving women's education and social rights. With 'liberation', it seems, those who bear the burden of the population boom take its control into their own hands.

The United Nations, for its part, convened an international conference on world population in Mexico City – the last one held in 1974 – this in itself being an achievement, given so many conflicting interests. A somewhat artificial distinction is sometimes drawn between the realms of public and private morality; the latter, ideally, is left alone by the state. To put it another way, it has been argued in the past that what people do in their bedrooms (assuming they are lucky enough to have them) is no business of the state, let alone international organizations; that family planning is a form of genocide promoted by the white races to repress the rest; that population policies merely divert resources from genuine programmes of economic development; and that birth-control methods are either dangerous or just plain wrong.

There are many ways of trying to regulate the population, some obvious and others less so. The four 'basic' ways are contraception, sterilization, abortion and infanticide. Socio-cultural factors can be involved – for example, the restriction of marriage, and procreation contingent on caste, tribe or taboos. Religious sanctions can be used, and laws can be passed to regulate 'promiscuity', prostitution, pornography, the age of 'consent' and marriage. Education and persuasion are often tried, with or without economic or other sanctions. Various attitudes, habits, beliefs and forms of behaviour can be made part of a cultural norm – for instance, attempts are made to desexualize society, especially women (as in China); to encourage or 'glorify' celibacy, abstinence and virginity and even homosexuality; to prevent the spread of Western 'decadence' and permissiveness; to restrict family size, prolong lactation and encourage breast-feeding; to discourage research and the treatment of infertility. These, finally, do little to combat starvation and extreme poverty, which by themselves cause sub-fertility, and such energies as are left are devoted entirely to seeking food. (We know, for instance, that anorexia nervosa – starvation, albeit self-induced – leads to emaciation and that periods cease, as does any interest in sex.)

Some of these methods of population control have been enshrined in legislation: but how far should legislation reflect the majority view, or set the trend for future change, or indeed be ahead of its time and 'public opinion'? This is not an easy matter to settle. Perhaps we get only the laws we deserve.

Although this book is primarily about abortion and how our own legislation developed in Britain, it is salutary to take a wider view and to examine what has been done, and is still being done, in other countries, in order both to compare and to contrast their aims and achievements with our own way of doing things and also to learn by others' mistakes and advances. It also helps to know about other countries, especially those in Europe, as any changes in abortion legislation in European countries will help us to predict how many foreign women will be coming to England for abortions. Obviously I cannot mention every country in the world – this chapter would degenerate into a tedious list – so I shall select various countries, both in Europe and elsewhere, for which there are reasonably well documented statistics. The situation in the USA provides one of the best examples of the complicated interplay of all the various factors to which I have already alluded.

Official statistics are available which tell us the country of origin of the non-resident women who come to Britain for abortions. The latest year for which a detailed analysis is available is 1982 (published in 1984). For comparison and to show shifting trends, I have chosen the year 1974 (see the table on p. 217).[2] The most obvious change has been in France and Spain, with a large decrease in the former and an equally big increase in the latter. There was also a more modest increase in the numbers of abortions in the British Isles. The rest of the world, proportionally, does not provide very many. In round figures, the number of resident women having abortions has gone up from 109,000 to 128,000, while over the same period the non-resident numbers have fallen from 53,000 to 34,000.

Abortion legislation in other countries

As already noted, changing attitudes to, and laws concerning, abortion are a complicated business, with many overtones. There are six main sets of factors, or social forces, which significantly affect abortion issues and which are not mutually exclusive. They can be summarized thus:

(1) neo-Malthusian;
(2) socialist-feminist;

(3) reformist;
(4) right-wing groups;
(5) religious groups;
(6) medical advances.[3]

Two of the main obstacles to abortion law reform are religious principles and the belief that abortion is detrimental to health (either physical or mental).

Over the past 20 years or so the abortion laws have been liberalized in many countries, partly to combat the high rates of illegal abortion and its complications but also in recognition of the fact that women now have more say in their own reproductive futures.[4] Since 1967 there has been a worldwide tendency towards the relaxation of abortion laws. Between 1967 and 1982 over 40 countries extended the grounds for abortion, and only three narrowed them. This means that in 1982 nearly two-thirds of women lived in countries where abortion was totally prohibited or permitted only to save the mother's life. A majority of countries in Africa, almost two-thirds of Latin America and the majority of the Muslim countries of Asia fall into the latter category. In 1981 these restrictions also applied to five countries in Europe – Belgium, Ireland, Malta, Portugal and Spain – but the position is rapidly changing.

The total number of abortions performed worldwide is very difficult to estimate. One such estimate made in 1982 was between 40 and 50 million, or three out of every 10 known pregnancies, half of them illegal. If the world annual growth rate were 80 million, in the absence of abortion this figure would reach about 120 million.

The pioneer country in introducing legalized abortion was the USSR, as long ago as the 1920s, followed by Japan. The first country to legalize abortions on medico-social grounds was Iceland, by Law No. 38, in January 1935. Abortion was then permitted up to 28 weeks' pregnancy if there was a threat to maternal health, either physical or mental.

Abortions in Britain, 1974 and 1982
(excluding England and Wales residents)

Country of origin	1974	1982
BRITISH ISLES	3,910	6,528
Scotland	1,026	898
N.Ireland	1,092	1,510
Irish Republic	1,421	3,653
Channel Isles and Isle of Man	371	467
OTHER EUROPEAN COUNTRIES	40,060	26,699
Austria	268	49
Belgium and Luxembourg	641	122
Denmark	4	–
France	36,443	3,825
German Federal Republic	5,991	365
Gibraltar	–	26
Italy	1,751	626
Malta	–	36
Netherlands	78	46
Portugal	59	50
Spain	2,978	21,415
Switzerland	618	106
Norway and Sweden	49	–
Others	180	–
REST OF THE WORLD	408	1,265
GRAND TOTALS		
Resident (England and Wales)	109,445	128,553
Non-resident	53,495	34,492
Total for year	162,940	163,045

The British Commonwealth

Most of the Commonwealth countries inherited the 1861 Offences Against the Person Act, but the most recent British legislation and case law have had their effects. Zambia was the first of the African Commonwealth countries to reform its restrictive laws in 1972 and come into line with the 1967 Act. Zimbabwe changed in 1977 and the Seychelles in 1981. A second group of nine African countries liberalized their laws along the lines of the *Bourne* case – to protect the woman's physical and mental health. A third group (Botswana, Malawi, Mauritius and Northern Nigeria) allow abortion only to save the life of the mother. In their final analysis of a total of 60 Commonwealth countries, Cook and Dickens[5] found that 18 allowed abortion to save the life of the woman, 30 permitted it to protect the woman's physical or mental health and 12 allowed abortion on wider grounds. A meeting of health and justice Ministers of 13 Commonwealth countries in Barbados in June 1979 proposed that abortion should be available on request during the first trimester of pregnancy.

The situation in Australia is complicated by its federal structure, with no supreme court, so that each of its seven states can decide its own law, as well as by the fact that in the country as a whole there is still a strong anti-abortion movement. However, the British 1967 Act has had an influence in helping to liberalize the laws, especially in South Australia, Victoria and Northern Territory. In New Zealand, after a centre was established in Auckland in 1974 to provide cheap abortions, there were a number of attempts to close it and much public and legal controversy. This led to the setting up of a Royal Commission (1975–7) which had a strong anti-abortion element. When it finally reported it proposed that abortion be allowed only for 'serious danger to the physical or mental health of the woman', with a committee system to decide on the details, although it did suggest that fetal abnormalities should also be a ground. However, strong anti-abortion pressure groups persuaded the Government to drop the fetal abnormalities suggestion when the law was passed (197). This law was very unpopular, and a 1978 amendment brought back fetal abnormality as grounds for abortion.[6]

In Canada there is an important and vociferous Roman Catholic population, so, not surprisingly, abortion legislation has had a turbulent history. The *cause célèbre* was the repeated prosecution in Quebec of Dr Henry Morgentaler, who carried out many abortions within (as he thought) the provisions of the Criminal Code. After several legal battles, in March 1975 he was sentenced to 18 months, 10 of which were to be spent in gaol. This did eventually lead to the law being amended slightly and to the setting up of the Badgley Committee, which reported in 1977. The Committee found that only 20 per cent of hospitals had formed abortion committees and that after a first visit it took an average of eight weeks to obtain an abortion. It also found that two-thirds of the hospital committees required the consent of the woman's spouse. For single women some committees even required the consent of the putative father. It was also reported that about one in six women wanting abortions went to the United States for them. Constant pressure has been brought to bear on these various hospital committees by locally organized anti-abortion groups, so that there is great variation in availability in different parts of the country.[7]

The Republic of India is officially a secular state. Abortion practices, dating from 500 years BC, are cited in Hindu literature. Susnuta, the ancient Hindu physician, was of the opinion that early termination was justified for the sake of the mother's health.

Under Imperial rule abortion was restricted by the provisions of Section 312 of the Indian Penal Code 1860: any contraventions of this were punishable by between three and seven years in prison. Under this code it was illegal for anyone voluntarily to cause an abortion in a pregnant woman.

In 1964 the Government of India appointed a committee to consider abortion legislation. It then estimated that 6.5 million abortions were carried out annually, of which approximately

2.6 million were spontaneous and 3.9 million induced. Few reliable statistics were available, but the impression was that abortion rates were lower in rural areas than in cities. Like China, India suffered from, and was concerned with, over-population; and in 1951 a birth-control programme had been instigated. The committee reported in 1966 and recommended a liberalization of the 1860 Code.[8]

The Medical Termination Bill was introduced in Parliament in 1969 and finally enacted as the Medical Termination of Pregnancy Act 1971. The law limited abortion to Western medical (allopathic) practitioners and required hospitals and clinics to be licensed. Termination was restricted to the first 20 weeks and on the following grounds: medical, eugenic, humanitarian, social, physical and mental health. Abortion was specifically allowed for contraceptive failure. The doctor was required to register the operation officially.

There were, however, problems over implementation, and illegal abortions continued on a large scale as a result. Such statistics as there are show that for the years 1972–3 in all India there were 24,298 abortions; for 1977–8 the figure was 221,488. A general survey showed that induced abortions certainly occurred in traditional villages but at a low rate (fewer than 5 per 100 pregnancies). They were more common in cities (at 10 per cent or more of pregnancies) but still low compared with many urban areas in other parts of the world. Also, the ratio of second-trimester to earlier abortions was still higher than in most other countries.[9]

Recent legal interpretations allow menstrual regulation to be practised. In Bangladesh artificial termination is permitted where there are strong health or social indications. In the late 1970s one quarter of all pregnancy-related deaths in Bangladesh were caused by illegal abortions.

As regards sterilization, this was particularly pushed during the 19 months of the Emergency, until March 1977. By this time 10 million had undergone tubal ligation or vasectomy. For a time these operations were made compulsory for parents of three or more children.[10]

Although child marriage was made illegal in 1929, it is still widely practised in rural areas and can occur when children concerned are very young indeed (*The Times*, 29 April 1985). When a little older, the girl is taken to her husband's home, where she is symbolically tied to him. The advantages of child marriage to the traditionally minded Hindu are many: it takes care of burgeoning female sexuality and the threat that that could imply for the status of the caste or sub-caste, for caste is transmitted by the father. If the women have children by higher-caste men, the children will have a ritual status higher than their mother's (and likewise lower if they marry lower-caste men). Thus child marriage protects the whole group from men of undesirable status, who might pollute it. Other advantages are mainly for the parents of bride or groom. It reinforces their authority, for instance; it also helps the young bride to adjust her behaviour to her in-laws' expectations before her own personality is fully mature. It is thought also to encourage the early birth of a son, so essential for the salvation of the parents, since only a son can perform the funeral rites for both parents; it ensures the consolidation of family property.

The United States of America

There is a wealth of documentation on the long and complicated history of abortion in the USA,[11] with its remarkable volte-face in 1900 and famous Supreme Court ruling of 1973. In the introduction to a scholarly review of the historical background up to 1900 Mohr[12] writes: 'In 1800 no jurisdiction in the United States had enacted any statutes whatsoever on the subject of abortion; most forms of abortion were not illegal and those American women who wished to practise abortion did so.' Yet by 1900 this had completely changed, and he offers a fascinating account of why and how this happened.

Before the American Medical Association (AMA) was formed in 1847 abortion was commonly done before quickening, and there was no legislation against this. As the century progressed, abortions were more openly performed and publicized until the AMA launched an anti-abortion drive in order to improve conditions and medical practice.[13]

By 1885 the religious press had joined in, and in 1869 there was the papal decree; finally Protestants also joined the debate. By 1900 abortions was illegal throughout the USA. Abortion was then driven underground for more than half a century until human rights activists, some leading physicians, lawyers and feminists, as well as family planning groups, led the struggle which ended in the momentous Supreme Court decision of 1973. Before then it was estimated that one out of every five pregnancies ended in an illegal operation.

Before considering in a little more detail some of the factors which helped to influence the 1973 ruling, it is worth pointing out some of the basic differences between the UK and the USA. The most important is the fact that the USA has a written constitution and the UK does not. Also, of course, the USA is a federation, so it has state laws and federal laws. There is also a much closer relationship between the law, politics and religion. In the American system it is possible to try to have a law annulled by a judicial declaration of unconstitutionality. How the Supreme Court is formed is also important: it has judges who are appointed for life by the President.

The sources of the various pressures which began to build up in the early 1970s against the anti-abortion policies inherited from the nineteenth century were the following. First, there was the fear of overpopulation, highlighted by the 1972 President's Commission on Population Growth. Secondly, more open concern was beginning to be expressed about the quality of life, as distinct from biological life itself (this was brought to a head by the thalidomide tragedy). Thirdly, the champions of women's rights changed their attitude towards abortion, particularly as it became a safer procedure. Most 'feminists' in the nineteenth century avoided the issue, but by the 1960s the doctrine began to emerge of a woman's inalienable right to control all her own bodily functions. Fourthly, there were important changes in medical opinion and practices: in the nineteenth century abortion carried high mortality and morbidity rates; later it became safer, in statistical terms, to have a first-trimester abortion than to have a full-term delivery. Fifthly, there was the increasing problem of numbers of illegal abortions and their consequences. The now classic study of Taussig[14] estimated that over half a million illegal abortions were taking place annually in the USA and that wealthy women were flouting the law. Last, the process of abortion policy-making had itself changed by virtue of the relatively new role of the federal Government, when such matters had previously been decided at state level. There was also the new role of public opinion as expressed by opinion polls, petitions, organizations, radio, TV and newspapers, and better education generally.

At the time of the Supreme Court decision (*Roe* v. *Wade*, 1973) 19 states allowed abortion to prevent grave damage to the mother's health. Some also permitted it in cases of rape and incest or if the child might be born handicapped, while 4 of the 19 did permit abortion on request although in practice these were often difficult to obtain. The other 31 states banned abortions: in 21 of these the statutes had not changed since 1868, the year in which the Fourteenth Amendment was ratified. No state had abortion laws as liberal as those which resulted from the Supreme Court's interpretation, so that suddenly the USA had one of the most liberal abortion policies in the world.

A pioneer in this direction had been California. In 1969 the California Supreme Court declared the state law unconstitutional, this declaration being precipitated by the trial of a doctor who had been performing abortions. In its decision the court defined the rights of a woman over her own procreation for the first time, and this was the first state Supreme Court decision in American history to declare an abortion statute unconstitutional. In 1970 legislation in the states of Hawaii and New York both gave women the right to choose an abortion during the early part of pregnancy.

So much has been written about the Supreme Court ruling of 22 January 1973 that it is difficult to summarize the essential issues. Officially the cases are referred to as *Roe* v. *Wade* (410 US 113 1973) and *Doe* v. *Bolton* (410 US 179 1973). In essence two litigants (given these pseudonyms), from Texas and Georgia respectively, challenged, on federal constitutional grounds, their states' statutes limiting the right of a woman to obtain a legal abortion. At the time Texas law prohibited abortion unless it was to save the woman's life on medical advice. In a word, 'Jane Roe' claimed that the Texas anti-abortion statute violated the US constitution. 'Wade' refers to Henry Wade, who at the time was District Attorney of Dallas County, Texas, where 'Jane Roe' lived.

It is now publicly acknowledged that 'Jane Roe' was Norma McCorvey, who at the age of 21 was raped by three men and became pregnant as a result. She married at the age of 16 but subsequently divorced. She came from a typical 'broken home', was a school drop-out and was generally unable to settle. By the time of the Supreme Court's decision her abortion had already been carried out. The other case (*Doe* v. *Bolton*) involved a very poor, married, pregnant woman, who also had her pregnancy terminated before the court ruling. More specifically, 'Jane's' case was that Texas statutes were 'unconstitutionally vague' and that they removed her right to personal privacy, as protected in the First, Fourth, Fifth, Ninth and Fourteenth Amendments of the Constitution.

The court ruled seven to two in favour of striking down the abortion laws, and Mr Justice Blackmun began by giving a summary of the historical origins of the laws then in force. One of the major factors invoked in favour of change was the right to privacy. Although not explicitly mentioned in the Constitution, it existed by implication:

> This right of privacy, whether it be founded in the Fourteenth Amendment's concept of personal liberty and restrictions upon state action, as we feel it is, or, as the District Court determined, in the Ninth Amendment's reservation of rights to the people, is broad

> enough to encompass a woman's decision whether or not to terminate her pregnancy. The detriment that the State would impose upon the pregnant woman by denying this choice altogether is apparent. Specific and direct harm medically diagnosable even in early pregnancy may be involved. Maternity, or additional offspring, may force upon the woman a distressful life and future. Psychological harm may be imminent. Mental and physical health may be taxed by child care. There is also the distress, for all concerned, associated with the unwanted child, and there is the problem of bringing a child into a family already unable psychologically, and otherwise, to care for it. In other cases, as in this one, the additional difficulties and continuing stigma of unwed motherhood may be involved. All these are factors the woman and her responsible physician necessarily will consider in consultation.

However, this right of privacy was not absolute. At some point in pregnancy, writes Justice Blackmun, 'A state may properly assert important interests in safeguarding health, in maintaining medical standards, and in protecting potential life.' Crucial to the outcome was whether the Fourteenth Amendment protected the unborn fetus from indiscriminate destruction. Justice Blackmun's solution was that the fetus was not a 'person' within the Amendment's protection. Taking note of previous philosophical, theological and other discussions on the point, the court simply asserted, 'We need not resolve the difficult question of when life begins' – but when does the state acquire a legitimate interest in protecting 'potential life'? Approximately at the end of the second trimester, when the fetus had become viable, was the court's ruling on this point. At this stage 'the state may, if it chooses, regulate, and even proscribe, abortion except where it is necessary, in appropriate medical judgment, for the preservation of the life or health of the mother.'

The court specifically ruled that in the first trimester 'the abortion decision and its effectation must be left to the medical judgment of the pregnant woman's attending physician' and again that before viability 'the abortion decision in all its aspects is inherently, and primarily, a medical decision, and basic responsibility for it must rest with the physician.'

The main effects and rationale of the *Roe* v. *Wade* decision in 1973 can be summarized as follows.[15] It endeavoured to resolve three conflicting principles:

(1) the right of the individual to privacy;
(2) the right of the state to protect maternal health;
(3) the right of the state to protect developing life.

It did this by dividing human gestation into three stages, thus adopting a 'gradualist' approach. During the first trimester of pregnancy the woman had a right to decide her own future privately, without state interference, and this took precedence over the other two rights. So during this time the court gave virtually an unconditional right to termination. In the second trimester, when the danger of abortion was relatively greater than in the first trimester, the right of the state to regulate and protect female health became 'compelling' but would still not deny her an abortion, insisting only on reasonable standards of medical procedure. As regards the third and final trimester, only then did the state's legitimate right to protect the developing life take precedence; only then might the state proscribe abortion except when necessary to preserve the health or life of the woman. On this latter decision the court placed great emphasis on 'viability' after approximately six months of intra-uterine life. The majority had defined viability as that point at which a fetus could live by itself outside the mother's womb, albeit with artificial aids, and implicitly denied that human life, in any legally meaningful form, existed prior to viability. Indeed, the court explicitly denied Texas the right to adopt a 'theory of life' which implied that it did.

A minority opinion was expressed by two of the Supreme Court judges, who objected, among other things, to the wide interpretation given, which they considered would virtually allow abortion on demand. The 1973 ruling seems, in retrospect, a masterly compromise, especially for such a pluralistic society, and a valuable effort to depoliticize the abortion issue, but the repercussions continue to this day with the warring factions quite literally coming to blows.

Before describing various attempts to alter this ruling, what do the statistics show after the 12 years 1973–1985? In the USA as a whole there are now approximately 1,600,000 abortions a year, and there have been 16 million abortions in these 12 years, involving some 10 million women. In 1976 the abortion rate was 23.3 per 1,000 women of childbearing age; in the same year in Britain it was 11.0 per 1,000. In 1979 17 per cent of all births were illegitimate. Abortion is now the most commonly performed surgical procedure in the USA. Every fourth pregnancy is terminated, and in New York City there are more abortions than live births. On average there are about 4,500 abortions a day. Put another way, each year 3 per cent of American women aged 15–44 have an abortion; 60 per cent of them were not using contraceptive devices when they became pregnant. About 30 per cent of all abortions are repeat ones. Proportionally, white middle-class women have most abortions. Many black Americans and other 'disadvantaged' groups cannot find the $200 or so to pay for an early standard termination. Free abortion is conditional on being a Medicaid patient living in a state which finances the operations.

One way of influencing abortion decisions is by controlling the financial aspect. There was another Supreme Court ruling in 1980 (*Harris* v. *McRae*) which stated that neither the federal nor the state Government have to pay for abortions for indigent women who are eligible under the federal state Medicaid program even if the abortions were 'medically necessary'. This decision was the culmination of nearly four years' litigation and by implication also applies to all women who obtain their medical care through programs that are partly or totally funded publicly, e.g. Indians. The decision was close, five to four, and it was made clear there were many reservations.[16]

Opposition to the more liberal abortion laws has come from the expected quarters but ways to implement proposed changes are limited. There are three basic ways of trying to do this. The first is 'political', in that, as already noted, the judges who constitute the Supreme Court are political appointments so that all new appointees could, theoretically, be selected for their anti-abortion views. This is now a distinct possibility with the emergence under President Reagan of the political New Right with its strong anti-abortion stance. Historically, though, the Supreme Court is extremely reluctant to change its mind on the principle that courts should honour the decisions of earlier courts. Also it is almost unique for a President to apply direct pressure on the Supreme Court in the way President Reagan is doing. For example, on 14 July 1985, the Reagan Administration directly asked the court to change its mind on the 1973 decision on the grounds that it was so sweeping that states were prevented from enacting their own abortion laws.

The other two ways open to the anti-abortionists are by altering the Constitution or by passing new laws. But amending the US Constitution is a difficult procedure as it requires a two-thirds vote of both Houses of Congress plus subsequent ratification by three-quarters of the states. Two types of amendment have been tried: one would have returned the power to approve or prohibit abortions to the states and the other, under various guises, would have guaranteed the 'right to life' from conception. To pass legislation is a more simple procedure as only a simple majority vote in each House of Congress is needed.

Examples of the latter are the 'Human Life Bill' (1981) which proposed that human life existed from conception. The Bill decreed that a fetus was a 'person' from conception onwards, so that abortion would then (legally) constitute the taking of human life. For the former an example was the 'Hatch Amendment' (1982) which tried to amend the Constitution to: 'A right of abortion is not secured by the Constitution. The Congress and several states shall have the concurrent power to restrict and prohibit abortion, provided that a law of a state which is more restrictive than a law of Congress shall govern'.

The most powerful pro-choice (abortion) lobby is the National Abortion Rights Action League, which is trying to prevent any congressional modifications of the 1973 decision. Its main concern is that the Supreme Court may think again on the subject, and as the judges are political appointees, this could happen.

The Roman Catholic Church and fundamentalist Protestant Churches form the backbone of the anti-abortion movement. In 1980 the population of the USA was 226,505,000. A 1981 estimate of the religious affiliations of the US population who were 'anti-choice' produced the following figures: out of 85 million Americans 50 million were Born-Again Protestants, 30 million morally conservative Catholics, 3 million Mormons, 2 million Orthodox and Conservative Jews.

Abortion vies with nuclear disarmament as the overriding moral issue of the US Catholic Church. There is unhappiness within the Church establishment over the grass-roots anti-abortion movement, and it took time for any denunciation of violence. Historically the Church has had a cautious fraternity with the Democrats, but paradoxically it has been the arch conservatives, including President Reagan himself, who have expressed most moral outrage against abortion.

The traditional Protestant Churches have tended to equivocate: for instances, the Episcopal Church – the sister church of the Church of England – emphasized the sanctity of life in a policy statement in 1976, but it did not seek to define at which point life began. Abortion as a means of birth control is opposed. The policy, in essence, is to allow a woman to decide to have an abortion after serious consideration of the issues, in conjunction with counselling from a minister. The Methodist Church issued what amounts to a pro-choice statement, supporting the option of abortion after counselling from a member of the clergy.

The main anti-abortion group is the National Right to Life Committee (NRLC) which, characteristically, trades most in emotive words like 'murder', 'holocaust' and so on and is now greatly relying on the publicity engendered by the showing of the film *The Silent Scream*.

The abortion debate in the USA is currently virtually deadlocked between the 'right to life' and the 'right to choice' movements, partly because of the constraints of the Constitution. This is in spite of the political bias of the Reagan Administration against abortion. In the (Reagan) presidential election campaign the two main issues were the economy and abortion. It is alleged that the pro-abortion stance of the Democrats, Mondale and Ferraro, lost them many votes (perhaps 3–5 million), with a consequent switch to Reagan–Bush.

In 1984 Congress banned federal funding through Medicaid for most abortions, consequently affecting the 'choice' for poor women, and the Senate rejected an attempt to permit federal funding of abortions for cases of rape or incest. The Administration now denies all aid funds to private overseas organizations which actively promote abortion. Ohio, steadfastly anti-abortion, tried to force women having abortions to take the fetus to a licensed funeral director. In his most recent State of the Union message (*The Times*, 8 February 1985) President Reagan is quoted as saying, 'Abortion is either the taking of human life, or it isn't – it must be stopped.'

It seems to me that the most worrying aspect of all this is the resort to violence, which was not specifically condemned by either the Roman Catholic Church or President Reagan until they were almost compelled to do so by the escalation of, and publicity over, the outrages. The 'right to life' groups deny either employing or encouraging violence, yet between 1977 and 1979 no fewer than 25 abortion clinics were firebombed, and the first arrest for such an offence was recorded only in 1979. In 1984, 24 clinics were wrecked or damaged in a continuing campaign by bombs and fire, and doctors and nurses were intimidated.

The National Right to Life Committee hopes to get the Constitution amended during President Reagan's second term of office. During his 1984 State of the Union message President Reagan appealed to Americans to find alternatives to abortion. He spoke, via loudspeaker hook-ups, to pro-life demonstrators outside the White House and expressed his support for legislation banning the use of federal funds to finance abortions for economically needy women. In January 1986, he repeated this message in exactly the same way.

Latin America

This continent still has a very high population growth, generally restrictive laws and an alarmingly high rate of illegal abortions.[17] In 1974 an estimate was made of 5 million illegal operations, with many tragic consequences. Two main factors that are most influential in deciding abortion policy are, first, the political nature of the regime currently in power and, secondly, the role of the Roman Catholic Church. Those priests in daily contact with the poor and needy have not always been able to support official Catholic teaching on contraception and abortion.

Of the 22 Latin American countries with populations over 1 million, in seven abortion is illegal in all circumstances, in six it is legal but only to save the woman's life, and in nine it is legal on broader medical grounds. Only in Cuba is abortion available on request. In Brazil, which is the largest Catholic country in the world, with an estimated population (1982) of over 125 million, about half of all pregnancies were terminated, according to a report in the *New York Times* (28 May 1977), with approximately 2 million illegal abortions each year. Up to 1974 birth control was available in only four of the 22 countries. In Mexico a family planning programme was started in 1975, and since then there have been efforts to liberalize the abortion laws. Many thousands of deaths a year have been reported, with only about 8 per cent of abortions done under medical supervision. A Bill was introduced in 1979 by the Communist Party but opposed by the President.

I should like next to consider how some of our traditionally Roman Catholic European neighbours have fared.

France

France in the nineteenth century was unique in Europe in having a low population growth. This may have had something to do with the widespread practice of coitus interruptus, first adopted by the aristocracy, for in the previous century their average family size was less than half that of the peasantry. This even received the tacit acceptance of the Church. There was also a liberal approach to abortion, and English women often travelled to France for their abortions. By the end of the nineteenth century there was a noticeable increase in the abortion rate, as judged from hospital admission figures.

The law dated from 1810 and was founded on the Code Napoléon, which prescribed between five and 10 years' penal servitude for abortion, although prosecutions were rare. This was still in force by the end of the First World War. One estimate put the annual number of abortions at between 100,000 and 500,000. In 1907, according to a report in the *Lancet*, French doctors were protesting that magistrates took too lenient a view of abortion and that upper-class women were open about their own abortions. It was also noted that English women, both unmarried and married, were still crossing the Channel simply to have an abortion. This continued until the 1930s, but by the 1970s it was French women who were coming to England for their abortions.

In 1939 the Code de la Famille was enacted: this prescribed between one and five years in prison, together with fines for abortionists, and even more severe penalties for recidivists. Doctors involved were disqualified from practice for a minimum of five years. Exceptions were made for therapeutic terminations to save the mother's life; also approved were hysterectomies and operations for ectopic pregnancy, which were also seen as licit by Catholic theologians.

However, Vichy France was very much more stringent, ranking abortion with treason and sabotage. A 1939 law stipulated the guillotine as a punishment for abortion – and it was used. Madame Giraud was a laundress who was tried and found guilty of performing 26 abortions. She was executed by guillotine in February 1942.

Since the end of the Second World War there has been a liberalization of attitudes. In 1950 2,885 people were prosecuted for abortion but only 471 in 1969 (*The Times*, 15 November 1974), though religious and political forces tried to retain restrictive practices. In 1971 over 300 French women signed a manifesto stating that they had had abortions and called for a repeal of the law. Among these women were the actress Jeanne Moreau, as well as a number of other women prominent in public life. None of them could actually be prosecuted, as the offences had been committed too long before. The direct challenges of the women's movement, supported by the political left, were crucial factors in producing change.

One case which received great publicity was the 'Bobigny Affair'. This concerned a 17-year-old girl who was aborted after being raped. Her trial took place at Bobigny (near Paris) in 1972. She was acquitted, her mother fined and the abortionist given a suspended sentence. In February 1973, 354 French doctors signed a manifesto confessing that they had taken part in abortions. Theoretically they were open to prosecution and risked up to 10 years in prison, but no action was taken.

Many French women with the means came to England but were said to be harassed by customs on their return to France, and some had their oral contraceptives confiscated and were fined. Public opinion, as reported in opinion polls, was also on the side of reform.

The first serious attempts at reform came in December 1973, when a Bill was introduced to legalize abortion for the sake of the woman's health, when pregnancy followed rape or incest and when there were fetal defects, but the Bill was bypassed by being referred to a committee. The Minister for Health at this time was Mme Simone Veil, who claimed that in spite of its illegality 300,000 French women had abortions annually. She also fought vigorously for a more liberal Bill, and by late 1974 public support was obvious.

France is nominally a Catholic country but at the same time has a strong tradition of atheism. The greatest Catholic support came from the rural areas. The French medical profession was also split, as organizations both for and against abortion were formed. One such was called the Association of Doctors Respecting Human Life, which was against liberalizing the law and was said to represent something like one in six practising doctors.

Finally, on 17 January 1975 the French parliament promulgated a law permitting abortion on request in the first 10 weeks after conception (12 weeks from the last menstrual period). Later in pregnancy termination was limited to cases involving a serious threat to the life of the woman or the strong possibility of a serious, incurable fetal malformation. However, conscientious objections could be raised, so that a whole clinic, hospital or institution could opt out on the decision of the medical director. Girls under 18 required the consent of one parent or legal guardian. Also the doctor concerned was obliged to discuss the medical risks involved, to give the patient a booklet explaining the law and help available for the unmarried mother and, finally, to send her to a counselling service. Along with her counselling certificate, the woman had to give the doctor written confirmation of her desire to have an abortion no earlier than one week following her first application. The number of induced abortions performed in a hospital or clinic was not to exceed 25 per cent of the total number of surgical and obstetrical operations performed. The law was also to be limited to French nationals only.

Although hedged about by all these bureaucratic conditions, the law was none the less a great advance, and it is of interest to note just how the voting went. The support from the left was more solid than it would be on abortion legislation of this nature in Britain or the USA. On a free vote 105 out of 106 socialists and radicals voted in favour. Similarly, 90 per cent of the communist members, but only 99 out of 291 members of the other three parties, voted in favour. The Government also set fees for abortion of between £40 and £70. The new law was initially introduced on a trial basis for five years.

As a consequence of this new legislation the number of French women coming to England for abortions dropped markedly. In 1979 the law was made permanent, although it was opposed by 20,000 feminists, who found it too restrictive. In 1982 the Government promised to cover the costs of abortion on the national health service.

Italy

There is evidence of abortion in Italy before the First World War: in a large trial in 1904 eight licensed midwives were convicted of what the *British Medical Journal* called 'abortion mongering'. It was not until the 1970s that movements for change began to be effective.[18] A Radical Party pressure group had been prominent in 1970 in bringing forward legislation for divorce, which was confirmed in 1974. In 1971 Professor Luigi de Marchi revised the Italian anti-contraceptive laws by means of an appeal to the Constitutional Court. By August of that year a draft Bill was introduced to permit abortion in cases of rape and incest, as well as for women who had five children and were unable to cope with more. This Bill made no progress.

In 1973 a socialist deputy, who had succeeded with the divorce laws, announced a Bill designed to permit abortions in hospital when approved for medical reasons by two doctors. This opened up public debate, and a referendum was held. The strength of the 1974 referendum vote to keep the divorce legislation encouraged further attempts at abortion reform.

Abortion referral agencies became bolder and the feminists more vociferous. In 1975, in a matter of six weeks, a petition carrying half a million signatures called for a referendum on abortion. Three estimates of the number of illegal abortions were published: the WHO estimate was 1.5 million for 1975, the Italian health authority's was 800,000, and the women's movement's was 3 million a year. It now seemed that the law would have to be changed, and some slight liberalization followed a Supreme Court decision in 1976.

Further scandals and press coverage hastened the process, and the main parliamentary parties began to draft abortion laws. The feminists, radicals and others combined (in Holy Year!) to form the most massive abortion reform campaign in Italian history. Changes in France also had some influence, as the two countries shared many similar political, legal and religious structures, but the campaign in Italy was more aggressive. Italian feminist groups began to refer women for abortions, and the Centro Informazione Sterilizzazione e Aborto (CISA) aimed to help women directly and to make the country face the issues (*The Times*, 15 April 1976). This movement was headed by a 55-year-old single woman, Adele Faccio, who at 36 deliberately bore a son. After more publicity she eventually got herself arrested. CISA had introduced abortion by suction and arranged with doctors to use this method if the woman was less than three months pregnant. If a woman was more than three months pregnant, she was sent to London for an abortion. In another incident a prominent gynaecologist and member of the Radical Party was imprisoned for two months, without trial, for performing abortions.

By the end of 1975 a draft Bill had reached the stage of detailed discussion of possible grounds for termination. Threats to mental or physical health, adverse socio-economic environment, as well as pregnancy associated with rape or risk to the fetus of congenital deformity were all accepted as grounds for abortion. This Bill might have become law except for the powerful intervention of the Church and a vehement outburst from the Catholic hierarchy. Eventually, at the end of April 1976, the inability to solve the abortion issue brought down the Christian Socialist Government. The crucial issue was the relationship between Church and State, this being highlighted by the Seveso disaster, when an explosion led to pregnant women being exposed to chemicals known to cause fetal abnormalities.

Less than one month before a referendum would have been mandatory, on 19 January 1977, the Italian parliament approved abortion during the first 90 days of pregnancy for reasons of mental and physical health. This measure finally became law in 1978 but was not fully implemented. What was intended was that up to 90 days abortions would be paid for by the state. A doctor's certificate had to be obtained, then the patient had to wait for a further week. Girls under age 18 (minors) needed the consent of parent, of guardian or of judge acting *in loco parentis*. Statistics were also required to be obtained from the various regions.

The Central Institute of Statistics (ISTAT) collected and published these regional figures.[19] The number of abortions per thousand live births rose from 171.7 in 1978 to 345.3 in 1980 and ranged from 206.3 in southern Italy to 471.1 in northern Italy. The abortion rate per thousand women in the age range 15–49 was 13.6 in 1979 and 16.1 in 1980. In 1978 only 4.1 per cent of all abortions were performed on women under 18; in 1979 the figure was 3.3 per cent, and in 1980 it was 3.6 per cent. As elsewhere, minors usually obtained abortions later in pregnancy. In 1978–80, 70 per cent of all abortions were obtained by married women: the majority had had primary school education and two live births. Terminations were usually done under a general anaesthetic, and women were hospitalized for more than one day. Conscientious objection in hospitals and authorized clinics was high. Among gynaecologists in six regions such objections ranged, in 1980, from 42.8 per cent in Tuscany to 75.7 per cent in Abruzzo.

After the failure to implement the 1978 legislation fully there were further pressures from various groups: the Church, feminist groups and the medical fraternity. In 1978 the bishops ruled that women having abortions would face automatic excommunication. None the less, by 1979, 188,000 legal abortions had occurred.

To try to settle the matter a referendum was called in May 1981, and voters were given three alternatives: to accept a restrictive law put forward by the pro-life movement, to leave the law as it was or to adopt the Radical Party's proposal to decriminalize abortion even for minors and to remove time limits. Both proposals for change were heavily defeated, proposal number one by 70 per cent and number three by 88 per cent. So the law remained as it was.

Spain

Abortion in Spain is, to this day, still the subject of lively controversy, and the legal position is not yet stabilized. Under Franco abortion, birth control and divorce were all illegal, and women found guilty of adultery faced a maximum prison sentence of six years. After his death a new Constitution was enacted which, in 1978, allowed birth control and divorce in 1981. Adultery was effectively repealed as an offence, but nothing was done about legalizing abortion. In October 1973 the Supreme Court sentenced to prison a Spanish couple who had obtained an abortion in London. However, this judgment was eventually overturned by Spain's Constitutional Court, which ruled that a Spanish woman who obtained an abortion abroad committed no crime. This was a significant ruling because it implied that a fetus could not be equated with a human being, whose inviolability is guaranteed by the 1978 Constitution. Equating a fetus with human life had been the basis of the conservative Roman Catholic opposition to any relaxation of the Franco regime's laws, which punished abortion in all circumstances. (The Pope supported such opposition when he visited Spain in 1982.)

The main pressures for change came from the women's movement as trials for abortion abounded. The well publicized trials of 11 women in Bilbao during 1979–82 caused the most furore. As in France, the most effective protests came from groups of well-known women, such as actresses and pop stars, who issued a signed public manifesto in 1979. Apart from saying that all who signed had had abortions, it also stated: 'Spanish justice is condemning women because they do not have the £250 which it costs to go to England for an abortion' (*Guardian*, 25 October 1979). After all this 10 out of the 11 women on trial were acquitted: the abortionist was found guilty but recommended for an immediate pardon. In 1980 an estimate suggested that 300,000 abortions a year were carried out in Spain.

In 1983 the newly elected socialist Government published plans to liberalize the law on abortion in cases of rape, fetal deformity and risk to the life of the woman, but these were rejected by the Constitutional Court, which ruled that the law did not sufficiently protect the right to life, guaranteed under Article 15 of the 1978 Constitution. This states: 'Everyone has a right to life and to physical and moral integrity.' The tribunal's decision, reached with the casting vote of its president, was greeted by the right-wing opposition as a moral and political victory and denounced by the socialists, communists and feminists. The opposition Popular Alliance has appealed against the law. The original (liberalizing) law was passed in October 1983 by a majority of 186 to 109 (*The Times*, 13 April 1985).

The guarantees that the Constitutional Court wanted to incorporate in any abortion legislation included the provision that two doctors instead of one should find serious risk of malformation and that operations should be done only in state or state-registered clinics. This decision to block planned legal reforms will certainly mean that more Spanish women will come to England for abortions – as many as 500 a week. In 1983 Home Office figures gave a total of 22,999 Spanish women undergoing abortions in British private clinics, mostly in London. Spanish feminist groups believe that the figure was even higher for 1984 and that it continues to grow. They also claim that each year more than 60,000 back-street abortions are carried out in Spain and that as many as 35 women die due to lack of adequate medical care (*Observer*, 14 April 1985).

The socialist Government has responded by suggesting, among other things, that it will start a 'pardon factory' to prevent women from being punished and has further vowed that there will be a relaxation of the tough rulings on the statute book by the end of 1985.

At the beginning of August, 1985, the law allowing abortion under certain circumstances – rape, mother's health in danger and risk of the child being seriously handicapped – was ratified. However, doubt was cast on the willingness of doctors to perform the operations. The first case under the law was that of a 22-year-old married woman, 12 weeks pregnant, who had been told that the child would very likely be born mentally handicapped like her other two sons. After four state-run hospitals turned her down another was eventually found, staffed by a volunteer medical team, who agreed to operate. Another woman, a drug addict with high blood pressure and poor physical health was also aborted.

Following a great deal of publicity over these cases it was reported (*The Times*, 14 August 1985) that anti-abortionists had taken out a writ in Oviedo against the doctors and health officials who both sanctioned and carried out the abortions. The anti-abortionists claimed the law had been infringed. Doctors have been claiming exemption both on the grounds of conscience and because of irregularities in referrals. In one province a 14-year-old girl, allegedly the victim of rape, was turned down by her local doctors.

To add to the difficulties in implementing the law the Church stepped in by excommunicating not only the first Andalusian woman to take advantage of the abortion law but also the medical team which performed the operation. This particular woman had contracted German measles during pregnancy (*The Times*, 23 August 1985). It looks, then, that in spite of a nominal change in the law, many thousands of Spanish women will continue to come to England for their abortions.

Scandinavia

The myth that there are free and easy abortion laws in Scandinavia is not actually true, but what the Scandinavians have produced is well designed follow-up studies (especially in Sweden) of what really happens to women who are refused abortion and, uniquely, of how the children born afterwards develop and grow up. In fact, the best study of this,[20] published in 1966, was done on 120 children who were subsequently born to mothers who had been refused an abortion. They were followed up until the age of 21 and compared with a carefully matched control group. The group of unwanted children were much more disturbed and were significantly worse off, compared with controls, on 11 important psychiatric and social variables. Further evidence on the risk of suicide in pregnant women has also been provided by Swedish work.[21]

Sweden first liberalized her laws in 1921, but illegal operations continued and, during the 1930s, resulted in about 70 deaths in a population of 6 million. A Royal Commission was convened in 1934, and the legislation was revised in 1938. There were further Abortion Acts in 1941, 1942, 1946, 1963 and 1974.[22]

The 1946 Act allowed abortion for illness, physical defect or 'weakness' in the woman, when birth or care of the child might severely endanger her life or health; for pregnancies under conditions which were illegal under the penal code (e.g. rape); and for cases when either the mother or the father might transmit a serious mental or physical defect or disease. The Acts passed during 1938–46 were much discussed and prompted a number of studies of the effects of unwanted pregnancies. The thalidomide tragedy led to further liberalization in 1963 with the addition of abortion for expected handicap or severe disease.

At this time there was no abortion for 'social' reasons, and patients spent a long time under investigation and in hospital. Also, Swedish women had been threatened with prosecution for going abroad (mainly to Poland) for abortions, on the grounds that it was illegal to do abroad what was illegal in Sweden (1964–5). This caused public concern, so a further committee was set up to consider the new evidence. From its studies emerged the current legislation, enshrined in the Abortion Act 1974, which permits abortion under the following conditions.

(1) A pregnancy may be interrupted, at a woman's request, before the twelfth week of pregnancy unless the interruption (because of illness in the mother) would constitute a serious risk to her life or health.
(2) If pregnancy has lasted for more than 12 weeks, it can be interrupted on the request of the woman if special investigations have shown there is no such risk as outlined in (1). There should also be a discussion with a social worker.
(3) After the eighteenth week of pregnancy an abortion is granted only for special reasons and after the consent of the National Board of Health and Welfare.

In 1980 yet another committee was appointed to evaluate how the new abortion law was working. It concluded that about 32,000 abortions had been performed annually since the law came into force. The actual rate has fallen a little – in 1982 it was 19.0 per 1,000 women of reproductive age, the lowest since 1974. There has also been a noticeable fall in the rate for teenagers from 28 per 1,000 in 1974 to 19 in 1982.

Nowadays most abortions are early ones and are done in outpatient clinics. The committee also confirmed that the abortion prevention measures introduced in connection with the 1974 Act had been successful, with available statistics on fertility and abortion showing no support for the idea that legal abortion had replaced other methods of birth control.

In Denmark a commission was set up in 1932 which reported and recommended changes in 1936. The law was promulgated in 1937 and became effective in 1939. It allowed abortion for the sake of the mother's health, in cases of rape and incest and for any potential fetal abnormality. In 1970 the Danish law was changed to allow abortion on request to all women living in Denmark who were over age 38 and for those who already had four or more children. In 1973 Denmark was the first Scandinavian country to introduce termination on request in the first trimester of pregnancy.[23]

In Norway the issue remains controversial. In 1977 King Olaf announced in the Norwegian parliament that a woman should have the opportunity to have an abortion in certain circumstances. A law was passed in 1978 that allowed abortion on request in the first trimester of pregnancy. Moves were made in 1981 to restrict the law again; legal, political and religious groups all joined in the controversy.

In Finland the abortion law was liberalized in 1951; by 1978 the time limit for legal aborting was reduced from 16 to 12 weeks. After this time an abortion could be obtained only with the agreement of the Board of Medicine. A feature of Finnish policy is that it legally requires abortions to be done at the earliest possible stage of pregnancy.

Czechoslovakia

Abortion on request was legalized in Czechoslovakia in 1957 but not all requests were granted. The main reasons for being denied an abortion included a gestation of more than 12 weeks, simultaneous occurrence of acute or chronic diseases which could increase the risk associated with abortion, and termination in the preceding six months. About 8 per cent of all requests are refused by district commissions. If the woman appeals, a special appellate commission hears her case and may or may not sanction the abortion.

These conditions were used by research workers to initiate an important follow-up study on what became of the children born to women refused abortion. An 'unwanted pregnancy' was then operationally defined as one that the mother was forced to complete after twice requesting an abortion and twice being refused. During the period of study about 2 per cent of the original requests were refused for the second time.

Only a very brief synopsis of this study is possible here which is reported in full, in English, by Z. Matéjček.[24] It has very similar aims to the only other study of this nature carried out in Sweden (see p. 241).

The number of children investigated was 220 which, by chance, was equally split between boys and girls. These were compared with a carefully matched control group. As with the Swedish study the 'unwanted' children compared very unfavourably in many areas of development and adjustment with the others. Detailed investigations were made when the children were aged 9, six years later, and a third follow-up study is still in progress with the children in their early twenties. Preliminary results show that 'the signs of social-problem-proneness are markedly prevalent among the former unwanted pregnancy group children. The less favourable psychosocial development of the unwanted children, as recorded in school age and adolescence, apparently continues into adulthood'.

The USSR

The USSR was the first country in modern times to legalize abortion, but unfortunately in more recent years it has been difficult to obtain information about both policies and practices. In 1930 the right of Russian women to terminate an unwanted pregnancy on health and other grounds was recognized in keeping with the 1917 Revolution, which implied feminine equality and freedom. The country was also faced with a birth rate of about 40 per thousand and a high rate of illegal operations. Abortion was unrestricted until 1936, when it was permitted for medical and eugenic reasons.[25]

These measures had important effects on the abortion debate in other countries because they demonstrated that change was possible, and they caused people to revise their estimates of the safety of the operation. The Russians published their results and sent a delegate to the First Congress of the World League for Sexual Reform in London. A report on a Russian series of 40,000 abortions, published in the *Lancet* in 1931, stated there were only two deaths.

The repeal of the law in 1936 was against the wishes of the people and was accompanied by financial inducements to have large families together with a crack-down on illegal abortions. The restricted Soviet law continued to allow abortions if pregnancy threatened the woman's health or if there was the likelihood of inherited disease. The change in the law was initially successful, with an estimated tripling of the birth rate in Moscow alone.

The law was once again liberalized in 1955 with two main aims: first, to reduce the harm done to women by abortions carried out outside hospitals and, secondly, to give women more choice in deciding their own reproductive futures. This liberal attitude towards abortion has been maintained and was adopted by most Eastern bloc countries except Albania; Romania and Hungary retain more restrictive practices in order to combat very low birth rates. However, their laws still allow abortion for broad health reasons and on demand to certain categories of women, such as those over the age of 40.

Since the late 1950s there has been a dearth of official statistics from the USSR. An article in *The Times* (11 May 1981) suggested that there were between 2.5 and 4 abortions to every birth and that each woman had an average of between 6 and 8 abortions in her lifetime. These high rates, together with fears of a declining population, were factors behind efforts to curtail abortions. Although it has been suggested that the socialist countries of Eastern Europe do not want women to use birth control because abortion can be controlled more easily to increase the birth rate when necessary, this does not seem to be the case in the USSR itself, where sex education and contraceptive advice are available. Theoretically the Malthusian hypothesis is contradictory to traditional Marxist teaching, but with two world wars and other social upheavals leading to a massive death toll, repopulation was to be encouraged, although it has not materialized.

China

Abortion was legalized by a directive from the Ministry of Health in 1957 in a further effort to control the size of the population which increased from 540 million in 1949 to 975 million in 1978. The official aim is to achieve zero population growth by the end of the century using all available methods.

According to Greer,[26] the campaign to limit population growth in the 1960s and 1970s was largely a campaign against sexual activity in itself. A low sex drive was considered normal, and signs on factory walls proclaimed: 'Sex is a mental disease.' Virtually no privacy was possible, and self-restraint was supervised by peer-group pressure and supervision of others.

The first campaign to control population growth was in 1954, but as there was a shortage of contraceptives, all restrictions on abortion, as the chief method of dealing with unwanted pregnancies, were removed in 1957. Opportunities to marry were restricted. After the Great Leap Forward vasectomy was promoted as an additional method of birth control. The number of abortions seems to have continued at about the same rate in the 1960s, with some instances of coercion being recorded.

Then came an insistence on one-child families, and family planning was supervised by the state right down to the local level of volunteers in production teams in factories. Individual menstrual charts were maintained, so that missed periods could be detected rapidly. Also, planned reproduction cards were introduced for each married woman, which formed the basis of reports passed up to the higher echelons of supervision. Although the emphasis was shifted away from abortion to sterilization and contraception, abortion rates continued to be high. For example, in one municipality

(Cheng-du) in 1979, 58 per cent of all pregnancies were terminated.

After the Cultural Revolution the push for family planning began again, this time adding the pill to other methods. The birth rate fell steadily: for instance, in 1978 8 million fewer babies were born than in 1971. By the 1980s great successes were claimed in the overall health programme, these being attributed to such things as 'political will', the role of the 'barefoot doctors' and the organization of the political and social structure right down to grass-roots level. Birth limitation was promoted as a way of improving the quality of life as well as safeguarding women's health, allowing them to participate more fully in production, which in turn would allow for study and political progress. Traditional techniques like acupuncture were combined with modern advances in surgery and drugs. By March 1980, 5 million couples had signed the one-child pledge; by 1981 this had risen to 10 million couples. These measures will, of course, have profound social consequences for family life and the age and sex structure of the whole society. Who will then look after the elderly? In 1979 between 6 million and 7 million sterilization operations and 5 million abortions were carried out. These reforms have been easier to enforce in the cities. The campaign in the countryside, where 80 per cent of the population live, has not been so successful. Here the concept of a one-child family is much harder to accept; there is also the continuing preference for a male heir and the tradition of female infanticide to contend with. In 1984 there were about 18 million births and nearly 9 million abortions.

Japan

Japan is certainly a country of interesting contrasts and contradictions. Religion and astrology are two influences to be taken account of in the history of abortion there. There are two major religions, Buddhism and Shintoism. Buddhism was adopted in the sixth century, Shintoism in the eighth century. Shintoism is indigenous to Japan; in fact, it is a kind of folk religion, so named (from the Chinese 'way of the gods') to distinguish it from Buddhism.[27] Its ceremonies are designed to appeal to the powers of nature, to invoke benevolent treatment and protection with the assistance of abstinence, offerings, prayers and purification. It also once claimed divine origin for the imperial family, although the idea of divinity was officially renounced in 1946 by Emperor Hirohito, who instead became a constitutional monarch.

Shintoism stresses the importance of purity, and since death and a variety of other pollutions are to be avoided, it is primarily concerned with life and the benefits of this world, which are seen as divine gifts. Ethically what was good for the group was morally proper. After the Second World War Shintoism lost its status as an official religion. Christianity, in the form of Roman Catholicism, was introduced in 1549 but Protestantism not until the nineteenth century.

That astrology is still a force to be reckoned with can be deduced from some interesting statistics. One belief held is that girls born in the Year of the Horse are bad-tempered, generally ill-natured and hence difficult to marry off. In 1906 and 1966, both Years of the Horse, falls in the birth rates of girls were recorded. This could have been achieved by a number of methods, such as selective infanticide or the parents' 'adjustment' of the birth dates of their female children born in those years. In 1966 the birth rate dropped precipitately from an expected 18.7 per 1,000 to an actual 13.7 per 1,000. At the same time the induced abortion rate rose from an expected 30.6 to 43.1 per 1,000 live births. The early neonatal mortality of girls rose from 5.17 per 100,000 live births in 1965 to 7.78 in 1966, when there was no such massive increase for boys: corresponding figures were 6.20 and 6.94.

The population of Japan in 1982 was about 118 million, with a growth rate of 0.6 per cent annually and with an average of 1.8 children per woman. At the end of the Second World War birth control was still illegal in Japan. Periodic abstinence was encouraged, but Ota rings (a type of contraceptive device) were used, and there was recourse to abortion. In 1947 the Japanese birth rate stood at 34.3 per 1,000; 10 years later it had been halved. This fall was due mainly to abortion, both legal and illegal.

The Eugenic Protection Law of 1948 recognized a number of grounds for legal abortion, including leprosy, but this limited sanction still meant a high incidence of illegal abortions. A 1952 Amendment Act then authorized abortions for economic as well as health reasons. The Japanese Family Planning Association was formed in 1955.

Researchers have inferred, by comparing the situation in the Ryukyu Islands (where abortion remained illegal) with Japan proper, that the decline in fertility would have occurred from illegal abortions even if it had not been permitted through doctors specializing in legal operations. In 1967, 1.7 million legal abortions were performed in Japan and possibly as many illegal ones. There was also a programme for the community-based distribution of condoms. These were distributed by means of 'love boxes', which were passed from house to house in villages. Couples took what they wanted from the boxes and left money in them for payment. The programme thus preserved privacy but at the same time exerted subtle peer-group pressure.

The condom is still the preferred method of birth control in Japan. In fact, around 80 per cent of couples have expressed this preference, making the Japanese users of one-quarter of all the condoms in the world! An IUD has been legal since 1974 but is used only by about 8 per cent. Another quirk is the fact that oral steriod contraceptives are not legal in Japan – although a small percentage are prescribed for gynaecological reasons – yet they are manufactured in Japan and widely exported. At the same time aid is provided for family planning in other countries (e.g. Indonesia).

It is alleged by Greer[28] that the medical establishment derives a huge income from abortions and, as a consequence, has blocked legislation for all other methods of contraception.

It is not known what the rate is for repeat abortions, but the rate for sterilization seems low. About 600,000 women were having legal abortions every year, and there is still a high rate of illegal ones.

More detailed statistics are now available[29] which show a gradual decline in abortions from a peak in 1955 when there were 1,170,143 abortions, which represented 50.2 per 1,000 women aged 15–49 or 67.6 abortions per 100 births to 1983 when corresponding figures were 567,539, 18.5 and 37.6 respectively. Practically all recorded abortions are done under Item 4 of Article 14 of the Eugenic Protection Law, which is loosely phrased and translated as: 'A mother whose health may be affected seriously by continuation of pregnancy or by delivery from the physical or economic standpoint'. An interesting fact of this law is that there must be consent of the spouse to abortion; this apparently can be got round by a wife whose husband will not give consent, by her obtaining readily available means of forging the legal documents required by using stamps of common family names. However, it is acknowledged that there is still widespread under-reporting of induced abortions.

The curious Japanese ambivalence is shown both in their attitude towards infanticide and in their religious doctrines. Before modern industrialization infanticide was fairly widely practised and given a horticultural name, *mabiki* or 'thinning out'. On the one hand, there seems to be little evidence of the Buddhist concern for life. The rationale of Shintoism is that the fetus does not have a spirit until it has seen the light, so the technique of abortion is considered to be sending a fetus 'from darkness into darkness'. Yet, on the other hand, many women visit temples to pray for the souls of their unborn children.

The religious concern for life can be adapted to fit cultural patterns. In this case, if life is seen as a unity, an aborted child is a part of existence that has never found expression, a lost soul called a *misogo*. Any clash between state and religion is not condemned; the fact and its symbolism are accepted and then dealt with. Many temples have walls lined with dolls and small offerings to commemorate the truncated lives of these *misogo*. Without such prayers and offerings, it is believed, misfortune could supervene, and barriers could form between the parents, their living offspring and, finally, enlightenment. All this is touchingly demonstrated in a book by the Japanese Buddhist Daryo Miura.[30]

7

Summing Up and the Future

Attempts to alter the Abortion Act 1967

Legislation very much reflects the state of society at the time it is made, and one reason why this particular Private Member's Bill was successfully transformed into the 1967 Abortion Act was because a 'liberal' atmosphere existed both in Parliament and in the country as a whole during the 1960s. It was a time of changing moral values, of 'swinging' London and the 'permissive society'.

The two Parliaments between 1964 and 1970 saw the passage of a variety of liberal reforms. Capital punishment was abolished by the Murder (Abolition of the Death Penalty) Act in 1965. Homosexuality between consenting adults was legalized (under certain conditions) by the Sexual Offences Act 1967. Censorship in the theatre was abolished by the Theatres Act 1968 and divorce significantly liberalized by the Divorce Act 1969.

None the less, the anti-abortion factions continued their activity, and there was soon an outcry about what some felt was too liberal an interpretation of the Abortion Act. It was partly to allay mounting public concern that a committee of enquiry was set up under the chairmanship of the Hon. Mrs Justice Lane.

This committee produced a long and detailed three-volume report in 1974.[1] Partly to placate feminists, who had always maintained that women were never appointed to influential committees in sufficient numbers or put in positions of power, no fewer than 10 of the 15 members of the Lane Committee were women. There was one (male) psychiatrist member.

Although their terms of reference precluded consideration of any fundamental changes to the Act, it was a thorough and far-reaching enquiry. The committee was generally satisfied with the way the Act was working but made a number of recommendations for improving this. The main one was that the upper time limit for the legal termination of a pregnancy should be 24 weeks instead of 28. Others were that the penalties for breaches of the regulations should be more severe; that certificates should be modified so that both doctors must examine a woman; that new legislation should permit the licensing of medical referral agencies; that the Chief Medical Officer should be empowered to give information to the General Medical Council in alleged cases of professional misconduct; and that menstrual regulation should be brought within the scope of the Act. Finally, the committee wished to see freely available contraceptive and counselling services. Unfortunately, the setting up of this type of committee is often used by the Government of the day as part of a delaying tactic in the hope that by the time it reports, public anxiety will be focused on something else. The committee's report can then safely be filed away to gather dust with so many others. A classic example of this arose over the anti-pornography laws, when the carefully evaluated recommendations of the Williams Committee (1979) were quietly shelved.[2] In the case of the Lane Committee very few of its recommendations were implemented, their general satisfaction with the Act being stressed instead.

The various political attempts to repeal or amend the Abortion Act, with interesting details of the pressure groups involved in these campaigns, along with their religious affiliations, are well documented in *Abortion Politics*.[3] Within five months of the Act being implemented the first attempt was made to amend it. Since then there have been 10 Amendment Bills, none of which has reached the statute book.

Between 1967 and 1975 there was a movement among MPs towards supporting amending legislation. However, after 1975 and until 1978 this pattern was reversed, and the support for amending legislation significantly declined. The proposal that was most fiercely fought, both in and out of Parliament, was Corrie's Amendment Bill. This was finally withdrawn in March 1980, when the House of Commons accepted as a compromise the recommendation that the upper time limit for abortion should be 24 weeks, but this never became law. A new Private Member's Bill in July 1981, proposing to make it obligatory for local authorities to provide free abortion treatment, was subsequently rejected. In December 1982 an Abortion Amendment Bill (Lord Robertson) had its second reading in the House of Lords. This was to amend Section 1 of the Abortion Act to read '*serious* risk to life or health' and '*substantially* greater than if the pregnancy was terminated', but again this did not succeed.

However, earlier in 1982 a new row blew up. This time it involved criticisms over what was seen as the Government's attempt (backed by the anti-abortion lobby) to amend and even curtail the Act by underhand means. This was done by the apparently innocuous method of requiring the DHSS to issue a modified form to be completed by the gynaecologist who carried out the abortion. The motive for doing so seemed suspect from the start because the change was brought about under a statutory instruments procedure. This is regarded as a notorious way of sneaking unpopular measures through Parliament, as one legal commentator put it. Also, there were no prior consultations with the appropriate medical bodies.

The form in question (HSA4) was a modification of the original notification form (HSA3), which is the one sent to the Chief Medical Officer at the DHSS and from which official statistics on abortion are derived. The 'official line' about the advantages of the new form was, first, that it would monitor changes in abortion practice such as day-care and agency arrangements between NHS and the private sector. Secondly, information on the period of gestation rather than the date of the last menstrual period would be used. Thirdly, there would be more detailed information on any medical conditions affecting the mother in addition to, or instead of, a suspected handicapping condition of the fetus. Last, the new form would save time by eliminating redundant questions and reducing the number of items of data collected.

Some gynaecologists saw this as an attempt to limit abortions done for psycho-social reasons, which were not necessarily affecting the woman's health at the time but might well do so if the pregnancy were allowed to continue. It seemed to be stating that a *medical* condition had to be present at the time of termination and, furthermore, that non-psychiatrically trained doctors should not be giving a diagnosis such as anxiety or depression. However, the Act is quite specific in that it states that the pregnant woman's environmental circumstances (i.e. social factors) can be taken into account in assessing the risks to her *future* health.

Two gynaecologists, to prompt a test case over the new form, deliberately put 'no medical reasons' on their forms but stated that there was an increased risk to future health if termination were not carried out, and so – legally – performed the operations. The Chief Medical Officer, on receipt of these forms, reported the matter to the Director of Public Prosecutions. After due consideration he declined to prosecute, thus ending this particular dispute.

The anti-abortion movement

The anti-abortion forces in this country are now grouped into two main organizations.[4] There is the Society for the Protection of Unborn Children (SPUC), which was formed as the result of correspondence in the *Church Times* in 1966. Originally, in an effort to forestall criticism, no Roman Catholics were allowed on the executive committee, although they were prominent members, but this rule was changed in 1975. One of its earlier and most famous recruits was the gynaecologist Aleck Bourne. SPUC tried to influence Parliament via lobbies, petitions and publications. By the 1970s it had become a highly efficient pressure group. It is more moderate in its views than some other organizations, as it agrees with abortions for medical reasons and to save the life of the mother.

The other main opposition group is Life or Save the Unborn Child. At the time of the 1967 Abortion Act, SPUC was the only organized anti-abortion pressure group. In 1970 it was joined by Life. Again Life's origins sprang from the correspondence columns of the religious press, and it takes a position very similar to that of the Roman Catholic Church. It has the aim of abolishing all abortions. Its most prominent advocate is Professor Scarisbrick, who has, among other things, talked of abortion as 'national suicide' and, in his 1971 pamphlet, argued that 'the unborn child has as much right to life as his mother has . . . It must be wrong deliberately and directly to kill either, even for the sake of the other.' He is even against abortion in rape cases. This group therefore takes an extreme absolutist position and is a direct challenger to the gradualist stance of the SPUC.

Such groups, though, tend to try to shock and to use the most emotive language possible. Many of their previous sensational campaigns have been discredited, the most notable example being the scurrilous book published in 1974 called *Babies for Burning*. This made unsubstantiated allegations, such as that 'abortion doctors' had strong Nazi sympathies, that malpractice by pregnancy testing agencies was rife, that an unnamed gynaecologist committed murder and that aborted fetuses were being used in the manufacture of soap.

The latest attempt to influence public opinion by dubious shock tactics is the distribution by the SPUC of video cassettes of a film called *The Silent Scream*. (I must say at once that I have not seen this film.) The original film, lasting about half an hour, was made in the USA, and shows the abortion of a 12-week fetus using an ultrasound scanner. It claims that the fetus is wriggling about in fear and pain and, when opening its mouth, is giving a 'silent scream'. (This is, of course, impossible, as you can scream only if you have air in your lungs.) When British gynaecologists tried to do the same type of scan there were no fetal movements, as, like its mother, the fetus was anaesthetized during the operation. In any case, such fetal movements do not necessarily indicate pain or fear.

As all the efforts of the anti-abortionists to alter or amend the Abortion Act directly have failed, more indirect methods have been tried: for example, the stirring up of old controversies under the Infant Life (Preservation) Act 1929 and attempts to get this amended. If it were to be annulled, it would certainly reduce the time limit on abortions but only in England and Wales, as the Act does not apply in Scotland.

Ultimately it is up to Parliament to determine whether the definition of viability should be changed. However, I would like to reiterate that as things stand at present (and things will improve only very slowly, or not at all, if further research is impeded), many prenatal tests, such as amniocentesis, cannot be undertaken until relatively late in pregnancy. If the time limit were reduced, even by eight weeks, more handicapped children would be born. For instance, in 1982 102 terminations of pregnancy were carried out after the twenty-fourth week of gestation, and although this was only a small proportion of all terminations, it does represent a large number of babies who might have been born handicapped if the law had been changed. In that same year a survey of more than 1,000 late abortions showed that if the 24-week limit had applied, about 26 abortions for severe handicaps could have been prevented. If a 22-week limit had been set, 77 such abortions could not have taken place.

The latest attempts have been even more indirect, as the controversies over research on human embryos have been exploited in attempts to influence the Government before it introduces comprehensive legislation in the wake of the Warnock Committee Report. I have already discussed the implications of this in the first chapter of this book.

Prevention of abortion

Even the most enthusiastic advocates of abortion would want to see more done in the way of prevention. Apart from the more obvious general measures, like improved education and medical services, the single most important factor is contraception. Ignorance of contraception, the use of unsuitable or unreliable methods or failure on a particular occasion are frequent findings in women who have pregnancies terminated. What can be done to improve this situation?

We immediately come up against our society's hypocritical and, indeed, often cynical attitude towards the availability of contraception. This is well exemplified by the ban on full-scale advertising of contraceptives, on television or radio, for instance, yet the advertisements that are shown, as well as many of the actual programmes themselves, dwell upon sexual titillation and women as sex objects. Talk about encouraging sexual activity!

Only very recently a public service announcement giving information to teenage boys about contraceptive methods was banned by the Independent Broadcasting Authority. It allegedly feared that broadcasting it might appear to be condoning promiscuity. Yet it did not seem to think that the average play or film shown on television depicting men leaping in and out of bed with various women without using contraceptives as 'macho' and admirable, is also condoning promiscuity!

Doctors too need to be better informed – for example, about postcoital contraception. The recent controversies over the long-acting contraceptive injection Depo-Provera have now been resolved. Further research into improved methods of contraception, both male and female, should also be encouraged and financed. More information about sterilization procedures would also help: sterilization is still so often confused with castration. Safe and reliable techniques which could actually be reversed should circumstances change in the future may eventually become a realistic alternative.

Britain's main contraceptive manufacturers are now funding a study, together with the Health Education Council and the Family Planning Association, to identify the 2 million women who are at risk from unplanned pregnancies. The Association estimates that there are about 200,000 unplanned pregnancies in Britain every year among 2 million women who are sexually active but do not practise reliable birth control. About 130,000 of the pregnancies end in abortion. Figures suggest that about 11.5 million women in Britain are in the fertile age range. About 6 million use reliable contraception, while another 3.5 million are either sexually inactive, sub-fertile, trying to conceive or pregnant. That leaves about 2 million at risk from unintended pregnancies.

In a market survey of fertile women a table of preferred methods of contraception was presented (*Observer*, 20 January 1985): sterilization – women 10 per cent, men 12 per cent; the pill – 27 per cent; IUD – 8 per cent; diaphragm and cap – 1 per cent; condom – 15 per cent; 'other' – 5 per cent; 22 per cent used none. However, the most recent work on the IUD suggests that it is unsuitable for women who have never been pregnant, as it doubles the risk of subsequent infertility. Plastic IUDs were found to be the most dangerous in this respect.

Another important aspect is to encourage more research into the attitudes of men both towards contraception and abortion. Some of the psycho-dynamic aspects involving men are outlined in a study on the effects of abortion on marriage.[5] An American survey has brought together research findings concerning men and abortion in a book bearing that title.[6] As regards contraception it is only too common for men passively to leave it to their female partners to take the pill. The Family

Planning Association's 'Men Too' campaign is to be welcomed and supported. On the other hand, there is still a great deal of ignorance over the benefits of the pill. Too many scare stories hit the headlines without recognition of the fact that research has been going on for a good number of years and there have been many advances: for example, we now have pills which in a whole month's supply contain only the same amount of hormones that a single pill contained 25 years ago.

How many young women know that the pill can actually offer protection against various diseases such as cancer of the uterus and ovaries? The recent cervical cancer scare, by the time it had been reported in the popular press and elsewhere, had become very distorted and made no allowances for some of the defects in the design of the study (e.g. that it did not take into account the amount of sexual activity). There is therefore still scope for reliable information setting out fairly the advantages and possible side-effects of all the different contraceptive pills currently available.[7]

The future

What can, and indeed should, be done for the future? I can offer here only a highly personal view of this. What I think is needed is a completely revised Abortion Act which takes into account recent advances in medical knowledge, techniques and practices. We must keep a clear head on this and not be swayed by polemics and emotive red herrings. The accent should be on the quality of life – of both mother and child – rather than quantity. It seems that our society generally now has a rather different attitude towards abortion, and I would like to see this reflected in legislation which, for instance, will help us to move away from the guilt-ridden approach that treats abortion as a potentially criminal act towards a more neutral, medico-clinical approach. Like any other form of treatment, abortion has its indications, complications and dangers which need careful evaluation. It should also be recognized that therapeutic termination of pregnancy, done by well trained doctors with the right resources, staff and atmosphere, is a safe and effective procedure which can do much to improve the mental health and happiness of properly selected women. However, no woman should undergo abortion without first having the chance to benefit from sympathetic, knowledgeable and unbiased counselling.[8]

As regards the legislation itself, this requires very careful drafting and, for this reason, should be a Government-sponsored Bill and not a Private Member's one, as then the best parliamentary advice and drafting could be brought to bear on it. The implementation and interpretations of the 1967 Abortion Act have shown that there is a shifting frontier between statutory interpretation and judicial law-making. The main function of the judiciary is to give effect to the intentions of Parliament, which should, in turn, try to make its intentions as clear as possible. Many statutes are couched in obscure terminology, so that their wording requires the minutest scrutiny. On the other hand, the law must be flexible and able to adapt to changing circumstances, as Parliament cannot be for ever amending legislation. A law that is unclear, ignored or largely unenforceable is a bad law and tends to bring the whole legal system into disrepute.

I would like to see the older legislation repealed – i.e. the 1861 Offences Against the Person Act and the 1929 Infant Life (Preservation) Act. Any offences or penalties can be built into a new Act without having to rely on outmoded laws passed over a hundred years ago. There has been only one (unsuccessful) prosecution since the 1967 Act became law, when a doctor was charged with attempted murder for carrying out an abortion after the legal limit (28 weeks) under Section 1(1) of the Criminal Attempts Act 1981. Abortion must be legally defined, with limits set at either end – that is, it must be determined when contraception ends and abortion begins and up to what stage of fetal development termination is permissible. (There are still doubts in judicial circles about the precise moment at which a child comes under the law of murder.) It would seem, for the former, that implantation of the fertilized ovum is a suitable dividing line, although the status of menstrual regulation still needs further clarification. Postcoital contraception should be recognized and defined, as should the matter of 'intent' and whether proof of pregnancy is required and, if so, how this should be established. This would also help to make clear what is entailed by a possible charge of attempted abortion or aiding and abetting one.

Abortion up to 12 weeks' gestation should be freely available on request after suitable consultation and counselling to make sure that it is the best course to take and that there are no compelling medical or psychiatric reasons why it should not be carried out. Between 12 and 20 weeks there would need to be definite medical, psychological and fetal reasons for recommending termination.

After 20 weeks' pregnancy more stringent criteria should be introduced, such as using modern techniques to establish the exact stage of gestation and state of the fetus, instead of relying on clinical criteria alone. Also the mother's or the fetus' current state, rather than a postulated future state, should be made the deciding factor, and a second specialist opinion should be required before abortion is carried out. If it was the woman's current physical health that was at stake, then a consultant physician or similar person would give an opinion on this. If her mental health were at risk, then a consultant psychiatrist would give his opinion. Similarly, if the fetus were endangered, a paediatrician or doctor specializing in developmental medicine should be asked. After 24 weeks abortion would be permitted only in more exceptional circumstances, such as to save the mother's life or for established fetal abnormality.

Apart from these suggestions of my own, there are signs, as previously noted, that the medical establishment is uneasy about the legal limit of 28 weeks, and some recommend lowering it to 24 weeks. Another argument for this is recent progress in keeping alive very premature babies: for example, one paediatrician has estimated that 60 per cent of premature babies can survive at 28 weeks and 30 per cent at 26 or 27 weeks. A World Health Organization recommendation that the legal limit should be 22 weeks could be too restrictive.

According to a survey of a total of 162,797 abortions in England and Wales in 1982, 836 were carried out in the twenty-third and twenty-fourth weeks of pregnancy and 102 between 25 and 28 weeks.[9] Of course, some sort of compromise is possible, such as that suggested in the Corrie Amendment Bill of 1979 – a legal limit of 20 or 22 weeks with an exception for cases of substantial risk of serious handicap in the child or of serious physical or mental harm to the mother. Another possibility is to distinguish between two very different grounds for abortion, with different legal limits for each. If suspected fetal abnormality were the reason, the limit should remain 28 weeks or should even be raised if prenatal screening demanded it. For those abortions where fetal abnormality was not suspected the legal limit could be lowered.

It is sometimes forgotten that late abortion for an abnormal fetus up until 24 weeks was suggested by the Lane Committee in 1974. Nevertheless, what has now (1985) happened is the adoption on a voluntary basis, and following the recommendations of the medical establishment, of an agreed policy to restrict the limit of legal abortions to 24 weeks instead of 28. Representatives of eight private clinics licensed to carry out abortions after 20 weeks have also agreed to this limit.

This restriction has resulted from detailed surveys of neonatal units which have shown that advances in modern technology make it necessary to revise the concept of viability as laid down in the Infant Life (Preservation) Act (1929). In other words, many babies born between 24 and 28 weeks can now be made 'viable', although no baby of less than 24 weeks has survived beyond a week of life in spite of anecdotal reports to the contrary.

In actual fact very few abortions are performed over 24 weeks on resident women; for example, there were only 238 in 1983, which represents less than 2 in 1,000 of all abortions.

From the medical point of view it is not so much the state of the brain or heart but that of the lungs which is the decisive factor for survival. Below about 24 weeks the lungs are too immature to function properly and nutrition proves impossible. To go further would involve the development of artificial placentas and wombs. So it can be seen that 'viability' is not fixed, it depends on technology.

This restriction to 24 weeks has been agreed voluntarily rather than risk having it imposed legally, as this in turn (at least in the view of those committed to abortion) could lead to a whole new re-appraisal of all related legislation with the possibility of ending up with even more restrictive laws. But sooner or later there will have to be more precise legislation on this thorny topic of viability with the proviso that it is not necessary to equate legal with biological viability. The ambivalent attitude towards this subject can be seen in the Department of Health's ruling that any private clinic authorized to perform abortions after 20 weeks must also have available means for resuscitating a liveborn fetus. At present, too, the law also requires the registration of a 'live birth' of whatever gestation length but does not define what is a 'live birth'. In practice, a birth is not registered before 28 weeks unless there are signs of breathing. There has been reluctance to register a very tiny baby of (say) 22 weeks solely because a transient pulsation occurred in the umbilical cord. On the other hand the WHO definition of birth includes any infant born after 22 weeks or weighing 500 grams or more, with signs of life which include cord pulsation even for a very short time.

The wording and clauses of the present Act require drastic revision. I am not a legal draftsman, so would not presume to offer any precise wording, but I simply give some general ideas for change. I would favour dropping two of the present four criteria for termination – those concerning risks to the mother's life or to any existing children. This would leave two main reasons for doing a legal abortion, namely, for the sake of the mother's physical or mental health and, similarly, for the sake of the fetus' expected health and development. Some sort of 'social clause' should be retained, as it is standard psychiatric practice to take into account a patient's social and cultural background when making a diagnostic assessment and prognosis. This clause could be something like: 'In assessing the risks to health all relevant background factors may be taken into consideration, including the current and foreseeable social situation.'

If the age of consent is to remain at 16 years, in spite of the earlier age of menarche and the increasing number of pregnancies in this very early age group, firm legal guidelines are necessary when it comes to consent to treatment and parental rights. The present situation puts doctors in a very difficult position, particularly in the case of children in care or the mentally handicapped and especially when the question of sterilization or long-acting hormonal contraceptive preparations are involved as well as abortion. What also needs deciding is whether a fetus has any legal rights and, if so, what these are and how best to codify them.

More contentious is Section 4 of the Abortion Act – the opting out and conscience clause. I would like to see this deleted. As already mentioned in chapter 4, this makes abortion unique in that no other type of medical treatment has this option built into it. It only adds to the already guilt-ridden and 'not quite right' sort of aura surrounding abortion, immediately making it divisive and unnecessarily emotive. In my view, a doctor should not impose his own values and religious views on his patients; instead he should take account of, and respect, the moral and religious views held by his patient. These should play a part in his overall assessment of her and her health problems and should be considered when he makes a final recommendation for treatment. If a GP is faced with such a situation and cannot bring himself to make an unbiased assessment, then he should tell his patient this and ask a partner or colleague to see her instead. I am very much against doctors hiding behind quasi-medical views (e.g. 'There are no psychiatric grounds for recommending abortion' or

'Pregnant women never commit suicide') when they are really against abortion on moral or religious grounds.

Most important of all, regardless of what law is actually passed, is that its provisions should be impartially administered via a free and comprehensive NHS. It should not matter where you live, or what sort of person you are, or what lifestyle you adopt.

The best way to resolve the acrimony between the NHS and the private sector is to improve NHS facilities. In a true democracy freedom of choice is vital, so instead of continually vilifying and trying to curtail the private sector, it would be preferable to make abortion truly and freely available to all who need it. This is the same sort of argument as that over private versus state education – both should be available, but the state system should be so good that only relatively few people need the other, which would then become simply an optional extra.

As regards abortion facilities, there is an increasing move towards out-patient and day-patient treatment, perhaps in special units run by part-time staff who want to do this sort of work. One or more such units could be made available in every health district, under the NHS, with back-up facilities in the local gynaecology unit for pregnancies more advanced than 12 weeks or other special cases, but it is also vitally important to have a freely available counselling service, not just to channel women into abortion but also to offer genuine alternatives and the necessary help and expertise to see these through.

If abortion is the eventual outcome, follow-up facilities must also be provided, and, among other things, further contraceptive advice must be given. This, hopefully, would offer the best chance of preventing further unwanted pregnancies.

Conclusions

There is no doubt that many further attempts will be made to alter or modify our abortion laws, either directly or indirectly, and I have myself suggested some ways in which this might be done. There is some reluctance to do this in some quarters in case we end up with more restrictive laws, and this certainly is a risk. However, what does seem clear is that some form of legal abortion is here to stay, and I am sure there are very few who would really wish to turn the clock back to the situation that existed prior to 1967.

There always tends to be a backlash after periods of apparent permissiveness, sometimes (paradoxically) exacerbated by scientific advances, particularly if their ethical implications have been outstripped. This seems to have happened over embryo research and surrogacy, so that these issues need to be resolved before further abortion legislation is proposed.

One way in which a society can be judged is by how it deals with the abortion issues outlined in this book. As these raise some of the most fundamental questions we have to face, like the nature of life and death, much anxiety and other powerful emotions are raised. The search for certainty and 'truth' will continue, and in the process extremists and fanatics, fundamentalists and absolutists of all sorts, will appear from time to time to offer us their solutions. Amid all this debate doctors still have to make difficult clinical decisions about their patients. This is not always easy, and there is no escaping the often appalling responsibility. The medical and the legal professions, while not immune to current trends and fashions, are generally conservative in approach and are often criticized for this. They need to stand firm and together in helping to plan and to put into practice humane legislation which is both workable and acceptable to the reasonable majority of the population.

References

The following references relate to the superior numbers used throughout the text. They are divided into the individual chapters.

Preface

1 Martin, A. (1982). Fetal rights: the legal dilemma. *World Medicine*, **17**, 60.

2 Warnock Committee (1984). *Report of the Committee of Enquiry into Human Fertilization and Embryology* (Warnock Report). HMSO, London.

Chapter 1

1 Williams, G. L. (1983). *Textbook of Criminal Law*, 2nd edition. Stevens, London.

2 Shain, R. N. (1982). Abortion practices and attitudes in cross-cultural perspective. *American Journal of Obstetrics and Gynecology*, **142**, 245.

3 Devereux, G. (1976). *A Study of Abortion in Primitive Societies: A Typological, Distributional and Dynamic Analysis of the Prevention*

of Birth in 400 Pre-industrial Societies. IUP, New York.

4 Whittaker, P. G. et al (1983). Unsuspected pregnancy loss in healthy women. *Lancet*, **1**, 1126.

5 Opitz, J. M. et al (1979). Genetic causes and workup of male and female infertility. (11) Prenatal reproductive loss. *Postgraduate Medicine*, **65**, 247.

6 Hook, E. B. (1981). Prevalence of chromosome abnormalities during human gestation and implications for studies of environmental mutagens. *Lancet*, **2**, 169.

7 de Cherney, A. (1984). Evaluation and management of habitual abortion. *British Journal of Hospital Medicine*, **31**, 261.

8 Craft, I. (1984). In vitro fertilization: clinical methodology. *British Journal of Hospital Medicine*, **31**, 90.

9 Trounson, A. A. (1984). In vitro fertilization: problems of the future. *British Journal of Hospital Medicine*, **31**, 104.

10 Cusine, D. J. (1984). In vitro fertilization: legal and ethical implications. *British Journal of Hospital Medicine*, **31**, 111.

11 Warnock Committee (1984). *Report of the Committee of Enquiry into Human Fertilization and Embryology* (Warnock Report). HMSO, London.

12 *The Use of Fetuses and Fetal Material for Research* (Peel Report) (1972). HMSO, London.

13 *Warnock Dissected* (1984). Save the Unborn Child (LIFE), Leamington Spa.

14 Grahame, H. (ed) (1983). *Postcoital Contraception: Methods, Services and Prospects*. Pregnancy Advisory Service, London.

15 ibid.

16 Editorial (1982). The law on menstrual therapies. *Lancet*, **2**, 422.

17 Lane Committee (1974). *Report of the Committee on the Working Party of the Abortion Act* (Lane Report), 3 vols. HMSO, London.

18 Baulieu, E. E. (1985). Contragestion by antiprogestin: a new approach to human fertility control. In *Abortion: Medical Progress and Social Implications* (eds Porter, R. and O'Connor, M.). Pitman, London.

19 Potts, M. (1985). Medical progress and the social implications of abortion. In *Abortion: Medical Progress and Social Implications* (eds Porter, R. and O'Connor, M.). Pitman, London.

Chapter 2

1 Francome, C. (1984). *Abortion Freedom: A Worldwide Movement*. George Allen and Unwin, London.

2 Callahan, D. (1972). *Abortion: Law, Choice and Morality*. Collier-Macmillan, New York.

3 Raphael, D. D. (1981). *Moral Philosophy*. Oxford University Press, Oxford.

4 Atkinson, R. (1965). *Sexual Morality*. Hutchinson, London.

5 Noonan, J. T. (ed) (1970). *The Morality of Abortion: Legal and Historical Perspectives.* Harvard University Press, Cambridge, USA.

6 Hare, R. M. (1975). Abortion and the golden rule. *Philosophy and Public Affairs*, **4**, 202;
Sen, A. and Williams, B. (eds) (1982). *Utilitarianism and Beyond.* Cambridge University Press, London.

7 Sumner, L. W. (1981). *Abortion and Moral Theory.* Princeton University Press, Princeton NJ.

8 Tooley, M. (1973). A defense of abortion and infanticide. In *The Problem of Abortion* (ed Feinberg, J.). Wadsworth International Group, London.

9 Tooley, M. (1983). *Abortion and Infanticide.* Clarendon Press, Oxford.

10 Moore-Cavar, E. C. (1974). *International Inventory of Information on Induced Abortion*. International Institute for the Study of Human Reproduction, Columbia University, USA.

11 Sumner, L. W. (1981). *Abortion and Moral Theory.* Princeton University Press, Princeton NJ.

12 Cross, F. L. (ed) (1958). *The Oxford Dictionary of the Christian Church.* Oxford University Press, Oxford.

13 Taylor, G. R. (1953). *Sex in History.* Thames and Hudson, London.

14 Dickens, B. M. (1966). *Abortion and the Law.* (MacGibbon and Kee) Granada, London.

15 Mahoney, J. (1984). *Bio-ethics and Belief.* Sheed and Ward, London.

16 Dunstan, G. R. (1984). The moral status of the human embryo: a tradition recalled. *Journal of Medical Ethics*, 1, 38.

17 Sumner, L. W. (1981). *Abortion and Moral Theory.* Princeton University Press, Princeton NJ.

18 Greer, G. (1984). *Sex and Destiny: The Politics of Human Fertility.* Picador, London.

19 Francome, C. (1984). *Abortion Freedom: A Worldwide Movement.* George Allen and Unwin, London.

20 Cross, F. L. (ed) (1958). *The Oxford Dictionary of the Christian Church.* Oxford University Press, Oxford.

21 Robinson, J. (1963). *Honest to God.* SCM, London.

22 *Towards a Quaker View of Sex*. (1964). Friends Home Service, London.

23 Hinnells, J. R. (ed) (1984). *The Penguin Dictionary of Religions.* Penguin Books, Harmondsworth.

24 Francome, C. (1984). *Abortion Freedom: A Worldwide Movement.* George Allen and Unwin, London.
25 Hinnells, J. R. (ed) (1984). *The Penguin Dictionary of Religions.* Penguin Books, Harmondsworth.
26 ibid.
27 Parrinder, G. (1980). *Sex in the World's Religions.* Sheldon Press, London.
28 Hinnells, J. R. (ed) (1984). *The Penguin Dictionary of Religions.* Penguin Books, Harmondsworth.
29 Parrinder, G. (1980). *Sex in the World's Religions.* Sheldon Press, London.
30 Dawood, N. J. (trs) (1956). *The Koran.* Penguin Books, Harmondsworth.
31 Hinnells, J. R. (ed) (1984). *The Penguin Dictionary of Religions.* Penguin Books, Harmondsworth.
32 Francome, C. (1984). *Abortion Freedom: A Worldwide Movement.* George Allen and Unwin, London.
33 Reynolds, V. and Tanner, R. (1983). *The Biology of Religion.* Longman, London.
34 Kolakowski, L. (1982). *Religion.* Fontana, London.
35 Batson, C. D. and Ventis, W. R. (1982). *The Religious Experience: A Social-Psychological Perspective.* Oxford University Press, Oxford.
36 Bullock, A. and Stallybrass, O. (eds) (1977). *The Fontana Dictionary of Modern Thought.* Fontana, London.

Chapter 3

1 Dickens, B. M. (1966). *Abortion and the Law.* (MacGibbon and Kee) Granada, London.
2 Means, C. (1971). The phoenix of abortion freedom. *New York Law Forum*, 17, 335.
3 Francome, C. (1984). *Abortion Freedom: A Worldwide Movement.* George Allen and Unwin, London.
4 Skegg, P. D. G. (1984). *Law, Ethics and Medicine.* Clarendon Press, Oxford.
5 ibid.
6 ibid., p. 26.
7 Hordern, A. (1971). *Legal Abortion: The English Experience.* Pergamon Press, Oxford.

Chapter 4

1 DHSS (1979). *Report on Confidential Enquiries into Maternal Deaths in England and Wales 1973–1975*. Report on Health and Social Subjects No. 14. HMSO, London.

2 Diggory, P. (1984). Safety of termination of pregnancy: NHS versus private. *Lancet*, **2**, 920 and 989.

3 Kleiner, G. J. and Greston, W. M. (eds) (1984). *Suicide in Pregnancy*. John Wright, Bristol.

4 ibid.

5 Kenyon, F. E. (1969). Termination of pregnancy on psychiatric grounds: a comparative study of sixty-one cases. *British Journal of Medical Psychology*, **42**, 243.

Kenyon, F. E. (1969). Psychiatric referrals since the Abortion Act 1967. *Postgraduate Medical Journal*, **45**, 718.

6 Kleiner, G. J. and Greston, W. M. (eds) (1984). *Suicide in Pregnancy*, p. 30. John Wright, Bristol.

7 ibid.

8 ibid.

9 WHO (1978). *Mental Disorders: Glossary and Guide to their Classification in Accordance with the Ninth Revision of the International Classification of Diseases*. WHO, Geneva.

10 Loeffler, F. E. (1984). Prenatal diagnosis: chorionic villus biopsy. *British Journal of Hospital Medicine*, **31**, 418.

McNay, M. B. and Whitfield, C. R. (1984). Prenatal diagnosis: amniocentesis. *British Journal of Hospital Medicine*, **31**, 406.

Nicolaides, K. and Rodeck, C. H. (1984). Prenatal diagnosis: fetoscopy. *British Journal of Hospital Medicine*, **31**, 396.

Smith, P. A. et al (1984). Prenatal diagnosis: ultrasound. *British Journal of Hospital Medicine*, **31**, 421.

11 Editorial (1985). When ultrasound shows fetal abnormality. *Lancet*, **1**, 618.

12 Campbell, A. V. (1984). Ethical issues in prenatal diagnosis. *British Medical Journal*, **288**, 1633.

13 Editorial (1982). No right to sue for 'wrongful life'. *British Medical Journal*, **284**, 1125.

14 Office of Population Censuses and Surveys:

Statistical Review, Supplement on Abortion (1974). HMSO, London.

Abortion Statistics 1975, Series AB No. 2. (1978). HMSO, London.

Abortion Statistics 1980, Series AB No. 7. (1981). HMSO, London.

Abortion Statistics 1982, Series AB No. 9. (1984). HMSO, London.

15 Ashton, J. R. (1983). Trends in induced abortions in England and Wales. *British Medical Journal*, **287**, 1001.

16 Cavadino, P. (1976). Illegal abortions and the Abortion Act 1967. *British Journal of Criminology*, **16**, 63.

17 Francome, C. (1984). *Abortion Freedom: A Worldwide Movement.* George Allen and Unwin, London.

18 Glass, D. V. (1940). *Population Policies and Movements in Europe.* Frank Cass, Leytonstone, London.

19 Francome, C. (1983). Unwanted pregnancies amongst teenagers. *British Journal of Biosocial Science*, **15**, 139.

20 Russell, J. K. (1983). School pregnancies: medical, social and educational considerations. *British Journal of Hospital Medicine*, **29**, 159.

21 Brahams, D. (1982). Whether pregnancy should be terminated and a contraceptive device fitted in a girl aged 15. *Lancet*, **1**, 1194.

22 ibid.

23 Teenage confidence and consent (1985). *British Medical Journal*, **290**, 144.

24 Latey Committee (1967). *Report of the Committee on the Age of Majority* (Latey Report). HMSO, London.

25 Honore, T. (1978). *Sex Law.* Duckworth, London.

26 Criminal Law Revision Committee (1980). *Working Paper on Sexual Offences.* HMSO, London.

27 Royal College of Obstetricians and Gynaecologists (1972). *Unplanned Pregnancy: Report of a Working Party.* RCOG, London.

28 Kenyon, F. E. (1972). The psychology of abortion. *Man and Woman*, **6**, 74, 2051. (Marshall Cavendish, London.)

29 Fowkes, F. G. R. et al (1979). Abortion and the NHS: the first decade. *British Medical Journal*, **1**, 217.

30 ibid.

31 Clarke, L. et al (1983). *Camden Abortion Study: The Views and Experiences of Women having NHS and Private Treatment.* British Pregnancy Advisory Service, London.

32 Joint Study of the Royal College of General Practitioners and Royal College of Obstetricians and Gynaecologists (1985). *Journal of the Royal College of General Practitioners*, **35**, 175.

33 Paintin, D. B. (1985). Legal abortion in England and Wales. In *Abortion: Medical Progress and Social Implications* (eds Porter, R. and O'Connor, M.). Pitman, London.

34 Lewis, T. L. T. (1980). Legal abortions in England and Wales 1968–78. *British Medical Journal*, **280**, 295.

Chapter 5

1 Millard, D. W. (1971). The abortion decision. *British Journal of Social Work*, **1**, 131.

2 Hamill, E. and Ingram, I. M. (1974). Psychiatric and social factors in the abortion decision. *British Medical Journal*, **1**, 229.

3 Waite, M. (1974). Consultant psychiatrists and abortion. *Journal of Psychological Medicine*, **4**, 74.

4 Hamilton, J. A. (1962). *Postpartum Psychiatric Problems*. C. V. Mosby, St Louis.

5 Kendell, R. E. (1985). Emotional and physical factors in the genesis of puerperal mental disorders. *Journal of Psychosomatic Research*, **29**, 3.

6 Pugh, T. F. et al (1963). Rates of mental disease related to childbearing. *New England Journal of Medicine*, **268**, 1224.

7 Snaith, R. P. (1983). Pregnancy related psychiatric disorder. *British Journal of Hospital Medicine*, **30**, 450.

8 Dean, C. and Kendell, R. E. (1981). The symptomatology of puerperal illness. *British Journal of Psychiatry*, **139**, 128.

9 Brockington, I. F. and Kumar, R. (eds) (1977). *Motherhood and Mental Illness*. Grune and Stratton, Orlando, Florida.

10 Brewer, C. (1981). *Psychiatric Problems in Women, Part 2: Some Psychiatric Aspects of Abortion and Contraception*. SK & F Publications.

11 David, H. P. (1985). Post-abortion and postpartum psychiatric hospitalization. In *Abortion: Medical Progress and Social Implications* (eds Porter, R. and O'Connor, M.). Pitman, London.

12 Brewer, C. (1978). Induced abortion after feeling fetal movements: its causes and emotional consequences. *Journal of Biosocial Science*, **10**, 203.

13 Savage, W. and Paterson, J. (1982). Abortion: methods and sequelae. *British Journal of Hospital Medicine*, **28**, 364.

14 Editorial (1981). Late consequences of abortion. *British Medical Journal*, **282**, 1564.

15 Editorial (1982). Legal abortions by hysterotomy. *British Medical Journal*, **285**, 446.

16 Editorial (1981). Nurses and the medical termination of pregnancy. *British Medical Journal*, **282**, 81.

17 Editorial (1981). Late consequences of abortion. *British Medical Journal*, **282**, 1564.

18 Joint Study of the Royal College of General Practitioners and Royal College of Obstetricians and Gynaecologists (1985). *Journal of the Royal College of General Practitioners*, **35**, 175.

19 Gandy, R. G. J. (1979). An estimate of the effect of abortions on the stillbirth rate. *Journal of Biosocial Science*, **11**, 173.

20 Kenyon, F. E. (1972). The present position of abortion. In *Psychiatric Aspects of Medical Practice* (eds Mandelbrote, B. and Gelder, M. G.). Staples Press, London.

Greer, H. S. et al (1976). Psychosocial consequences of therapeutic abortion. *British Journal of Psychiatry*, **128**, 74.

21 Kenyon, F. E. ibid.

22 Handy, J. A. (1982). Psychological and social aspects of induced abortion. *British Journal of Clinical Psychology*, **21**, 29.

23 Berkeley, D. et al (1984). Demands made on general practice by women before and after abortion. *Journal of the Royal College of General Practitioners*, **34**, 310.

24 Joint Study of the Royal College of General Practitioners and Royal College of Obstetricians and Gynaecologists (1985). *Journal of the Royal College of General Practitioners*, **35**, 175.

25 Brockington, I. F. and Kumar, R. (eds) (1982). *Motherhood and Mental Illness*. Grune and Stratton, Orlando, Florida.

26 Donnai, P. et al (1981). Attitude of patients after 'genetic' termination of pregnancy. *British Medical Journal*, **1**, 62.

27 Lloyd, J. and Laurence, K. M. (1985). Sequelae and support after termination of pregnancy for fetal malformation. *British Medical Journal*, **290**, 907.

28 Brewer, C. (1977). Third time unlucky: a study of women who have three or more legal abortions. *Journal of Biosocial Science*, **10**, 203.

29 Richards, J. R. (1982). *The Sceptical Feminist: A Philosophical Enquiry*. Penguin Books, Harmondsworth.

30 Greer, G. (1984). *Sex and Destiny: The Politics of Human Fertility*. Picador, London.

31 Joint Study of the Royal College of General Practitioners and Royal College of Obstetricians and Gynaecologists (1985). *Journal of the Royal College of General Practitioners*, **35**, 175.

32 Cooper, J. E. et al (1985). Effects of female sterilization: one-year follow-up in a prospective controlled study of psychological and psychiatric outcome. *Journal of Psychosomatic Research*, **29**, 13.

33 Gath, D. and Cooper, P. J. (1982). Psychiatric aspects of hysterectomy and female sterilization. In *Recent Advances in Clinical Psychiatry* (ed Granville-Grossman, K.). Churchill Livingstone, Edinburgh.

34 Editorial (1980). Sterilization of mentally retarded minors. *British Medical Journal*, **281**, 1025.

35 Berg, I. (1975). Sterilization of Children. *British Journal of Psychiatry*, (News and Notes) November.

36 Craft, A. and Craft, M. (1981). Sexuality and mental handicap: a review. *British Journal of Psychiatry*, **139**, 494.

37 ibid.

38 Wolfers, H. (1970). Psychological aspects of vasectomy. *British Medical Journal*, **4**, 297.

39 Wilkins, A. J. (1985). Attempted infanticide. *British Journal of Psychiatry*, **146**, 206.

40 Butler Committee (1975). *Report of the Committee on Mentally Abnormal Offenders.* HMSO, London.
41 Wilkins, A. J. (1985). Attempted infanticide. *British Journal of Psychiatry*, **146**, 206.
42 Resnick, P. J. (1970). Murder of the newborn: a psychiatric review of neonaticide, 1751–1968. *American Journal of Psychiatry*, **126**, 1414.
43 Wilson, P. (1971). *Murderess.* Michael Joseph, London.
44 Mason, J. K. and McCall Smith, R. A. (1983). *Law and Medical Ethics.* Butterworths, London.

Chapter 6

1 *World Development Report* (1984). Oxford University Press, Oxford.
2 Office of Population Censuses and Surveys (1974). *Statistical Review, Supplement on Abortion.* HMSO, London.
Office of Population Censuses and Surveys (1984). *Abortion Statistics 1982, Series AB No. 9.* HMSO, London.
3 Francome, C. (1984). *Abortion Freedom: A Worldwide Movement.* George Allen and Unwin, London.
4 Potts, M. et al (1977). *Abortion.* Cambridge University Press, Cambridge.
Tietze, C. (1981). *Induced Abortion: A World Review*, 4th edition. World Population Council, New York.
Tietze, C. (1983). *Induced Abortion: A World Review*, 5th edition. World Population Council, New York.
Tietze, C. and Lewit, S. (1969). Abortion. *Scientific American*, **220**, 21.
5 Cook, R. J. and Dickens, B. M. (1983). *Emerging Issues of Commonwealth Abortion Laws.* Commonwealth Secretariat, London.
6 Francome, C. (1984). *Abortion Freedom: A Worldwide Movement.* George Allen and Unwin, London.
7 ibid.
8 Dutta, R. (1980). Abortion in India with particular reference to West Bengal. *Journal of Biosocial Science*, **12**, 191.
9 ibid.
10 Greer, G. (1984). *Sex and Destiny: The Politics of Human Fertility.* Picador, London.
11 Francome, C. (1983). *Abortion Freedom: A Worldwide Movement.* George Allen and Unwin, London.
Gebhard, P. H. et al (1959). *Pregnancy, Birth and Abortion.* Heinemann, London.
Means, C. (1971). The phoenix of abortion freedom. *New York Law Forum*, **17**, 335.

Sarvis, B. and Rodman, H. (1974). *The Abortion Controversy*. Columbia University Press, USA.

Shain, R. N. (1982). Abortion practices and attitudes in cross-cultural perspective. *American Journal of Obstetrics and Gynecology*, **142**, 245.

12 Mohr, J. C. (1978). *Abortion in America: The Origins and Evolution of National Policy 1800–1900*. Oxford University Press, Oxford.

13 Shain, R. N. (1982). Abortion practices and attitudes in cross-cultural perspective. *American Journal of Obstetrics and Gynecology*, 142, 245.

14 Taussig, F. J. (1936). *Abortion: Spontaneous and Induced*. C. V. Mosby, St Louis.

15 Mohr, J. C. (1978). *Abortion in America: The Origins and Evolution of National Policy 1800–1900*. Oxford University Press, Oxford.

16 Rosoff, J. I. (1985). Politics and abortion. In *Abortion: Medical Progress and Social Implications* (eds Porter, R. and O'Connor, M.). Pitman, London.

Grimes, D. A. (1985). Provision of abortion services in the United States. In ibid.

17 Francome, C. (1984). *Abortion Freedom: A Worldwide Movement*. George Allen and Unwin, London.

18 Tosi, S. L. et al (1983). Abortion in Italy. *New England Journal of Medicine*, **308**, 51.

19 ibid.

20 Forssman, H. and Thuwe, I. (1966). One hundred and twenty children born after application for therapeutic termination refused. *Acta Psychiatrica Scandinavica*, **42**, 71.

21 Kleiner, G. J. and Greston, W. M. (eds) (1984). *Suicide in Pregnancy*. John Wright, Bristol.

22 ibid.

23 Francome, C. (1984). *Abortion Freedom: A Worldwide Movement*. George Allen and Unwin, London.

24 Matějček, Z. et al (1985). Follow-up study of children born to women denied abortion. In *Abortion: Medical Progress and Social Implications* (eds Porter, R. and O'Connor, M.). Pitman, London.

25 Shain, R. N. (1982). Abortion practices and attitudes in cross-cultural perspective. *American Journal of Obstetrics and Gynecology*, **142**, 245.

26 Greer, G. (1984). *Sex and Destiny: The Politics of Human Fertility*. Picador, London.

27 Hinnells, J. R. (ed) (1984). *The Penguin Dictionary of Religions*. Penguin Books, Harmondsworth.

28 Greer, G. (1984). *Sex and Destiny: The Politics of Human Fertility*. Picador, London.

29 Muramatsu, M. (1985). Abortion law and abortion services in Japan. In *Abortion: Medical Progress and Social Implications* (eds Porter, R. and O'Connor, M.). Pitman, London.
30 Miura, D. (1984). *The Forgotten Child*, trs. Cuthbert, J. Aidan Ellis, Henley-on-Thames, Oxford.

Chapter 7

1 Lane Committee (1974). *Report of the Committee on the Working Party of the Abortion Act*, 3 vols. HMSO, London.
2 Williams Committee (1979). *Report of the Committee on Obscenity and Film Censorship*. HMSO, London.
3 Marsh, D. and Chambers, J. (1981). *Abortion Politics*. Junction Books.
4 Francome, C. (1984). *Abortion Freedom: A Worldwide Movement*. George Allen and Unwin, London.
5 Mattinson, J. (1985). The effects of abortion in marriage. In *Abortion: Medical Progress and Social Implications* (eds Porter, R. and O'Connor, M.). Pitman, London.
6 Shostak, A. B., McLouth, G. and Seng, L. (1984). *Men and Abortion*. Praeger, New York.
7 Cooper, W. and Smith, T. (1984). *Everything You Need to Know about the Pill*. Sheldon Press, London.
8 Cheetham, J. (1978). *Unwanted Pregnancy and Counselling*. Routledge and Kegan Paul, London.
9 Alberman, E. and Dennis, K. J. (eds) (1984). *Late Abortions in England and Wales: Report of a National Confidential Study*. Royal College of Obstetricians and Gynaecologists, London.